NICK NAYLOR THE SPACEMAN WHO LIVED NEXT-DOOR

— NICK NAYLOR —

The Spaceman Who Lived Next-door

By Nick Naylor

Illustrated by Nick Naylor

Cover concept Nick Naylor & Rob Hick

Cover illustration by jacquiedwards.com

ISBN:9798767249374 (paperback)

For the Dreamers of the World

TABLE OF CONTENT

– 1 –

MOVING HOUSE

JONATHAN WAS A dreamer. He spent most of his life dreaming. When he was tucked up in bed and the Sandman paid a visit, he would be having the most wondrous, magnificent dreams that a child could ever have. Even when he was eating his breakfast, he would be daydreaming about the dream he had just had.

It didn't stop there. When he went to school, he would daydream all through his lessons too. All the other children would watch him staring blankly out the window, wondering what he was dreaming about. A tropical island with the waves gently lapping on the shore or some far-off galaxy on the other side of the known universe. For Jonathan, there was no better thing than dreaming. That's the beauty of it. You can make anything come true, even the most impossible things. All you have to do is apply a little elbow grease, a bit of imagination, a spot of determination and stand well back and watch your dreams grow. It doesn't matter how big or how small they are; just know that they can become real.

It was one Saturday morning when Jonathan's life changed forever. That was the morning he and his family moved to their new home. Squeezed into the back seat of the car, he and his sister waited for their parents to finish locking up. There was two years' difference between Jonathan and his sister. He was nine and Liz was seven.

Jonathan didn't know what was wrong with their old house. He liked it. However, his mother said it was time they moved somewhere bigger, somewhere with more space. She was Headmistress at the big school, and his dad was a nurse who worked very long hours at the hospital.

It was getting hot sat in the back of the car, and Jonathan's sister began to complain as to why it was taking so long.

"Can't we get going?" she grumbled.

"Just one minute!" said their father, busy making sure they had not forgotten anything.

Now, normally Jonathan would be quite content to sit daydreaming but with the sun beating down on them, things were beginning to get unbearable.

"Dad!" yelled Jonathan.

Their father raised his hand, pleading for his son to be patient with him.

Both Janathan and Liz were squashed like sardines in between the house plants, suitcases, and Tessa the cat, who sat in her basket looking rather worried. Finally, the house was locked up and his parents got into the car.

Waving and cheering they shouted "Bye!" to the house before taking one last look at it.

Their new house was all the way across the city. Jonathan had only seen his new home once before and didn't have a strong recollection of it.

"Mum, what's our new house like?"

"Well, it's big and it's old," said their mother turning round to face them.

"How old?" Jonathan asked. His mother thought for a moment.

"Oh … probably a hundred years old."

"Are there any ghosts in it?" his sister asked.

His mother, caught up in the excitement, laughed. "I don't know … maybe."

"I don't like ghosts," replied his sister.

"Me neither," added Jonathan who didn't like spooky places.

"Don't scare the kids, Carol," pleaded their father, looking somewhat exasperated at their mother for winding the children up.

"Oh, what's wrong with you? I was only having a bit of fun."

"Well, let's not make this move any scarier than it is," he added, as he concentrated on his driving.

Their new house seemed miles away. As they drove through the city, they passed unfamiliar-looking places and, after what felt like forever, their dad finally announced that they had arrived.

The house was built of red brick and the top half was covered in gleaming whitewash. From the roof protruded two extremely tall chimneys, also made of red brick.

"I thought you said this house was old?" chirped up Liz, as she got out of the car to stretch her legs.

"It is," her mother told her.

"It doesn't look old to me," she replied huffily, somewhat disappointed that it didn't look like a castle. Lifting the pet carrier from the back seat, their father made sure the cat was alright while their mother unlocked the front door of their new home.

Inside, the house felt very bare. There were no carpets, and everything echoed as they ran around exploring all the rooms. All their furniture and possessions had been piled up in various rooms by the removal men and as their parent's unpacked things, Jonathan and his sister took the chance to look around the house. Charging upstairs, they went to find out where they would be sleeping.

"I want to sleep in this room," declared his sister, claiming the small bedroom at the front of the house. Jonathan was sure that his parents would want the bedroom next to hers as it was the biggest, so while his sister got used to her room, he went to explore the rest of the house.

The back bedroom looked down upon the garden which was overgrown with trees at the far end. Jonathan thought they would make an excellent place for building a den or hanging a rope swing.

Out on the landing, there were yet more stairs. He wondered where they went. Perhaps an attic? Jonathan decided to investigate.

Making his way up the stairs, he found another bedroom. It smelt rather odd, like old mothballs, but he didn't mind as the view was much better than the other bedroom. From out of the window, he could see right across the city, all the way over to where he used to live. He could even see straight into the garden of the house next door. Unlike all the other houses on the road, it looked like nobody lived there. The grounds were so overgrown that the house was barely visible through the trees. Only the very top of the house could be seen with its copper-clad tower peeking out from between the trees.

As Jonathan worked out where he was going to put his bed and have his computer, he heard his dad shouting to him from downstairs.

"Jonathan, Jonathan, can you come down here and help, please?" Jonathan rushed downstairs to find his father carrying a box full of stuff through into the hallway.

"Ahh…there you are," said his dad smiling.

"Can you look after Tessa for me?" he asked. "Don't let her out of her basket though, we don't want to lose her, eh?" he stressed nodding in the direction of the cat. Tessa looked overwhelmed by everything that was going on. Jonathan thought he'd take her somewhere quiet, somewhere out of the way of all the noise.

The only room where there didn't seem to be any crashing or banging going on was the kitchen. Jonathan set Tessa's box down on top of the kitchen table.

Wishing to help, he thought his parents might appreciate a drink, so he took the kettle out of one of the boxes and filled it up with water. That's when Tessa began to meow loudly.

"What's the matter eh, girl?" he asked looking at her through the wire door of her basket.

"Would you like a saucer of milk?" he asked. Jonathan remembered what his dad had said about not letting her out of her basket, but what harm could it do? He was sure she would like something to drink.

Finding a saucer, he put it down on the floor and filled it up with milk. Then he opened the cage door and the black and white cat leapt off the table and onto the floor.

Turning his attention away from that of the cat, Jonathan busied himself pouring cups of tea as well as two glasses of juice, one for him and one for his sister. Placing them on a tray he then carried them through to the front room, leaving the cat to finish her milk.

"Here you are," he said, announcing his arrival and handing his parents their drinks.

"Oh, oh, thank you dear. What an angel you are!" said his mother, messing up his hair affectionately.

Jonathan then called to his sister upstairs that he had made her a drink. Hearing this, she came charging downstairs, her footsteps echoing off the bare walls.

His dad was sat in one of the chairs that had been dumped in the living room while his mother sat on top a packing box.

"So, what do you think of your new home?" asked his mother, leaning forward and cradling her tea in both hands. Jonathan didn't know what to say; it was all a bit strange and seemed a bit new to him.

"It's alright, I suppose…," he said taking a gulp of juice from his glass.

"Alright? Alright?" his dad joked. "Have you seen the back garden? It's so big that we can have ourselves a proper football pitch out there. And I bet you'd like a swing, wouldn't you?" He said turning to Liz.

"What? We can have a swing?" she beamed.

"Course you can, my dear," replied her mother, inviting her to sit on her knee.

"Have you decided which bedrooms you want yet, eh?" asked their dad, his feet dangling over the arm of the chair.

"I've got the one at the front above the door," replied Liz.

"And what about you, Buster. Which one have you chosen?" Asked his dad as he looked over at Jonathan.

"I like the attic room. You can see our old house from there and all the city too."

"So, you've got the crow's nest, eh?" joked his father.

"I think this house will take a bit of work to bring things up to scratch, but it's nothing we can't manage, eh? What do you think, love?" His father looking to Jonathan's mother for a reply.

"No, it's nothing we can't manage. But you're not going to get anything done sitting there all day," she teased, encouraging him back to work.

Leaving his parents to get on with the unpacking, Jonathan took the empty mugs and glasses back into the kitchen. It then dawned on him that he had completely forgotten about the cat. Looking around he found she was nowhere to be seen. He checked the pantry and all the cupboards. Then he noticed the cat flap in the back door!

Oh, no! he thought. Rushing outside into the garden, he desperately shouted for the cat, but she did not respond to his call.

The garden had plenty of places for a cat to hide, she could be anywhere. Nervously he checked over his shoulder hoping that his parents hadn't heard him calling her, as he would be in big trouble. Jonathan scouted around and, after some rustling, Tessa emerged from some bushes.

"Come here girl!" he called, trying to encourage the cat to come back to him, but Tessa thought it all was a big game. Leaping playfully from flowerbed to flowerbed, she escaped Jonathan's clutches. Arching her back, she stuck her tail straight up in the air as if to say, "Catch me if you can!" then she decided to make it more fun by jumping up on to the fence. Jonathan froze in terror. *No*, he thought, *don't go into the next door's garden!* Trying to coax her back down he called her name, but the cat wasn't having any of it. Turning her back to him, she leapt off the fence and disappeared into the next-door neighbour's property.

Jonathan put his head in his hands. He imagined all the trouble he was going to get into. He tried jumping up, but the fence was far too tall for him to see over. Then, running up and down its length, he looked for a place to get in. Nothing. By now his heart was pumping hard, and he knew the trouble he was in.

"Tessa, Tessa," he called in desperate hope that she might return. Running along the fence, Jonathan snagged his foot in the brambles and stumbled. Reaching out to save himself, he grabbed at the fence, but suddenly found himself flat on his back underneath an old willow tree.

As he lay there on the soft green grass feeling slightly dazed, he realised he was holding a plank in his hand. How did that happen he wondered? Then it became clear that when he fell over, he had grabbed at the plank, and it had come away in his hand. As he sat up, he found staring back at him, a boy-sized gap in the fence, just big enough for him to squeeze through.

Jonathan wondered whether he should go after Tessa. He might get into more trouble. What if the neighbours were to find him? He would have to explain to his parents, not only that Tessa was missing, but also that he had been trespassing on the neighbour's property, and what if there was a nasty dog too? All these questions raced through Jonathan's mind.

Weighing everything up he knew the only way to get Tessa back was to go after her. With his decision made, he cautiously stuck his head through the gap in the fence. His neighbour's garden was far more overgrown than theirs. Trees towered high above him, huge bushes reached for the sky, while a profusion of petals carpeted the ground. It looked so enticing. It was just begging to be explored.

Squeezing through the gap, Jonathan let his foot fall silently onto the carpet of moss, not wanting to arouse the suspicion of his neighbours or any large, angry dog that might be lurking.

There was an air of stillness to the garden as it was slowly being re-claimed by nature. Careful not to stray too far from the path, he stumbled across a carved gargoyle covered in moss and red creepers. Jonathan wanted to investigate further but knew he didn't have time. If he was not back soon, his parents would be looking for him. So, making clicking noises with his tongue he tried enticing the cat towards him.

"Tessa..., Tess...," he called out quietly. Then from behind a tangle of bushes, she came strolling out, looking all pleased with herself.

"Just where do you think you're going?" Jonathan scolded her as she came over to see him, rubbing herself against his leg. "You could have landed me in a whole load of trouble," he said, scooping her up in his arms.

Back in the house, Jonathan had just got in when his dad came walking into the kitchen.

"I thought I told you not to let her out of her basket," said his dad, with a stern expression on his face.

"I…I…just let her out for a saucer of milk," Jonathan said quick as a flash, not wanting to let on as to what he'd been up to.

After a long day of unpacking, it was time for bed and Jonathan's mother came upstairs to see if he was alright.

"Are you sure you'll be okay up here all on your own?" She asked. Jonathan gave a satisfied nod.

"Once we've got settled in, we'll get some curtains for you, and we'll give this whole room a good lick of paint. It could do with it." She said running her hand over the wallpaper. "You know your father and I are only downstairs if you need us," she added reassuringly.

"No, I'll be fine, Mum," Jonathan replied with smile. Pulling the covers up tight, his mother switched off the light before pulling the door shut.

Jonathan couldn't sleep that night. After the excitement of the day, he was far too lively. Instead, he lay in the dark listening to all the strange sounds that the new house made. The creaking of the floorboards, the tick, tick, tick of the radiators and a whole host of other strange noises that he had never heard before. It was late when his parents came to bed. Hearing them climb the steps, he listened to them talking for a while. Then it all went quiet. He assumed they had gone to sleep.

Lying there awake, it must have been well past midnight when he heard a strange noise coming from outside. At first, it was a faint hum, but as time passed it seemed to be getting louder. Interested to see what it was, Jonathan got out of bed to investigate. Looking out of his window he found there was little to be seen in the dark, but it seemed as if the noise was coming from his next-door neighbour's property.

The noise grew louder and louder until it was like that of a fast-approaching train. He thought about waking his parents, but surely, they must be able to hear this too? Outside the leaves on the trees began to thrash wildly about as if being blown about by some invisible force, and the vibrations grew so strong it was if the whole house was shaking. Jonathan had no idea what was going on.

Squinting into the darkness, he saw a light appear from between the trees. At first it was only faint, but then it grew and grew until it was that bright, it was like looking at the sun. Then, with a sudden flash, the blinding light shot up into the sky and exploded like a firework turning night to day. For miles around it lit up everything as far as the eye could see in a multitude of fantastical colours. Jonathan wondered what could be capable of such a magnificent feat. He had never seen anything like it in his life. However, as suddenly as it had started, it all came to a halt. The light blinked out and everything fell silent apart from a strange whining noise that could be heard coming from over the fence next-door.

Jonathan tried to make sense of what he had just seen. What could be capable of such immense power and dazzling beauty? He had no idea what was going on in his next-door neighbour's garden but swore to himself that he was going to find out.

~2~

DR FIFE

W HEN JONATHAN CAME home from school, he found the house all quiet. His dad was at work, his mother was busy in her study and Liz had gone to play with one of her new friends. Not wanting to be stuck inside on his own, Jonathan decided to explore the neighbourhood on his bike and see if he could find the source of the terrific light he had seen.

Rummaging around in the garage, he found his bike stacked at the back. Wrestling it free from all the junk, he dragged it out and set out along the pavement to see what he could find.

Cycling along he stopped outside the gates of his next-door neighbour's house. Getting off his bike he leant it up against the low wall and peered through the railings. Around the gates was fastened a large padlock while either side of the gates stood two stone pillars with the words 'Sunshine Villa' inscribed on them. To Jonathan it didn't look very sunshiny at all. To him it seemed rather gloomy and foreboding, not at all a place welcoming of guests.

There was little to be seen from the road as the grounds were so overgrown. He could just make out the old, run-down house sticking up from between the trees but that was it. There was no sign of what had caused the magical light. He was sure if he wanted to find out more, he was going to have to sneak through the gap in the fence again. Not fancying his chances of tangling with a nasty dog or irate neighbour he thought it best if he leave his investigations to another day.

With no luck in finding the light and with nothing else to do he decided to time himself just to see how fast he was on his bike. Head down and peddling as hard as he could he raced furiously along the pavement. Up and down the road he went however, he was not paying as much attention as he should and hit the kerb sending him flying headfirst over the handlebars.

Coming round he found himself lying on the floor in a tangled mess, when he heard a voice calling to him.

"Are you alright, laddie?"

Jonathan groaned and looked up to see an elderly gentleman rushing towards him dragging a shopping trolley behind him. He had no idea who the man was or where he came from, but he was glad to see him.

The old man offered Jonathan a hand to get up off the pavement.

"Well, you've certainly made a mess of yourself, haven't you?" he said, looking Jonathan up and down. With blood coming from his hands and knees, Jonathan could see that he had scraped himself badly.

"We'd better sort you out. That looks nasty," said the man nodding to the injuries.

Jonathan replied that he was fine not wishing to inconvenience the gentleman any further.

"No, no, no. We can get you cleaned up in a jiffy. This is my house here," he said pointing to the high railings that ran along the pavement. Jonathan looked up and saw that they were outside the unwelcoming mansion that the strange light had appeared from.

"No, it's fine really. I only live next door," Jonathan protested, but the man was resolute in his desire to help.

"Tell me what sort of person I would be if I couldn't help a neighbour out?" Then, with a courteous bow, he presented himself to the young boy.

"Dr Oban Fife at your service."

The Doctor had a kindly face, a gentle smile and sported a pair of wire-rimmed spectacles. His hair was peppered with grey and was neatly swept to one side. Smartly turned out, he wore a white starched collar, an olive knitted tie, a tweed jacket and matching waistcoat.

It was then Jonathan's turn to introduce himself. "Jonathan Bawtry aged nine!" he said picking his bike up off the ground.

The Doctor chuckled. "Well Jonathan Bawtry aged nine, let's get you cleaned up." He then took a small key from his waistcoat pocket and un-locked the padlock on the tall iron gates, encouraging Jonathan to follow him inside. As he locked the gates behind them, Jonathan had an uneasy feeling.

"What…what are you locking the gates for?" stammered Jonathan who could hear the voice of his parents ringing in his head, telling him not to go with strange people. The Doctor, however had a more down-to earth explanation.

"Unfortunately, my dear Jonathan, there are some people who find it amusing to break into my property, vandalise my house and throw stones through my windows."

Making their way up the overgrown path, Jonathan leant his bike against the steps while he followed the Doctor as he made his way awk-wardly up the steps, dragging his shopping trolley behind him. Reaching the top, the old man paused to regain his breath. Then, taking his keys from his pocket, he unlocked the large wooden door to the house. Pushing it open with a gut-wrenching creak he invited Jonathan to step inside. In the darkness of the hallway, Jonathan felt something furry rub up against his leg and immediately leapt into the air with fright.

"What was that?" squealed Jonathan.

"Ajna!" glowered the doctor as a big fat ginger tomcat ran between his legs nearly tripping him up. "Don't worry," he reassured him. "That's just my cat."

Closing the door, the Doctor took off his jacket and hung it over the arm of a stuffed bear that stood in the corner of the hallway. Wearing a maroon-coloured fez it was conveniently being used as a hat stand and had a selection of umbrellas neatly hung over its arm. Jonathan found it all rather odd and quickly scuttled past the bear just in case it wasn't dead.

The house was all shuttered up with only a faint chink of light piercing the overwhelming gloom. Jonathan looked around. Stacked in the hallway were piles of newspapers and many weeks of unopened mail scattered across the floor. As he followed the Doctor inside, his attention was drawn to something sat on top of a pile of opened letters.

"What's that?" he asked pointing, his voice going all high pitched and wobbly.

"That's my paperweight," the Doctor replied.

"But isn't it a human head?"

"Well observed." Said the Doctor.

Jonathan leapt up in the air in fright for the second time in just as many minutes.

"Here," said the Doctor placing the ashen-faced head in Jonathan's hands as he stowed his shopping trolley away in a cupboard.

Shrunk to a miniature size and with a grim look on its ghastly face, its lips were sewn shut and it had coarse black hair sprouting from the top of its head. It looked like a grizzly coconut. Juggling it wildly between his hands, Jonathan was repulsed by the ghoulish article.

"Why…why…have you got a human head as a paperweight?" he stammered placing the head back down on top of the pile of letters as quickly as he could.

"My parents brought it back from one of their many travels," the Doctor explained. "It's a shrunken head from one of the indigenous tribes of the Amazon."

"But…but… why are you using it as a paperweight?"

"Why not?"

Jonathan wiped his hands on the seat of his shorts repulsed by what he had unknowingly handled.

"Urgghh!" he groaned in disgust while the Doctor seemed indifferent about the whole matter.

Shuffling around in the dim light of the hallway, the Doctor lit the wick on an old oil lamp and turned up the flame to shed some light on his mysterious inner world. Even though it was daylight outside, the house was in complete darkness save for an eerie glow that cast long shadows into the rooms that lay beyond.

Just as Jonathan was recovering from the shock of the shrunken head, he spied something equally disturbing. There, sat on a table next to the lamp, was a wizened, shrivelled, severed hand.

"Why is … th…there a dead person's hand on your table?" Jonathan stammered, his hand shaking with fright as he pointed to it.

"That's where it got to. I wondered where I had put it," said the Doctor picking it up to inspect it.

"Ah yes…" he said scratching his head with it. "It fell off my mummy when I was last cleaning it."

"You've got a mummy, here in the house?"

"It's just a mummy, Jonathan. It's nothing to get excited about."

"But you've got a dead person in your house!"

"Jonathan, I wish you'd stop being overly dramatic. It's only a hand, it's not like the person needs it anymore."

Jonathan stood in the hallway unable to comprehend that his neighbour was in possession of an actual mummy!

"Look. I'll show it to you later, but right now we really need to get you sorted out,"

Following the Doctor through the oppressive gloom, he passed old paintings and chandeliers covered in cobwebs as well as odd bits of furniture covered with dust sheets. The house had the appearance it was not lived in.

Reaching a huge carved wooden staircase, the Doctor announced, "This way," as he opened a heavy, wood panelled door into what looked like a library. The room was bright and airy in contrast to the rest of the house.

Blinking in the light Jonathan took a minute to get over the size of the room. From floor to ceiling, the walls were covered with nothing but books. There was even a ladder running around the room on brass rails so the Doctor could reach the books on the very top shelves.

"Welcome to my home!" the Doctor beamed as he threw his arms open wide. "You'll find books here on anything you could ever imagine. And…" he continued, "…if you can imagine more than that, then there's always the secret library up here," he said tapping the side of his head with a wry smile. Jonathan had no idea what the doctor was on about.

"Secret library?" Questioned Jonathan.

Dr Fife turned and smiled. "The secret library, my friend, is a place that doesn't exist. Think of it as a repository of all knowledge. It's where all the information that has ever been and ever will be is kept," he winked.

"You see I am an inventor, and the secret library is one of my many inventions," he admitted, elaborating further. "It is a holographic storage system that allows the user to download information straight out of thin air and into their mind."

Jonathan wasn't entirely sure what the doctor was talking about but smiled politely and nodded as if he understood.

"In the meantime, do make yourself at home while I just nip next door and get the first aid kit," said the Doctor patting a red leather chaise longue. Jonathan had never seen one before and to him it looked like a cross between a sofa and a bed.

Left alone in the room, Jonathan wandered around looking at all the strange things there were to see in the library. On the writing desk was a plastic pipe for blowing bubbles, which the Doctor used for when he was deep in thought. An ice maker that looked like a snowman for putting ice in his drinks and a model train that ran around the top of the bookshelves. And there right at the very back of the room was a large double bed. *How peculiar*, thought Jonathan. *A bed in a library?*

The door opened and in came Dr Fife carrying with him a first aid box and a bottle of antiseptic. Intrigued to know why there was a bed in the room, Jonathan asked the Doctor what it was doing there.

"I'm afraid you have to have deep pockets to run a house like this," sighed the doctor, looking rather despondent. "The upkeep is never ending, and as I don't have much money, I find it easier to live in just these two rooms, the library and the kitchen where it's nice and warm." He explained.

Now let's have a look at those cuts of yours," he said ushering Jonathan over to the red leather chaise longue.

On his knees, the Doctor rummaged through his box of bandages while the cat rubbed itself against Jonathan's leg. Relaxing for the first time since he had got there, Jonathan gave the cat a hearty stroke. Ajna arched his back and purred loudly with pleasure.

"I have a cat called Tessa. What's your cat's name?"

"This is the Emeritus Professor Ajna," the Doctor proudly announced.

The cat, as if it knew it was being talked about, rubbed its whiskers with its paw before giving the fur on its chest a preening lick.

"That's an odd name for a cat, isn't it? Is he a real professor?"

The Doctor looked down at the cat with affection. "I like to think so. To me, he's smarter than a lot of humans. He's content to sleep anywhere he can. He's friends with anyone who wants to stroke him, and he doesn't worry about a thing, which in anyone's book seems like a good way to live."

"How old is he?" Jonathan wanted to know.

The Doctor scratched his head and thought for a moment.

"I'm not sure, come to think of it. Ajna was a stray when I found him. He was wandering round the grounds looking hungry, so I offered him a home and something to eat, and he's been here ever since."

Feeling more at ease, Jonathan was content to sit and stroke the Emeritus Professor Ajna while the Doctor got on with tending to his wounds.

"Now this might sting a little." the Doctor warned him. Jonathan winced. Once he had his cuts cleaned, Jonathan asked the Doctor a question.

"Are you Scottish?" having noticed the Tartan curtains in the hallway.

"In name only. My great, great grandfather left Scotland many years ago. He owned and ran a huge factory here and became incalculably wealthy. He built this house that you see before you. However, times have changed and there is little left of that great fortune now. I try to make do with what I have, scrimping and saving where I can," he said without any hint of regret.

Ajna stared intently at them while the Doctor finished bandaging his hands and knees.

"I wish I was like you and Professor Ajna," noted Jonathan glumly as he watched the Doctor dress his wounds.

"Why, what do you mean?" he asked.

"I mean I wish I was intelligent like you. I'm no good at school and I'm terrible at maths and I hate doing sums. The only thing I'm good at is dreaming."

"Dreaming!" exclaimed the Doctor, as if he had just struck gold. "Dreaming is the finest profession going. I consider myself to be one of the world's greatest dreamers!" he said puffing his chest out with pride. "Where would we be, Jonathan, if it wasn't for dreaming, eh? Some of the greatest inventions have been created by dreamers: the telephone, the light-bulb, the internet! Good gracious, Jonathan, if it wasn't for dreamers we would be still floundering around in the dark ages! There's nothing wrong with being a dreamer, let me tell you! And I'll let you in on a little secret: all the best dreams in the world start with the ocean," winked the Doctor.

"Tell me. What's the most important thing in the world?"

Jonathan gave a shrug as if to say he didn't know.

"A smile!" answered the Doctor merrily. "Did you know a single smile can change the whole world?"

Jonathan shook his head.

"You see, it's no good being intelligent if you can't be happy. The happiest people I know are the ordinary, everyday people: the people who clean the streets, pack your groceries, drive our buses and trains, and look after the elderly. They know that the key to a happy life is a smile, and a smile can raise the spirits of even the meanest and saddest of people. That's what makes the world go round, not the fact that someone can add up or spell correctly," he said wagging his finger to reinforce how important it was.

"Happiness can be found in the most unlikely of places my friend," he continued. "A song playing on the radio, the tweeting of a bird, the smile of a dog, the green shoots of a tree when spring is about to burst forth, and my particular favourite…a sunset. Oh, and not forgetting when the fog hangs low in the valley on a morning," he added with a contented smile. "You must take time to enjoy these things, Jonathan. It's what life's all about.

Jonathan did his best to raise a half-hearted smile.

"That's better!" enthused the Doctor giving him a reassuring pat on the shoulder. Getting to his feet, the Doctor then asked Jonathan if he would like to see the rest of the house.

Strolling through the great hallway, past huge gilt mirrors and tribal masks that hung from the walls, the Doctor turned to Jonathan. "You know it's a long time since I've had guests here. In fact, it's so long that I've forgotten how many rooms this place has got."

Jonathan felt sorry that the Doctor had no friends who wanted to visit him.

"Don't you have any family, or someone who lives with you?"

The Doctor sighed. "I am afraid that after my parents died, I have been the sole incumbent here at Sunshine Villa and now I only have Ajna for company."

"What? Don't you have any brothers and sisters?"

"I am an only child, Jonathan. My parents were so busy traveling the world collecting antiquities that I fear sometimes even I was too much of a drain on their precious time."

He showed Jonathan into a long room. Pulling back the shutters, light flooded in to reveal a mothball-clad world of dust blankets and faded glory. Removing the sheets that were draped over the furniture the Doctor allowed Jonathan to peruse what lay underneath.

There were Greek and Roman busts of important men and women from history, works of art painted by great masters, suits of armour, antique curios filling glass cases, and more rare stuffed birds and animals than Jonathan knew existed. The Doctor walked over to a glass case.

"You see that tiny piece of insignificant stone here, the one with a pointy end?" Jonathan nodded. "Well, that is one of the oldest pieces of man's history."

"What is it?"

"It is a tool used for shaping other stones and it's over two million years old."

"Really?" said Jonathan in disbelief.

"And that lump of rock there, that is a fossilised dinosaur egg."

"A dinosaur egg!" Jonathan squealed with glee. "Could I hold it please?"

The Doctor lifted the lid of the glass case and handed the egg to Jonathan. "Careful. It's heavy," he warned.

Jonathan felt the great weight of the fossilised rock and couldn't believe he was holding in his hands the actual egg of a dinosaur.

"How old is it?" he asked.

"Approximately one hundred and fifty-four million years old," the Doctor stated in a matter-of-fact way.

"One hundred and fifty million years old!" exclaimed Jonathan in awe as he held the rock in his hands, just to feel what one hundred and fifty-four million years felt like.

Sauntering into the room, Professor Anja came to join them. After rubbing himself against the leg of the wooden display case, he jumped onto the glass case next to them.

"Do be careful, Anja!" the Doctor cautioned his most esteemed companion as his attention was drawn to yet another lump of rock.

"See this? This is a meteorite from space."

Jonathan placed the egg back carefully and picked up a black, pitted lump of rock to examine.

"WOW. Is this really from space?" cried Jonathan, his head nearly exploding with amazement. "Gosh it's heavy!" he exclaimed almost dropping it on the floor.

"That's because it's made of iron and if you thought those other bits of rock were old, that's nothing. That lump of rock you're holding right there is four point five billion years old."

Jonathan didn't know what to say. He couldn't imagine anything ever being that old. His Grandpa was eighty-seven and already looked pretty old to him.

"Would you like to see the mummy now?" The Doctor asked. Jonathan nodded excitedly.

Leaving the room behind, they walked along the dark, cavernous corridors and up the many stairs with only Professor Ajna and the faint echo of their footsteps for company. Jonathan wanted to ask the Doctor about the dazzling light that he had seen coming from his back garden but wasn't sure how he would react. Suddenly, without thinking, he found himself blurting out his question. Stopping dead in his tracks the Doctor turned to him with a stern expression on his face.

"Have you seen my light?" he asked with a seriousness that Jonathan had not previously seen in the Doctor.

Jonathan nodded and bit his lip nervously. Maybe he wasn't supposed to have seen the light.

Bending down the Doctor looked him directly in the eye. "The light has been my life's work. It has been my essence, my reason for being for the last fifty years. Do you understand?" He paused, taking a deep breath.

"I have devised many earth-shattering inventions in my time, but nothing comes close to this. It is so fantastical that it will change the world as we know it. However, there are still some final adjustments to be made before

I can reveal my greatest work. May I count on you not to say a word?" He asked with a sincerity that the boy had rarely heard in a grownup.

Considering his options, that he was in a strange house with someone he barely knew Jonathan concluded that he didn't really have much of a choice.

"Yes, I'll keep your secret," agreed Jonathan.

The Doctor immediately leapt into the air cheering. "Good boy, good boy!" He yelled pacing up and down the corridor excitedly and rubbing his hands together. Then, spinning on his heels came striding back towards Jonathan.

"For your loyalty, Jonathan, I will reward you with a visit to my laboratory. I will show you the many wondrous things I have been working on. I think you'll find it quite something," declared the Doctor skipping along the corridor merrily.

"But first, this way," he instructed. Turning a big brass doorknob on one of the many rooms, the Doctor disappeared inside.

Following behind, Jonathan found himself in a huge gallery overlooking the great hall. Amongst the shadows, he could tell it was crammed full of artefacts. Flicking on the lights, the entirety of the Doctor's Egyptian collection came into view.

There were battle chariots, strange-looking carved dogs covered in gold, busts of Pharaohs and images of long forgotten gods sat astride thrones. But there in the centre of the room was the most impressive piece. Sat behind a glass case was a bejewelled sarcophagus complete with its bandaged mummy.

"Well, what do you think?" Yelled the Doctor from across the other side of the room. Jonathan didn't know what to say.

"I'd like to introduce you to Tadi-tata-bethen!" He said making his way over to the glass case that held the remains of the mummy.

Jonathan pressed his face up against the case, his breath steaming up the glass in front of him.

He couldn't believe he was face to face with a mummy. He had only ever read about them in books. All Jonathan could do was stare obsessively at the elaborately adorned death mask. The deep black gaze of its obsidian eyes and the radiant glow of the worked gold mesmerised him. Entranced by its beauty, Dr Fife pulled him away insisting on a full tour of all the artefacts.

It was a good hour later when the doctor looked at his watch. "Won't your parents want to know where you are?"

Crumbs! thought Jonathan. Thanking the Doctor for his hospitality and treating his wounds he rushed home, filled with excitement at the prospect of telling his family about what he had seen.

-3-

THE LABORATORY

AROUND THE DINNER table that evening, Jonathan excitedly told his mother and sister about meeting their mysterious next-door neighbour and all the amazing things he'd seen. However, as he told his story his mother began to look concerned.

"I'm not sure I want you going round to a strange man's house that I don't know."

"But Mum…," complained Jonathan.

"Don't but Mum, me," she replied as she served out the spaghetti and meatballs.

"He helped me after I fell off my bike."

His mother threw him a stern look and put her spoon down.

"You didn't tell me about falling off your bike. Are you alright?"

Jonathan nodded and showed her the bandages on his knees. He then explained that he had been timing himself when he fell off his bike.

"What have I told you? You should really be paying more attention, Jonathan," was his mother's response as she enquired as to who this man was.

"He's our next-door neighbour. His name is Dr Fife…and he has a cat called the Emeritus Professor Ajna."

Liz let out a giggle when she heard that. "Nobody calls their cat that. It's a silly name."

Ignoring his sister, he explained that the Doctor was an inventor and, made all sorts of earth-shattering discoveries and inventions, even telling them about the light he saw from his window.

"Well, I don't care if he's fixed the hole in the ozone layer. He can't go around accosting children on the street!"

"He didn't, Mum. It wasn't like that. He helped me after I had fallen off my bike."

"Well, I'm still not happy with you going round to a strange man's house."

Knowing that there was no point arguing with his mother, he thought it best if he wait till tomorrow to tell his father.

The following morning Jonathan couldn't wait to tell his dad about the mummy and everything that he had seen. Rushing downstairs, he found his dad still in his nurse's uniform busy making everyone breakfast.

"You'll never believe it, Dad, but the Doctor next door has a real mummy in his house!"

"Really?" replied his dad from over his shoulder whilst stirring his tea.

"He has a gold coffin, and it's all wrapped up in bandages, and he had chariots and all sorts of amazing stuff. He even had a dinosaur egg and a meteorite... and the tiny head of a dead person!"

"Really, dear, I do think you are imagining things," interrupted his mother. "Nobody has the head of a dead person in their home."

"Dr Fife does. He said it's from an Amazon tribe or something like that."

"You mean a shrunken head? Cool!" remarked their father who was now interested in what his son had to say.

"Oh, don't go encouraging him, dear," came his mother's response. "I mean, we should really be asking ourselves, is this the sort of person that we want our son engaging with?"

His dad shrugged. "Hey, if the guy has a collection of severed heads in his home, who are we to question why?"

Their mother did not look impressed.

"Yesterday, our son had a nasty accident on his bike and all you're interested in is a severed head?"

"Did he?" asked Jonathan's father in surprise.

"Jonathan, show your father where you cut yourself," insisted his mother. Examining the bandages, his father said he had made a good job of it as he looked at the bandages with an expert eye.

"We should really get him a gift or something as a thank you. What about a box of chocolates?" Suggested his father.

"Mmm, I suppose that's a good idea," said their mother begrudgingly.

"And make sure Jonathan apologises to him for being so much trouble," she added quickly gulping her coffee and checking her day's schedule on her phone.

When Jonathan got home from school that afternoon, he found a box of chocolates on the kitchen work top and a note from his dad saying it was for the doctor.

"Have you seen the chocolates and the note?" asked his mother when she came home from work.

"Well, I want you to go round and apologise to the Doctor for being a nuisance to him and give him those chocolates, do you hear?"

"Yes, Mum." he replied

Jonathan didn't mind going round to the Doctor's house. In fact, he was looking forward to it. After all, the Doctor had promised to show him his laboratory and Jonathan couldn't wait to find out what mind-boggling inventions the Doctor had hidden away. If he was lucky, he might even find out more about the mysterious light he had seen.

"Don't forget, I want you home for dinner by six," his mother called out as she made her way upstairs to her study.

Making his way down the garden, Jonathan pushed back the flowing limbs of the old willow tree that hid the gap in the fence and squeezed through.

Giving three loud knocks on the front door he waited for an answer, but there was no response. He tried peering through the windows, but the shutters inside were closed.

Round the back he tried the kitchen door. Finding it open he called the Doctor's name, but there was no answer. He thought better of venturing inside uninvited, besides the Doctor might be in his laboratory.

Unsure as to where the Doctor's laboratory was, he guessed it must be somewhere in the grounds. Making his way past an overgrown tennis court, rusting cars and disused swimming pool, he found a well-trodden path that led through a tunnel of overgrown bushes, into a clearing beyond.

Standing in front of him was an old Victorian greenhouse built of red brick and acres of glazed panels. The greenhouse was huge. From a central rotunda, four long arms ran off it where the plants had once been grown. However, it now looked somewhat sorry for itself. Paint flaked off the woodwork and there were tell-tale signs of neglect, with cardboard squares replacing missing panes of glass.

Gazing upwards, Jonathan's eyes were met with something that he had never seen before. It was spellbinding, it looked so beautiful.

There, stood atop of the rotunda, was a circular mirrored disc. Smokey in colour and with a hole in its centre, it was the most dazzling thing he had ever seen. Mesmerised, Jonathan stood there rooted to the spot.

He wasn't sure how long he'd been there when he heard the Doctor calling his name.

"Jonathan, Jonathan, over here!" Came the voice.

"How did you get in?" enquired the Doctor pushing his glasses back upon his head and blinking like a mole emerging into the sunlight. "The gates are locked."

"Through a gap in the fence," said Jonathan, pointing back to the way he had come.

"I didn't know there was a hole in the fence. Oh well, never mind," he said with a wave of the hand.

As Jonathan made his way over to see the Doctor, he was greeted by the Emeritus Professor Ajna who had been busy sunning himself in one of the flower beds. Nosing through long-stemmed daisies, Ajna slid up beside Jonathan and rubbed himself up against him.

"Oh, don't mind him. He'll be anyone's friend for a good stroke," chuckled the Doctor, beckoning Jonathan inside.

"I've brought these for you," said Jonathan holding out the box of chocolates for the Doctor to take.

"For me!" he exclaimed. "What are they for?"

"My Dad bought them for you. He said it was for doing such a good job of looking after me. He says you're as good as him at putting dressings on and he's a nurse."

"My, that is praise indeed," said the Doctor, "but there was really no need. I was only doing what anyone would do. Anyway, come in, come in," he said ushering the young boy in through the door.

"Welcome to my world," declared the Doctor beaming with pride.

Jonathan surveyed his laboratory and didn't think much of it. He couldn't tell what was junk and what was an invention.

"What does this do?" asked Jonathan pointing to a strange mechanical device.

"That, my friend, is the next millennium's most sought after device. It's a zero-point energy generator!" the Doctor exclaimed with glee.

"It's a what?"

"A zero-point energy generator! It creates limitless energy from nothing, merely by the flow of subatomic particles across energy states."

"It looks like a piece of junk to me," puzzled Jonathan as he cast his eye over the series of concentric rings and cathodes that stuck out from the generator.

"Well, thank you for your vote of confidence, young man, but this, I hasten to add will revolutionise the world. One day everybody will have access to free, abundant energy. There will be no need for dirty big power stations and all this pollution. Petrol and every other sort of fuel will be a thing of the past. This will provide for everyone. From the world's most modern cities to the most remote desert."

Jonathan poked at it with his finger and screwed up his nose. "Are you sure?"

"Absolutely positive! Come," he instructed, clearing a space in amongst all the junk for them to get through.

Long wooden benches flanked either side of the greenhouse, stacked high with all sorts of scientific equipment. There were glass flasks full of brightly coloured liquids bubbling away and spiral tubes connecting to glass stills. Oscilloscopes flashed rhythmically away while highly sophisticated equipment blinked on and off.

It was at this point that Jonathan decided to ask about the mirrored disc he had seen outside. Spinning on his heels, the Doctor stopped dead in his tracks and grabbed him by the shoulders.

"That, my boy, is the most important, most special thing in the whole wide world ever, in fact, the universe! Remember the secret I told you about? The light? Well, that's it!" Whispered Dr Fife in a reverential tone, his finger pressed to his lips. "From that, the light you see at night is emitted. It is the most extraordinary invention that I have ever worked on!"

"What does it do?" asked Jonathan innocently.

Taking the young boy into his confidence, the Doctor looked over his shoulder checking no one was about.

"I can't really say too much, but for someone such as yourself, a dreamer, you're going to love it!" he said tapping the side of his nose and winking.

"Can I see it?" enquired Jonathan tentatively.

"Not just yet. It's not finished, but when it's up and running you'll be the first to see it, my dear boy. I guarantee it!"

"Really?" gasped Jonathan excitedly. "What is it called?"

Taken off guard the Doctor stroked his chin as he thought about the matter. "To tell the truth, I haven't thought of a name for it yet. But when I do, I'll let you know."

"Anyway, enough about that. Right now, I've got something else I want to show you, which I think you might like." The Doctor beckoned for Jonathan to follow him as they made their way into another wing of the greenhouse.

As Jonathan followed the Doctor along a narrow walkway between benches, the doctor explained to Jonathan what he did in this area. "This wing of my greenhouse is dedicated to the preservation of the Earth and all living things in it. I'm working on all sorts of new ideas that will help humans live more harmoniously with their environment."

Suddenly Jonathan got a whiff of something foul. "What's that?" he squealed, pulling a funny face, and sniffing the air in front of his nose.

"What's what?" asked the Doctor spinning round.

"That smell!" gasped Jonathan trying to hold his breath.

"Ah, that's what I call my micro biotic polymeric semiconductor-metal-based nanoparticles or, if you can't manage that mouthful, you can just call them Fug Munchers as I do."

"Fug Munchers!" said Jonathan laughing. "You can't call them that," he chuckled, unable to stop himself from laughing.

"Why not? It's pretty much what they do, and it's easier to say. Look, come and see," said the Doctor, pulling out a stool for Jonathan to sit on. Leant over the bench, he then explained what he was doing.

"This microscope here allows you to see particles two hundred times thinner than a human hair."

"Really?" asked Jonathan, getting excited and trying to see what the Doctor was talking about.

"But why do they smell so bad?"

"It's not the nano particles that smell so bad. It's what they're eating that does." Replied Dr Fife.

"Why, what do you feed them on?"

"Here, come see." Inviting Jonathan to have a look down the lens of the microscope. Squinting hard, Jonathan strained to make out what the Doctor was on about.

"Are those hairy little things Fug Munchers?"

"Yes, those are my little beauties. Aren't they something special?"

Under the magnification of the microscope, Jonathan could see what looked like hairy little creatures going about their business, chomping their way through anything that stood in their path.

"What do they eat?"

"That's the good bit," the Doctor added. "Look at this."

Pulling himself away from the microscope Jonathan took a closer look. On the floor was the foulest, smelliest bin of mush you could ever imagine. The smell was so bad that it nearly knocked Jonathan off his stool.

"You see, everything that we humans throw away as rubbish goes in here. You name it: food waste, plastics, car tires, metal, chemical waste. It all goes in, and the nanoparticles munch their way through it. They break down all the bad stuff into its individual chemical components, which comes out of this tap here at the bottom of the drum. Then I filter out the particles so I can reuse them. Anything that's left over is just harmless organic waste that can be used as fertiliser for farming."

"That's amazing." gasped an astounded Jonathan.

"So, no more pollution," noted the Doctor proudly.

"What? We can live in a world where no one dumps rubbish anymore and there's no more plastic in our oceans?"

"Exactly. And it's all thanks to these little Fug Munchers here," he said tapping the side of the microscope affectionately.

"Here," said the Doctor, in need of a sit down. "I have one last thing that I want to show you before we have a cup of tea and open those chocolates of yours, eh?"

"This way," he said while checking his reflection in the glass to make sure his bow tie was on straight.

Leading him into what looked like an old potting shed, they stepped through a door and down a couple of steps into a darkened room. Taking a moment or two for his eyes to adjust to the darkness, Jonathan saw a pair of glowing glass orbs sat on a bench in front of him. As he cast his gaze around, he noticed that sat on the shelves were more of the globes, all giving off the same beautiful blue light.

"What are they?"

With his hands in his pockets, the Doctor looked on at his invention with paternal pride. "Just in case the worst should happen, and we humans do not change our ways, I've taken a few safeguards to make sure the planet keeps on going even if we mess it up. What you see here are biospheres that I have created. Each one has everything in it to make sure we can kick-start life again long after we have gone the way of the dodo."

"How does it work?" Jonathan wanted to know.

"Think of it like an incubator for a baby," he smiled. "With a pipet of water, a bit of warmth, a few threads of long strand protein and some amino acids, you're ready to go," he said casually while inspecting his lab coat for dirt.

"Go on, take a closer look," motioning for Jonathan to step forward.

Standing on his tippy toes Jonathan strained to see inside the two beach-ball-sized globes.

"What's inside this one?" Jonathan enquired peering into the glass bowl.

"I like to think of it as an oceanarium."

"What, a fish tank?"

"You could say that, but it's a bit more than that. In fact, I have recreated every ocean-based environment from tropical reefs to kelp forests and everything in between. Here, take this; it might help you see better," said the Doctor handing him a magnifying glass from out of his pocket. "If you take a closer look, you might find it a little more interesting than your average fish tank."

Straining to see, Jonathan moved the magnifying glass closer to the bowl.

"There's a whale!" he cried.

"And a humpbacked one at that," noted the Doctor, leaning over Jonathan's shoulder to see better.

"What's in the other one?" he enquired moving over to get a better view of the other orb.

"That is what I like to call my Giant Redwood biosphere. In there you will find the biggest trees that stand here on Earth today."

"But they look the size of matchsticks," complained Jonathan.

"True, but remember, they are in my specially designed biosphere. In real life they are as tall as a football field is long, and if you were to leave the lid off the jar they would grow to their actual size."

Jonathan was astounded.

"Now let's have that cup of tea I was taking about. All this excitement has left me rather tired."

The Doctor trudged out of his potting shed and retraced his steps, passing through the central atrium and into yet another wing of the glass house. Running the entire length of the wing was a black-and-white checkerboard floor and dotted every few feet stood carved marble statues.

"What do you use this room for?" Jonathan asked.

"This is my thinking room, where I do all my best work," the Doctor told him.

"I can sit here for hours and not do a single thing. Most people would call me lazy, but even when I'm sat here doing nothing I am working, busy thinking of things." The Doctor pulled out a white wicker chair for Jonathan to sit on.

"Here I can watch my mind. The view from it is simply amazing, like a peerless blue sky with only the odd cloud scurrying by as thoughts."

Rinsing off a selection of dirty teaspoons he threw the old teabags into his compost bucket. Jonathan was intrigued to know who the statues were of. Pausing as he filled the kettle, the Doctor turned to Jonathan.

"They are my inspiration," he declared. "They are a mix of great thinkers and humanitarians."

Jonathan looked down the long line of exquisitely carved marble figures.

"I think they would inspire me too," he added.

While the kettle boiled, the Doctor opened the box of chocolates. "Do thank your parents for their gift," he said allowing Jonathan to take first pick.

"I'm afraid I only have tea. I'm out of juice. Will that do?" Jonathan nodded in appreciation as the Doctor fussed about trying to find a clean mug for the young boy.

"What are those on the wall?" Asked Jonathan pointing up at two picture frames. One looked like an envelope in a frame and the other was a photograph of an astronaut.

"As you can see, the statues are all people from the past, but these are some inspiring people from more recent times." Reaching up he took the pictures down and handed them to Jonathan.

"That there is a first issue envelope cover signed by the very first men to land on the moon." Jonathan looked at the faded postmark. It read 'Washington D.C July the 20th 1969' and on the cover was a picture of the Earth.

"What does it say below?" asked the Doctor. "Read it to me," he begged.

Tracing the words with his finger Jonathan read it aloud, slowly, "WE CAME... IN PEACE... FOR ALL MANKIND."

"Oh, joy of joys! That's music to my ears," whooped the Doctor. "You see this photograph here?" showing Jonathan the picture of an astronaut on the moon.

"This is the very last man to have walked on the moon. Sometimes I sit here for hours and have entire conversations with Gene."

"Who's Gene?"

"Gene is the man in the picture," said the Doctor pointing to the astronaut.

Reaching under the bench the Doctor pulled out a milk bottle from a small fridge and began to pour. Handing Jonathan, a chipped and slightly mottled mug, the Doctor then examined the tray of chocolates as he took a seat.

"Mmm. I think I'll have that one," he decided. Biting into it and holding the remaining half between his thumb and forefinger, he proceeded to talk with his mouth full.

"You see, humans, Jonathan, were meant for more than this," he said holding his mug aloft whilst chewing at the same time. "Tell me what's the most powerful force in the universe?" asked the Doctor as he polished off his chocolate.

Jonathan looked down at his mug of tea and thought. "Gravity?" he said, unsure of himself.

"Now most people would have you believe that, wouldn't they?" the

Doctor giggled, putting his tea down on an old box that was acting as a makeshift table. "But they'd be wrong," he laughed. "It's LOVE! Plain and simple, good old-fashioned love."

Jonathan watched the Doctor as he turned around in his chair and prodded the wall behind him. With a look on his face that half expected his hand to disappear through the wall, the Doctor turned to him.

"You see this," he said indicating to the wall, "this amazing holographic projection. This illusion of reality. This life. … This was created solely for one purpose and for one purpose alone, that is, to experience the giving and receiving of love. Not just the kind of love between two people, but the love between all living things. Do you get me, Jonathan?"

Jonathan was listening, but at the same time he was having trouble poking a toffee out from behind one of his teeth.

"Here. Have another chocolate" said the Doctor pushing the tray in Jonathan's direction. As the young lad picked out another chocolate, he was quite content to sit there and listen to what the Doctor had to say.

"Now you get all these bigwigs with certificates and letters to their names pretending they're all holy moly, talking about the meaning of life and what's our purpose here," said the Doctor wagging his finger wildly, "but they don't have a clue what they're talking about. Otherwise, they'd be helping to make the world a better place rather than listening to the sound of their own voices."

Jonathan let out a small titter of laughter. "How do you know all this?" he asked as he picked out another chocolate.

The Doctor looked at him over the top of his glasses.

"Strange as it may seem, Jonathan, I am traveller of both space and time and I have been around for rather quite some time in one form or another," he said matter-of-factly. Jonathan looked shocked for a moment.

"What? You're a spaceman?"

"Something like that," replied the Doctor, picking up his mug and taking another sip.

Jonathan couldn't believe he was sat next to a spaceman. "Are you an extra-terrestrial? Do you have a spaceship?"

The Doctor looked at him with kind eyes. "It's not quite like that. I prefer to see myself as a traveller between lives… I go wherever I'm needed." Thumbing his way through the tray of chocolates, he looked for his favourite. Finding a hazelnut swirl, he bit down hard on it.

"You see, Jonathan, I have been sent here for the advancement of humanity. Earth is the most violent planet in the universe, and it is my duty to help humans live peacefully with each other and coexist with other life-forms out there. It is many lifetimes ago since I lived as an extra-terrestrial…" he added.

"…but I do hold on to some of my spaceman like abilities."

"What like?" Asked Jonathan.

"Oh, this and that," remarked the Doctor being coy about his inner secrets.

"Tell me. You have a sister, don't you?" asked the Doctor as he inspected the other half of his chocolate. Jonathan nodded.

"Well next time you come round, bring her along with you. I might have a little surprise for the both of you." Then, as if remembering something, he stuck his finger in the air.

"Oh, and can you bring your rubbish with you? It can be anything you like, any old junk you have lying about. I think we'll have ourselves a little experiment. What do you say?"

Jonathan was excited that the Doctor might have something interesting planned for them. Then, suddenly realising what time it was he jumped to his feet spilling the remainder of his tea. "Whoops, I nearly forgot. I'll be late for dinner," he said as he made for the door.

"It was a pleasure having your company, Jonathan. Do feel free to pop in anytime." The Doctor called after him as the young boy made his exit.

– 4 –

SECRET WORLD

AFTER SCHOOL, JONATHAN met up with his sister to walk home. As they walked along together, Jonathan couldn't wait to tell her what he had found out about the Doctor.

"He told me he's a *spaceman*!" He said telling her of what he knew. His sister looked at him with disbelief.

"He's not a spaceman; nobody has a spaceman living next door to them." She argued.

Jonathan had to admit she did have a point.

"I know it sounds weird, but he does seem to be telling the truth."

"Does he look like a spaceman?" Liz wanted to know.

"No, not really, he looks pretty normal to me."

"Well, he can't be then!" stated Liz as though she was an authority on what spacemen looked like.

"How do you know what they look like? Not all of them are green and have antenna coming out of their heads. Besides, he didn't really say he was a spaceman in the normal sense. He said something about being a traveller between lives."

Liz looked at her brother mystified.

"Are you sure he's telling the truth and not having you on?" She asked. Jonathan shrugged.

"He says you can come with me to see him next time." He said hoping his sister would believe him if she met him.

"He has all these amazing inventions, and he says he's working on his greatest invention yet. You know, the one I told you about, the light?"

Suddenly Liz became more interested in what her brother was saying.

"I think he wants to show us something, one of his new inventions maybe. And do you know what else?" He elaborated.

"He has these glass orbs that have mini worlds inside them?"

Liz looked at her brother with suspicion.

"He doesn't." She replied not believing him.

"He does so! The Doctor says it's just in case humans make a mess of the planet," argued Jonathan.

"Well, what do they do?" Liz wanted to know as she kept pace with her brother.

"They are like a tiny version of Earth. He says if we humans destroy the planet, he will have all the ingredients to start the world over again."

Liz still wasn't convinced that her brother was telling the truth, but she was quite happy to listen to his tall tales as they walked home together.

A few days later Jonathan invited his sister to accompany him to meet the Doctor. With their parents out at work, it gave them the perfect opportunity to see him.

"He told us we had to bring our rubbish with us and any old junk we had lying about." Jonathan told her as he searched the kitchen cupboards for a fresh refuse sack.

"Why does he want our rubbish?" asked Liz looking puzzled.

"I don't know," he replied as he grabbed the refuse bag from the bin and tied a knot in it.

The pair of them made their way down the garden towards the old tree that hid the gap in the fence. Jonathan threw the refuse sack over and it landed with a thud on the other side.

"Are you sure it's alright to do this, I mean sneak through the fence?" Liz asked hesitantly as she poked her head through the gap.

"Course I am. The Doctor doesn't mind."

With her brother's reassurance, she breathed in and squeezed through the gap. For a brief moment she stood there all alone, looking up at the trees and exotic plants that were festooned with flowers of every different colour.

"It's magical!" She said to her brother as he pushed his head through the gap.

"I've never seen anywhere so beautiful!" She remarked taking a deep breath whilst surveying the carpet of multi-coloured petals that covered the ground.

"It's like a dream," she said as her brother clambered through using her shoulder to steady himself on.

Jonathan led the way through the grounds of the old house, past the rusty old cars, the overgrown tennis court, and on through the bushes to the old greenhouse that lay beyond.

Peering through the glass, they found the Doctor asleep in his thinking room with Ajna curled up on his knee. Giving a loud knock on the glass, they startled the cat, which leapt from the Doctor's lap in fright, rousing the old man from his slumber.

"I was only taking a nap!" The Doctor declared holding his hand up as if guilty of a crime. Motioning to the side door, he opened it and looked at the children with a perplexed expression.

"My goodness, what have you brought me?" he asked spotting the refuse bag.

"You told us to bring our rubbish with us next time we came to visit," replied Jonathan.

"So I did, so I did," recalled the Doctor brushing the biscuit crumbs from his cardigan and offering them a welcoming hand.

"And this must be your sister?" he remarked, adjusting the glasses on his nose so he could see better.

Liz overcome with shyness was unable to bring herself to speak. The Doctor sensing this bent down and held out his hand for Liz to shake.

"Hello, I'm Oban," he said shaking her hand.

"My name's Liz," she replied, blushing ever so slightly.

"Well, don't stand outside. Come in, come in," he said ushering them through the door.

"You can put the rubbish down there," he said instructing the children to leave the refuse sack by the door. Inside, the Doctor excitedly told the children what he had in store for them.

"I've got something rather special planned for the both of you," he declared giddily.

"But first, how about a spot of refreshment, eh? And as I knew you were coming; I've bought a few things especially for you."

The Doctor ushered them through into his thinking room.

"How about a nice glass of pop and a bag of crisps, or perhaps a strawberry milkshake and a biscuit, what do you fancy?" Liz looked to her brother unsure of what to say.

"I'd like a milkshake, please," replied Jonathan.

"And what about you Liz, what would you like?" asked the Doctor. Still too shy to speak Liz grabbed hold of her brother's arm. Recognising she was overcome by shyness; Jonathan spoke on her behalf. "She'll have the same please."

While the Doctor fixed them a drink and put some biscuits on a plate, Liz spent her time studying the doctor carefully.

"What's wrong with you?" whispered Jonathan, noticing that she was staring.

"Is he really an alien?" she whispered making sure the Doctor didn't overhear.

"He doesn't look like one," she added.

The Doctor encouraged Jonathan to pull up an empty tea chest for them to sit on while he settled down in an old wicker chair. By now, Ajna was busy rubbing himself up against their legs in the hope he might get a stroke.

"So, Liz, how do you like my laboratory?" asked the Doctor. Liz didn't say a word as she stared at all the marble statues and the checkerboard floor that seemed to run on into infinity.

"Whatever's the matter?" Sensing that the little girl seemed on edge. Knowing that she was feeling nervous, Jonathan explained what was wrong.

"I told her you were a spaceman and I think she's worried you're some sort of creature from outer space with eight legs and claws."

"Ah-ha, that explains it!" noted the Doctor clapping his hands together and sitting back in his chair, chuckling in amusement.

"Well, Liz if you'd like to know, I'm as human as the next person. It's just that I've lived many, many lives and transcended the far reaches of the universe to be here, in this life as a human being, but in reality, I'm just a silly old fool who likes to help people out, that's all," admitted the Doctor.

Liz looked at him nervously as she took a sip of pink milk from her glass.

"Biscuit, anyone?" asked the Doctor offering the plate around and trying to break the tension.

"If you would like to know…" said the Doctor leaning forward as if confiding in Liz.

"…when I did live on another planet, I had a rather large pear-shaped head and big black glossy eyes. However, I can assure you all traces of my past are now gone. I am a regular human being just like you," he said reassuringly.

"I say, have you seen my latest invention?" asked the Doctor rummaging around the back of his chair as if looking for something.

"Ahh, here we are," he exclaimed pulling out what looked like a half-made jumper.

Silver in colour and catching the light in a remarkable way, the Doctor held up his latest creation for the children to examine.

"See this?" he asked while holding onto a pair of knitting needles.

"This will be what everyone will be wearing in the future. It is what I call my atomic clothing range," he said chuckling away to himself.

"Sounds rather good, doesn't it?" he said winking and leaning over to address Liz personally.

"It's made of thread that is only one atom thick, that's a million times thinner than the hair your head. Not bad, eh?" He said sounding proud of his efforts.

"Now where are my readers? Ahh here they are!" he exclaimed digging out his prescription spectacles from his pocket and slipping them on.

"You see what I have done is atomically scan my entire body to create a pattern to work from…," he said holding the garment up for them to inspect.

"… and if I've got a spare minute to myself, I like to get on with a bit of knitting."

The Doctor leant forward and handed it over for Jonathan to examine as he explained its miraculous properties to him.

"You see it repels dirt and water, and is self-regulating temperature wise, so when you're hot it's cool and when you're cold it keeps you warm… and the thread is made of a synthetic metal polymer so it withstands abrasions; you could fire a bullet at it, and it wouldn't penetrate the material. And as it is an atomically perfect fit, it's all day comfortable and doesn't weigh a thing!" Jonathan held it up against him for size.

"Could you make me one please?" he asked. The Doctor laughed, explaining that it might take some time as it had taken him ten years just to make the thread for this one jumpsuit alone.

As the two children finished their milkshakes, the Doctor encouraged them to put some biscuits in their pockets for later.

"Come on help yourselves, I bought them for you." He said pushing the plate towards them. Getting up from his chair, he then invited them to follow him through to one of the other wings of the greenhouse.

"Now the reason I asked you to bring your rubbish with you was for this." Patting a rather large, shiny stainless-steel drum that sat on the floor.

"You see, I really want you to experience my Fug Munchers at work."

Even though Liz was only seven and had never heard of a Fug Muncher, she thought what the Doctor was saying sounded pretty crazy and gave Jonathan a look that said as much.

"Bear with me, please," the Doctor begged catching her gaze. Taking the clasps off the drum, he removed the lid, and a foul stench. filled the room. Pinching their noses, the children held their breath going all red in the face.

Putting on a big black rubber glove that ran the entire length of his arm, the Doctor went to get the bag of rubbish from outside. Holding it at arm's length, he gently lowered it into the drum, while still holding on to it. The two children peered over the edge.

"Not so close," the Doctor warned.

"When these little blighters get hungry, they'll eat anything," he informed them. Liz and Jonathan took a step back as they watched the Doctor lower the rubbish into the drum. The refuse sack was only part way in when they saw it disappear, reduced to nothing more than a fine dust. The Doctor then lifted out what remained of the bin liner and held it aloft. As they stood there, Jonathan and Liz watched the bag vanish right before their eyes while the Doctor held it at a cautionary arm's length.

"You see, I told you they're veracious little feeders, didn't I?" said the Doctor looking slightly nervous.

"If I let them, they'd eat this entire glove off my arm and the clothes right off my back," he continued.

"So, I think it's prudent if we leave them to it." With that, the Doctor cast what remained of the refuse sack into the drum. Liz then peered in wanting to know what all the noise was.

"Ahh, that my dear are the blessed little Fug Munchers farting and belching away. They are quite repugnant in their manners, but extremely useful at cleaning up after us." The Doctor tittered as he stood back to watch the spectacle.

"Now that's not the only thing I brought you here to see," said the Doctor with a mischievous grin.

"I have something far more astonishing, something that I think you'll like." He said pulling the rubber glove from his hand and discarding it on the bench.

Leading the way, he picked his way through the assorted junk. Then reaching the far end of the greenhouse he stopped and turned to them.

"Now Jonathan, you've seen this before, but Liz I think you're going to love what I'm going to show you."

Opening the door, he stepped down into the darkened room that was the potting shed. At first Liz was nervous, but as her brother made his way down the steps, she followed. The room was pitch black and as she looked up, all she could see were rows upon rows of glowing spheres sat upon shelves. Liz stared in amazement.

"What are they?" she asked, her curiosity overcoming her fear.

"Those, my dear, are my worlds in a bottle," replied the Doctor.

"See I told you I wasn't lying!" crowed Jonathan, pleased to be proved right.

As Liz looked at the rows and rows of beautiful blue glowing orbs, she carefully read the labels under each one.

"Savannah," read one. Then next to that, "Polar Ice cap." then "Mediterranean Garden." Each one containing a miniature eco-system inside.

"I thought you were teasing me," she whispered to her brother.

"What are they?" she asked, her curiosity getting the better of her.

"Ahh, they're my latest invention," The Doctor noted, reaching up and taking one down off the shelf that was full of stars. Jonathan had not seen this particular orb before, and even he was astounded by the Doctor's latest work.

"Beautiful, aren't they?" remarked the Doctor modestly as he set it down on the bench in front of them.

"I have gone one step further with my biospheres. I have started working with the very stars themselves," he said, looking over the top of his glasses at them.

Jonathan and his sister were speechless as they watched the magnificent beauty of a galaxy full of stars slowly revolve inside a glass bottle.

"Truly stunning, isn't it? There is no other word for it." The Doctor said as he wistfully looked on.

"If only the rest of humanity could see this, I'm sure they'd be moved to tears too," he added going misty eyed.

The three of them stood there in silence for a moment as they watched the movement of the heavens take place before their very eyes. The Doctor, taking a handkerchief from his pocket, removed his glasses to dab at his eyes.

"Do forgive me…" he said to the children.

"…but I get a bit teary when I see the true nature of creation revealed in all its glory. It really is quite something to behold is it not?" he said putting his glasses back on and making a sniffing sound with his nose before giving it a good blow. After regaining his composure and examining the contents of his handkerchief, he then explained that he had something else that he wanted to show them.

"I think you might like this," he said rummaging around under the bench. Pulling out an old newspaper, he let it drop on to the concrete floor. Then with great care he removed one of the spheres from the shelf and set it down on top of the newspaper. Urging the children to sit down, he insisted they sit in a circle.

"That's it, circles are good; it's what the universe is made up of,"

he said to the mystified looking children, who did not have a clue what he was talking about.

Unsure of what was expected of them, they gathered round the globe with their legs crossed.

"I'd like to teach you something," said the Doctor in a hushed voice, as he shuffled around on his bottom.

"I'd like to show you how you can make the universe work for you,"

Liz and her brother looked at each other and then at the Doctor, wondering what on earth he was talking about.

"You see, each of us is a tiny part of this magnificent whole, and although we are all different, we are all the same," the Doctor explained.

"And as you are part of the very stuff the universe is made up of, you can attract the universe to you, but only if you're a kind-hearted person," he said shuffling around with his legs crossed trying to get comfortable.

"Here," he said, nodding to the bowl.

"I have what I call my Boreal Forest biosphere. It's one of my favourites!" he declared with a twinkle in his eye.

Jonathan and Liz leaned forward and peered in. It seemed like there were a thousand thin, needle-like pine trees clamouring for space.

"Do you know why I like my Boreal Forest biosphere so much?" The children shook their heads.

"You see, although there are thousands of trees here, and they all stand on their own, and all look different, underneath they are all connected by the same root system; they are all one, they are all interlinked," the Doctor let on with a secretive smile.

"And, say if one tree is not getting enough water, it sends out a message to all the other trees and they transport water to help it survive. They're all interconnected, you see; they can talk to each other through their root system. Pretty impressive huh, don't you agree?" said the Doctor. Jonathan and his sister had to agree.

"Anyway, back to making the universe work for you!" said the Doctor shaking his shoulders loose as if in preparation for something big.

"What we want to do is encourage it to snow inside this biosphere. You could say it's a bit like doing a rain dance," he said tapping on the side of the glass with his long, thin finger.

"But in order to do that, we first we must clear our heads of everything." Sitting there on the cold concrete floor, Liz and Jonathan shook all their thoughts from their mind.

"What we then do is ask the universe to make it snow for us. Now you can't demand that the universe does this as it doesn't work that way; it is more like a partnership, do you understand? So, let's close our eyes." Jonathan and Liz looked at each other, unsure as to what the Doctor was telling them was the truth, but they went along with it anyway.

For what seemed like an age, they sat in the dark with their eyes closed and every so often Jonathan would take a peek. With nothing happening, Liz got bored and opened her eyes to find the Doctor still sitting there with his legs crossed. After some shuffling about on her bottom, the Doctor finally stirred, coming to with a sigh.

"Has anything happened yet?" he asked looking over at his two companions. The children both shook their heads in reply.

"Patience," he said with a sage-like grin. Then Liz thought she noticed something.

"What's that?" she called out as her brother huddled over the globe to see better.

"Just as I thought," announced the Doctor with a smile.

"It's snowing!" Liz was unable to believe that the power of thought alone had managed to do this.

Inside the biosphere, big white fluffy clouds dumped handfuls of snow onto the stunted trees covering them in a fine, white blanket, just like icing sugar.

"It's amazing!" declared Jonathan congratulating the Doctor.

"The best is yet to come; just you wait and see."

Jonathan and his sister sat there mesmerised as they watched the marvellous scene unfold. It was then that Liz noticed something happening to the globe.

"Look, it's changing colour!" she said unable to believe what was taking place.

Around the top of the biosphere, a light began to slowly pulse and resonate with a multitude of colours as they gasped with excitement.

"What's that?" asked Liz looking to the Doctor for an explanation. The Doctor smiled back.

"That is the Aurora Borealis my dear, or as it's more commonly known the northern lights." Jonathan leant over and gently tapped the Doctor on the elbow.

"Did you do this?" he asked. The Doctor shook his head.

"No. *WE* did this," he answered emphasising that they had all played a part in this.

"It's magic!" declared Liz. The Doctor laughed shaking his head.

"Magic," he uttered with a genial smile.

"There we go with that word again. That's all we ever hear these days: it's magic 'this' and magic 'that.'" He laughed chuckling away to himself.

"I prefer to call it what it actually is, and that is higher-level consciousness,"

"What's consciousness?" asked Liz looking bemused.

"It's what we all are, my dear. It's what everything is made up of; it's like water," the Doctor explained in a down-to-earth manner.

"It fills the many shapes that are here on this planet, from the birds and the trees to the rocks and the animals, even the very earth that we walk upon, including us. It is all one giant energy field," said the Doctor putting his hand on the young girl's shoulder. Then with the squint of a wise old sage, he further elaborated.

"Magic suggests that we don't understand what's going on. When all we are doing is projecting our consciousness on to what we call reality," he added giving the children a knowing wink.

"You see when you have sat for as long a time as I have, you become aware that the universe is not as rigid as it would first seem. Reality can be rather bendy, rather malleable in fact, and all sorts of weirdness and high strangeness can occur."

"Like what?" asked Jonathan. The Doctor leant back on the shelf behind him and gave Jonathan a knowing smile.

"Like all sorts of odd things…" he said tapping the side of his nose as if he had a thousand and one secrets up his sleeve.

"… and *I* can tell that you two have got the magic in you," nodding in the direction of the children.

"Us…really?" asked Jonathan, in disbelief.

"Course you have! Both you and your sister have what we say…a *glow* about you," he noted as he searched for the right word to best describe what he wanted to say.

With his legs crossed and his face illuminated by the faint glimmer of the light from the globe, the Doctor leant forward.

"Now you see, when you have the glow, you can't go around telling everybody, do you understand? It has to be a secret." The two children gave a solemn nod to say they understood.

"…I bet the pair of you can read each other's thoughts, can't you? And I bet you know what each other is thinking, right?" he asked, leaning forward. The children looked at each other and nodded.

"I thought as much," said the Doctor chuckling happily away to himself. Putting his arms around them, he brought them into his confidence.

"Look, things will be different for the both of you," he said.

"As you grow up, you will begin to notice that the glow becomes more apparent, and you will be able to do things that not everybody else can. It's nothing to worry about, it's just higher-level consciousness at work *or* 'magic' as everyone likes to call it,"

"You see, some people can build houses, some people can make furniture and some people drive buses; it's no different from that… it's just you'll have a special talent that not very many people will have seen that's all.

"However…" He said raising his eyebrows.

"…some people can get funny about it and that's why you have to be careful who knows about your glow."

"What we have to keep it a secret, right?" said Liz making sure she understood.

"That's right, but it doesn't mean you have to hide your glow completely; just be careful of how you use it that's all. I have a glow all of my very own…" added Oban.

"…and I use it to create all of my amazing inventions. That way I can help the world and so can you."

~5~

How to Make
a Biosphere

IT WAS DARK as Jonathan lay in his bed staring up at the ceiling. Well past midnight his parents had long since gone to bed when he heard a noise coming from the Doctors house. He knew it meant that the light was soon going to show itself and he wanted his sister to see it for herself.

Pulling back the covers, he popped on his slippers and wrapped his dressing gown round him. Making his way silently downstairs, he opened the door to his sister's bedroom and crept in. Gently shaking her by the shoulders, she awoke. Surprised to see her brother standing there she knew not to make a sound when she saw him with his finger pressed to his lips.

"What's the matter?" she whispered sleepily.

"I thought you might want to come and see the Doctor's new invention…" said Jonathan keeping his voice low. Liz nodded and got out of bed. Helping her on with her dressing gown, they crept past their parent's room and tiptoed upstairs.

Peering out into the night, they could hear a low rumble coming from next-door. Liz wanted to know what it was. Jonathan told her it was the Doctors new, earth-shattering invention. After several minutes the vibrations grew so strong that they were coming through the floor and shaking the very foundations of the house. Liz thought the house was going to fall down. Then, with a rush of energy the trees outside began to thrash about wildly and the vibrations could now be felt in their chest.

"Wait till you see this," Jonathan told her excitedly. Liz pulled up a chair so she could see better.

"What are we looking for?"

"You'll see," said Jonathan nudging her with anticipation, excited for his sister to witness what he had seen.

Patiently they waited, then in the distance they glimpsed a light cutting through the trees. No bigger than a beach ball, it gave out a terrific light, like that of the sun. So bright was it that they had to shield their eyes from its brilliance, only daring to look at it for a second. It was so amazing that around the edges all the colours of the rainbow shimmered this way and that, glowing as if it were on fire.

Then with a sudden explosion of energy, the light shot up into the night sky and spread out across the horizon as far as the eye could see. It was as if night had turned to day, making the whole world come alive.

"Wow! It's amazing," said Liz, who was astonished by what she saw.

More colours than she could ever imagine raced across the sky like someone had taken a giant bolt of electricity and mixed it with an artist's palette. She could barely contain herself she was so overcome with excitement. The sky turned all the colours of the rainbow, flashing the most amazing light. It was so unique and brilliant that it was hard to describe the miraculous event.

However, the experience did not last long. As suddenly it appeared it disappeared as if nothing had ever happened.

"Wow, what was that?" asked Liz, barely able to believe what she had seen.

"It's the Doctors new invention, it happens every night, like magic," her brother told her.

"But what do you think it is?" she asked, her eyes as large as saucers. Jonathan shrugged, unsure of what it could possibly be.

"I don't know, but whatever it is the Doctor says it is going to change the world," he said trying to shed some light on the true nature of the Doctor's invention.

"What if it's something to make people happy?" his sister suggested, taking a wild guess.

"Maybe…" he said wondering if his sister's theory was correct.

With nothing more to see, Jonathan led his sister back to bed.

"I'll never be able to sleep after that; it was fantastic," she whispered keeping her voice down. Jonathan smiled, holding his sister's hand as he helped her down the stairs. Even in the dark, Jonathan could tell she was excited.

The following day after school they made their way over to the Doctor's house, having been invited to partake in one of his experiments.

"Do you think he wants to show us his new invention, the one we saw last night?" asked Liz squeezing through the gap in the fence.

"I don't know," replied Jonathan.

"No one is supposed to know about it, so you better not mention it!" he said, hastily making his way through the gap in the fence.

The Doctor was in his laboratory when they called on him. Wearing his white lab coat, he was busy mixing chemicals and playing with strange-looking scientific equipment, creating all sorts of interesting concoctions.

"Aah, there you are!" he beamed, stopping what he was doing and bounding over to greet them.

"I'm glad you came round. I've something rather special for you!" Liz's ears immediately pricked up. Was he going to show them his super-secret invention that they had witnessed last night? The Doctor however had other things on his mind.

"Tell me, who fancies making a biosphere?" he asked, looking for volunteers. Jonathan's hand shot up like a rocket.

"And what about you Liz, do you fancy making a biosphere?" Hiding her disappointment that she wasn't going to find out about the light she still managed to raise a smile and give a polite nod.

"What fun we're going to have!" declared the Doctor throwing one of his magic potions into the flame of a Bunsen burner, and letting it explode like a firework.

Then, issuing them with two white, oversized lab coats and a set of safety goggles each, the Doctor began sizing up the right sort of glass bowl for his experiment.

"Let's see, what have we got here," he muttered to himself as he scrabbled around on his hands and knees under the bench, rummaging through a bunch of cardboard boxes.

"This should do," he said pulling out two dusty-looking goldfish-sized bowls from underneath the bench. Getting to his feet, he then turned to the children.

"Right, it's time we made scientists of you," he said standing in front of them with a big grin on his face and brushing off the fluff from his knees.

He then handed Jonathan a shovel while he found himself an empty bucket.

"First, we need some good old-fashioned muck. There's nothing like a bit of muck to get things going, is there?" The two children looked blankly at each other.

Leading them out into the garden, and whistling as he went, he cast his eye over the ruinous garden as he sought out some suitable earth for his experiment.

"Here!" he declared, digging his heel in the ground. Jonathan placed the shovel where the Doctor instructed him. Then putting all his weight on the spade, the blade disappeared into the ground. With a bit of wiggling and to'ing and fro'ing, Jonathan lifted out a shovel full of soil and deposited it in the doctor's bucket.

"That should do, my dear boy," he said with a giddy smile, patting him on the back.

Carrying the bucket back inside, the Doctor instructed Jonathan to leave the spade by the door. As he fiddled around with his equipment, he asked the children if they knew what type of biosphere they would like to make.

"You can make anything you want, anything at all," said the Doctor inviting them to be inspired by the world around them. Immediately, Jonathan blurted out that he wanted to make a galaxy full of stars after having seen the one in the Doctor's potting shed. Dr Fife looked at him over the top of his glasses.

"I thought you might; they're pretty impressive, aren't they?" he said knowing full well what an impact a bottle full of stars had over a young mind.

"And what about you Liz, what would you like to make?" Liz didn't know and stood there thinking. To help her the Doctor gave her a little encouragement.

"Tell me what's your favourite animal in the whole wide world, eh?" he asked. Liz put her finger to her lips as she thought.

"I like parrots, they're my favourite animal," she replied.

"Then parrots it is!" the Doctor cheered.

"What do you fancy, an outback biosphere or a rainforest biosphere as they both have parrots?"

"A rainforest!" replied an eager Liz.

Springing into action, the Doctor cleared away a whole host of junk that was lying about and sorted out a couple of stools for the children to sit on. With their safety goggles on, they awaited their instructions.

"Right," began the Doctor.

"First, we need to sieve all this dirt before we can start," he told them as he handed them a sieve a piece.

"This is the first step in the process of making any orb. Muck is essential to any experiment. It holds everything needed for life," he told them.

After Liz and Jonathan had thoroughly sieved the soil, the Doctor inspected it before sticking it in his microwave.

"That's it, we need to kill off any of those nasty bugs that might be lurking in there," he said as the microwave pinged and he removed a plateful of hot steaming earth. Carefully weighing it out into two glass petri dishes, he then broke into song.

'Think…think of a circle,'

'A circle so radiant and bright'

'A circle so full of life'

'Mix it with some light, a touch of zing, a bit of bling'

Liz and Jonathan both looked at each other; wondering if the Doctor was feeling alright, but as he looked okay, they didn't want to stop him mid-song to ask.

'Take a pinch of life, a spot of fun!'

'Some nucleic acid and see what's begun,'

'A dash of protein and then it's done, and hey presto be amazed with what has become.'

Singing and dancing merrily around his laboratory with jars of chemicals in his hands, he leapt sprightly into the air. To finish, the Doctor then threw in half a can of fizzy pop, some mints, and a whole load of baking soda into the glass bowls.

Bubbling away, the mixture frothed, boiled, and spat over the lip of the bowl forming a giant foam bath in the laboratory. Liz and Jonathan found it highly amusing as the foam spilt onto the floor and crept along between the benches. Fighting his way through the waist high foam the Doctor then handed a test tube full of clear liquid over to Liz.

"What's this?" she asked.

"This is the exact ratio of proteins, carbohydrates and amino acids that will give us a beautiful rainforest. Now don't spill it," he advised her.

"Otherwise, we'll have trees and bushes growing everywhere." Liz looked at him dubiously.

"No, really," nodded the Doctor. "It's potent stuff this," he added as he handed over the test tube.

Meanwhile, Jonathan watched transfixed as the gases inside his biosphere made beautiful, marbled patterns. Pressing his nose up to the glass, he could see tiny sparks of light suddenly coming to life.

"What are those?" he asked as the Doctor came rushing over to his side.

"Those, those are nebulae forming... they are the very place from where stars are born," he told him.

Like fireworks, they fizzed and popped into existence, flashing brightly before exploding into astonishing supernovae. The Doctor, as if he had something to tell them, beckoned for the two children to lean in closer.

"Now, they tell you that this is where all life comes from, these fantastical, wondrous stars, but they're wrong," he whispered in a secretive manner.

"Nothing comes into existence without this," said the Doctor tapping the side of his head.

"Thoughts you see, conscience! It's what I was telling you about before." The children could tell the Doctor was excited by this as his voice ever so slightly trembled as he talked about it.

"You see, you can have all these chemicals swirling about the universe, but without thoughts they are nothing. It's thought that gives them shape," he marvelled.

"Remember that I told you that the universe is made of circles?" said the Doctor jogging their memory.

"Well, in order to make a fully functioning biosphere, we have to think of circles, beautiful circles, like that of a kaleidoscope – all overlapping," he said pulling up a spare stool and sitting down in between them.

"So, let's just sit here for a moment and think, think of those circles and how marvellous we want our biospheres to be."

Taking hold of the children by the hand the Doctor closed his eyes encouraging them to do the same. The three of them sat there in silence until the Doctor let out a long-drawn-out sigh.

"Ahhhh, I think our job here is done," he said letting go of their hands.

"Now that we've injected a little bit of amazingness into our experiments,

I think we should have ourselves a couple of fully functioning biospheres," he said proudly, rolling down his sleeves and buttoning up his cuffs.

"But there is one thing I must warn you about..." he said, straightening his collar and smoothing out the creases in his lab coat.

"...and I cannot stress how important this is." He continued to caution them.

"Once we've put the tops on these bowls, you MUST NEVER take them off or drop them. Otherwise, we could end up with all sorts of disastrous consequences," he said, raising his finger in the air as if to emphasise his point.

"Why, what could happen?" asked Jonathan innocently.

"Oh, you don't to even want to think about it!" replied the Doctor, shaking his head.

"A black hole could escape and swallow up everything and I mean everything. Just imagine you and your whole house disappearing in the blink of an eye along with the rest of the street and the entire planet. That's why I'm entrusting these to you for their safekeeping. Remember they're not everyday playthings," he warned.

With enough fun for one day, the Doctor cast aside his lab coat and put on his old, threadbare cardigan before giving Liz a hand down off her stool.

Helping Liz with her biosphere, the Doctor carried it under his arm while she held the door open for them.

"I'll let you out of the front gate. You'll never get through that gap in the fence with these," said the Doctor holding the glass flask under his arm and rummaging around in his pocket for his keys. Leading the way, Jonathan was careful not to trip up, remembering what the Doctor had said could happen if the bottles were to be opened or smashed.

Putting the globe down and balancing it on top of a pile of old leaves, the Doctor took hold of the padlock and with one quick twist of the key, the chains swung loose around the gates.

"Now remember..." said the Doctor as he pulled aside the rusted gate.

"NEVER, and I can't stress this enough, NEVER leave the top off the biospheres – is that understood?" The two children looked up at the Doctor.

"We promise," they both replied.

"Good, that's what I like to hear."

The Doctor held the gate open for them as they squeezed through with their precious cargo. As he locked the gates behind them, he called out to them.

"Keep an eye on them; you should notice some results in about a week or so," The children thanked the Doctor and made their way home.

As they pushed the front door open Jonathan called out to his mother, careful to make sure she did not see what they were carrying. Fortunately for them, she was upstairs busy in her study.

"Dinner won't be long," she called out as she peered over the top of her glasses at her computer, too busy to notice what the children were up to. Creeping across the landing, the children scurried into Liz's room where once inside they were safe from their mother's prying eyes.

Breathing a sigh of relief, Jonathan asked his sister where she thought they should keep them.

"We don't want Mum and Dad to know that we've got them, do we?" she said, realising how much trouble they would get in if their parents found out they had a super massive black hole in their house.

"Why don't we hide them under our beds?" she suggested. After giving Liz a hand to hide her biosphere, Jonathan sneaked upstairs to hide his own.

The following morning as he got ready for school, he took a peek at his new galaxy before rushing downstairs for breakfast. That was when he overheard his parents talking in the kitchen.

"Colin, I'm not sure that our children should be spending so much time with a strange man who we haven't met," he heard his mother say. Hesitating Jonathan clung to the handrail at the bottom of the stairs while eavesdropping on their conversation.

"I don't know what all the big fuss is about, Carol. The neighbours seem to think he's harmless enough and wouldn't hurt a fly."

"All the same I'm not sure about letting our children spend time with him," he heard his mother say.

"Yeah, but the kids seem to enjoy being with him and he seems to be good for them."

"That's not the point," she said her voice now beginning to grow louder.

Jonathan, perched on the bottom step, listened intently to their conversation, worried that his parents might want to stop them from seeing the Doctor.

"Well, why don't we invite him over, then you can check him out?" suggested his dad who was immediately interrupted by his mother.

"We can't just knock on his door and say, 'by the way we would like you to come round to our house so we can vet your suitability to be with our children, and make sure you're not an axe murderer,'" his mother snapped.

"Why not?" quipped his father, who was more interested in getting his breakfast.

"You're not taking this seriously, are you?" complained his mother, giving Jonathan's father a hard stare.

"Look, why don't we invite him round for dinner one evening? That way we can say it's a housewarming party and it doesn't sound strange. He gets a nice meal, and we get to check him out. How does that sound?" suggested his dad. To Jonathan, that seemed to be a good idea.

Coughing loudly and making his presence known, Jonathan entered the kitchen. Acting as if nothing had happened, his mother pushed her hair behind her ear and asked what he wanted for breakfast.

"We were just talking, weren't we?" said his dad looking over at Jonathan's mother.

"We thought it might be nice if we invite the Doctor over for dinner, what do you think?" Jonathan said nothing; he just gave a polite nod and a mutter of agreement. Inside he was secretly pleased that they hadn't banned him from seeing the Doctor.

"Your mum will write the invitation, and you can take it over to him," his father added.

"That's right," his mother agreed.

"That way, we can get to meet our new neighbour," she remarked pleased at getting her own way, and unaware that Jonathan had overheard the entire conversation.

As the week went by, Jonathan kept a check on his biosphere. After the initial chaos, everything was beginning to settle down in his galaxy;

however, Liz's rainforest was a different story: everything was romping away, and things were beginning to sprout out everywhere.

"Jonathan come and look at my orb," said his sister from round the corner of her bedroom door. After checking that the coast was clear Jonathan slipped inside and got down on his hands and knees as he slid under the bed.

"Look at this," she whispered with her finger to her lips. Jonathan looked closely at the glass sphere.

Glowing blue, hot humid clouds billowed up from the jungle floor while the entire surface of the orb had been taken over by a green carpet of towering trees and vines that pushed their way towards the light.

"It's amazing, isn't it?" said his sister. Jonathan didn't know what to say; he was taken aback by how much it had grown. From nothing it had turned into a full-fledged biosphere in little over a week.

As they lay in the darkness underneath her bed, Jonathan let his sister in on what he had overheard.

"You know Mum and Dad want to meet the Doctor,"

"Why?" asked his sister.

"Well, they think he might be a bit weird or something, and they're not sure they want us seeing him."

"Well, he is a bit weird, isn't he?" came his sister's reply.

"Yeah, but he's not 'weird' weird if you know what I mean; he's 'nice' weird," said Jonathan jumping to the Doctor's defence.

"Whatever we do we can't let on that the Doctor's…you know…different," said Jonathan searching for the right word to best describe him.

"You mean we can't tell them he's a spaceman?"

"No, we definitely can't tell them he's a spaceman or we'll never be allowed to see him ever again, and that'll be the end of our globes…and you don't want that to happen, do you?" he said stressing the seriousness of the situation. Liz thought about it, and although the Doctor was not like ordinary people she knew, she didn't want her parents to judge him just because he was different.

-6-

WHAT A CALAMITY

I T WAS SATURDAY evening round at the Bawtry household and everyone was settled in front of the TV, eating boiled eggs, toasty soldiers
and crumpets with jam. Asking to be excused, Liz went upstairs to wash
her hands when something grabbed her attention. Feeling like she was being watched, she turned around, and there sat on the landing was a jaguar
looking directly at her.

Liz rubbed her eyes just to make sure she wasn't seeing things. With
its coat a resplendent gold and covered with a multitude of black spots, the
jaguar stood there staring intently at her. Unable to believe what she was
seeing, she rushed downstairs, checking over her shoulder to make sure she
was not being followed. Back In the living room everyone was gathered
round the TV. Trying not to draw attention to herself, she sat down on the
sofa next to her brother.

"Jonathan," she whispered in his ear.

"I need you to come with me, it's urgent!"

"But I'm watching TV," Jonathan protested unaware of his sister's predicament. Liz tugged at his arm.

"No, this is really serious," she said, motioning with her eyes for him
to meet her outside. It was then that her brother realised there must be
something wrong.

Making their excuses, they left the room, their parents barely noticing
they were gone. Once outside, Liz was desperate to tell her brother what
she had seen on the landing.

"Don't say anything but I think something's happened to my biosphere."

"Like what?" asked Jonathan, immediately sensing something was not right.

"Well…there's something upstairs." Motioned Liz, wincing as if she knew she was in trouble.

"Why, what is it?" asked her brother who was becoming increasingly suspicious that there was a problem.

"There's a jaguar upstairs on the landing!" she whispered.

"A what?" he remarked.

Grabbing him by the wrist, she dragged him upstairs to see for himself. When they reached the very top, she poked her head over the lip of the step, but there was nothing to be seen.

"It was here a minute ago!" she said looking for signs of the animal.

"What would a jaguar be doing here?" asked her brother trying to get to the bottom of it.

"I didn't mean to," she confessed.

"Didn't mean to what? Why, what have you done?" Asked Jonathan, who could tell something was wrong.

"I only wanted a parrot," she said with her bottom lip out.

"You didn't leave the top off the biosphere, did you?" said Jonathan sensing at what might have happened.

"What did the Doctor tell you? He said NEVER leave the top off your biosphere, didn't he?" snapped Jonathan despairingly.

"I thought I'd put the top back on, but I must have left it off." Jonathan shook his head. Then from over his shoulder, he heard a roar come from their parents' bedroom.

"What was that?" he squealed taking cover behind the handrail on the stairs. There was little point blaming his sister now as they had something bigger to deal with. There was a fully grown jungle cat in their parents' bedroom.

Now Jonathan was not the bravest of people, but he knew they were going to have to lock the jaguar in his parents' bedroom if they stood any chance of solving this problem.

With his legs quivering and his tummy doing flip flops, Jonathan dug deep and gathered his courage. Quietly he crept across the landing. Peeking through the gap in the door, he could see the animal laid out on his parents' bed taking a nap. Slowly, without making any noise, he pulled the door shut and breathed a sigh of relief. It was then as he tip-toed across the landing that he got an even bigger shock.

Rooted to the spot he motioned for his sister to join him. When she saw what he was looking at, she didn't know what to say.

There in her bedroom were giant trees, plants and creepers sprouting out everywhere. The trees were so big that they had pushed through the ceiling and were sticking out of the roof so daylight could be seen through the missing tiles.

"Oh crumbs, we're done for now!" moaned Jonathan putting his head in his hands. He knew they were going to be in serious trouble if their parents found out. There was no way on earth that they could hide all this mess.

Trying to recover from his despair his gaze was met by a large, orange-shelled snail that was making his way up the door frame. Liz tapped her bother on the arm. In her bedroom a flock of red and green parrots were circling the room.

All this commotion wasn't just confined to the bedroom. There were now animals everywhere. Hummingbirds were darting this way and that. A bird of paradise was roosting on the handrail that ran up to Jonathan's bedroom, a sloth clung to the banister. There was even a troop of golden lion tamarins drinking from the toilet bowl in the bathroom and a toucan was perched on the windowsill. Jonathan watched on in horror as a giant anteater made its way across the landing flicking its tongue back and forth.

Every second that they stood there, more animals were beginning to appear, and it wasn't just animals that were the problem; there were plants invading too.

Realising the enormity of their problem, Jonathan knew there was only one way they were going to resolve this problem.

"We're going to have to get the Doctor!"

"How are we going to keep it a secret though?" Liz wanted to know as she looked around at all the animals that were now taking over the house.

"Look!" said Jonathan grasping her firmly by the shoulders.

"Whatever you do, you've got to keep Mum and Dad in the front room. You can't let them find this lot, otherwise we'll be in more trouble than you could ever imagine." Aware of the desperate state of things, Liz rushed downstairs to keep her parents from finding the truth.

Meanwhile Jonathan ran as fast as his legs would carry him. Out the back door, down the garden, through the gap in the fence and through the tangle of overgrown bushes as he made his way over to the Doctor's house. Peering through the window of the library he found him seated on the floor with his legs crossed and eyes closed. Jonathan knocked loudly on the glass, but the Doctor did not respond. It looked like he was asleep. Banging and shouting as hard as he could, he saw him casually open one eye and then the other. Realising the urgency etched on Jonathan's face, the Doctor slowly rose from his position of repose and made his way towards the back door.

Out of breath, Jonathan ran around to the kitchen door where he was greeted by Ajna and the Doctor, who was surprised to see him at such a late hour on a Saturday evening.

"Good heavens, whatever seems to be the matter?" the Doctor asked.

"Lots of animals and plants have escaped and they've taken over the house," he gasped with barely time to catch his breath. The Doctor calmly took his glasses off and gave them a rub on the corner of his cardigan.

"And what sort of animals are we talking about?" he enquired placing his glasses back on his nose.

"Big ones. Ones with teeth!" He told him. Jonathan was by now getting frustrated by the Doctor's lack of urgency and begged him to come quickly.

"All in good time my dear boy. Let's not rush things,"

"Liz wanted a parrot as a pet you see…" Jonathan explained.

"…and she left the top off her biosphere and now all the animals have escaped!" Jonathan told him hoping that the Doctor was not going to be too mad at him.

"Ahh…now I see," replied the Doctor calmly.

"Now I'm not going to admonish you as that would be a pointless task and it doesn't solve anything. What we must do is sort out this incident as quickly and quietly as possible. Are your parents aware?" Jonathan shook his head to say no.

"Good, good," nodded the Doctor.

"Well, that's the way we like to keep it, eh?" he said giving Jonathan a wink.

"Grownups only get in the way of things and blow things out of all proportion, I find," he added as if he had an inside knowledge of the strange workings of parents.

"If you just bear with me one minute while I get my jacket on, I'll be right with you."

Jonathan couldn't wait that long and knew that with every second they wasted the animals would be wandering about the house unhindered, getting into all sorts of trouble.

"Can't we hurry up?" asked Jonathan hopping from one foot to the other with impatience. The Doctor looked at him as he put his arms through his jacket.

"I don't think a few seconds here or there is going to make much difference, do you?"

Appearing at the door in his tweed jacket, the Doctor signalled that he was ready.

"Don't you need any of your special equipment with you, you know your science stuff?" Jonathan quizzed him. The Doctor calmly turned to him.

"Science is only half of it my boy, what we need is a bit of magic," winked the Doctor with a twinkle in his eye.

"I thought you didn't approve of the word magic?" remarked Jonathan recalling what the Doctor's feelings were on the matter.

"There are times when a bit of theatricality is called for. Anyway, let's go, we haven't got all evening, have we?"

Squeezing through the gap in the fence, the Doctor followed closely behind as they made for Jonathan's home. For an old man, the Doctor was surprisingly sprightly and had no problem keeping up with Jonathan's young legs. Pushing the back door open, Jonathan put his finger to his lips signalling for the Doctor to be quiet. Tiptoeing stealthily past the living room where his parents were watching TV, the Doctor followed him upstairs. Reaching the top of the of landing, the Doctor was taken aback.

"My, my…it has turned out rather well, hasn't it?" he commented as a toucan landed on his shoulder and an anteater wandered past sniffing at his socks. The Doctor tucked his thumbs behind the lapels of his jacket with a proud smile.

"The good thing about this mess is at least we know my biospheres work. Just in case there is ever an emergency here on earth," Tugging at the corner of his jacket, Jonathan tried to get the Doctor's attention.

"There's a jaguar in my parents' room," he told him nervously.

"Is there now?" replied the Doctor with a raised eyebrow.

"How are we going to get rid of it?" Jonathan wanted to know, sounding somewhat distressed by the whole situation.

"Don't you go worrying about that mi' laddie," replied the Doctor.

"We'll use a bit o' this!" he answered, tapping the side of his head and looking to Jonathan for a prompt.

"Errr…higher-level consciousness?" stammered Jonathan.

"Correct!" remarked the Doctor, raising his finger in the air as if signifying a light bulb moment.

"We'll have no problem making them disappear, for they are just projections upon our own consciousness. But first, we will need more than just the two of us. We'll need the help of your sister too; after all, we'll be using some serious thought power for this!"

Jonathan rushed downstairs and burst into the front room drawing the attention of the whole family upon him.

"Where have you been?" enquired his mother demanding an answer.

"Nowhere, just upstairs in my bedroom," he said without hesitation.

"Well, you're missing your programme you know," she added, looking over her shoulder and flicking her hair behind her ear in an irritated manner.

Standing in the doorway, Jonathan stared intently at his sister. Sensing her brother's gaze, Liz got up off the floor saying that she needed to go to the bathroom.

"What is it with you two tonight, can't you sit still?" moaned their mother.

"Oh, leave them to it," replied their father turning down the TV.

"They're not doing any harm."

"What do you mean they're not doing any harm. I know what children are like. I'm an educator and I know when they are up to something!" said their mother.

"Well, whatever they're up to I'm quite happy to leave them to it." answered their father as he turned up the TV.

Outside in the corridor Liz was desperate to know if Jonathan had managed to get hold of the Doctor.

"He's upstairs waiting for us," he told her.

"He says he needs some more thought power to sort this problem out."

"Has he seen my room yet?" she asked as they made their way upstairs. The Doctor, however had overheard what had just been said

"What's this?" he enquired; his interest now piqued. Jonathan explained that his sister's room now resembled a jungle.

"My oh my, I must see this!" he grinned rubbing his hands together with glee. Taking a peek behind the door, the Doctor slowly pushed the handle down and opened the door ever so slightly, letting out a silent gasp.

"What a magnificent sight!" he muttered breathlessly as he peered into the room. With Jonathan and Liz hanging on his coat tails, they too stuck their head round the corner of the door.

The entirety of her bedroom was now covered with a thick layer of plants in every shade of green imaginable. Trees that would have taken many lifetimes to grow were now pushing their way through the ceiling, and the din from all the chirping insects was almost deafening.

"Marvellous, absolutely marvellous!" grinned the Doctor from ear to ear, hardly able to contain himself.

"It takes my breath away to see the resilience of nature," he said, overcome with emotion.

"But what about my bedroom?" pleaded Liz.

"Ah yes…that, right then let's get down to business," he said closing the door gently behind him and straightening his bow tie.

"First, we need to make sure that all the animals are here. We don't want any wandering off downstairs, do we now?" said the Doctor clearing his throat.

"Can I keep a parrot as a pet?" pleaded Liz.

"I'm afraid not. We must be like the wind; we cannot seem to have been here at all. Otherwise, your parents will begin to suspect something."

Loosening his bow tie and hanging up his jacket on the balustrade, the Doctor kicked off his shoes.

"First, let's get down to business, eh?" he said as he sat down at the top of the landing, shooing a resting monkey off the lampshade.

Stretching his arms and clicking out the joints in his fingers, he encouraged the children to sit down in a circle next to him.

"Right," he declared in an authoritative tone.

"I want you to think of absolutely nothing; the more nothingness the better," he said as he sat back, closed his eyes and relaxed. It was hard for Jonathan and Liz to do the same as they were not used to having a house full of strange animals wandering about.

After some time, Jonathan was getting worried and was hoping that the Doctor was going to hurry up, sure that his parents would be getting suspicious.

With no choice, but to resign themselves to the Doctor's wishes, the children closed their eyes and focused on nothing. They sat there with not a single thought passing through their heads and then out of the complete and utter nothingness they felt something. Something incredible, as if the universe was talking to them. Like clouds being blown away on a stormy day, the nature of the universe revealed itself to them as a beautiful blue sky.

Jonathan opened his eyes and found to his astonishment that all the animals had disappeared; not one was left. The Doctor let out a long sigh like a deflated balloon, as Liz peered round at an empty landing.

"Have they gone?" she asked her brother. Jonathan nodded and then pointed to the Doctor.

"I'd better take him home though. We don't want mum and dad to find him." Nodding to the Doctor who looked like he was dead. Eager to wake him up, Jonathan gave him a gentle nudge.

"Doctor are you awake?" asked Jonathan. The Doctor did not respond.

"Doctor," said Jonathan one more time trying to wake him up by giving him a good shake. The Doctor let out a deep sigh, one that seemed to come from the very pit of his stomach, which scared the life out of the children.

"Are we done?" he gasped, coming to with a start. Liz nodded.

Taking a look around, he was pleased with his efforts.

"Looks like we've done our job here, eh?" he chirped, slipping his shoes back on and putting his arms through the sleeves of his jacket.

"However, I think the concrete test is if we take a peek inside your room, what do you say Liz?" The Doctor then opened the door.

Gently, the door swept against the soft carpet and to the children's astonishment, the room was back to the way it was before the biosphere had spilled out into the room. There were no holes in the roof, no giant plants, no vines trying to escape and best of all there were no birds flying about and no wild animals.

"That's better," declared the Doctor with a satisfied smile. Scurrying under her bed, Liz went to check on the biosphere. Pulling the glass jar out, she was surprised to see that it was completely empty, and everything had disappeared.

"Ah…just as I thought, we have returned everything to its original form, that of nothingness," said the Doctor with a look of relief on his face.

Opening the door to his parents' room, Jonathan peeked cautiously round the corner. To his relief, the jaguar was gone and all that was left was a large imprint on the bed where it had been laid out. So, with a good shake of the duvet, Jonathan smoothed out the sheet leaving no trace of the big cat.

"I think my work here is done," noted the Doctor pulling down his waist coat and extending his neck in a proud fashion.

Thanking the Doctor for his help, the children escorted him back downstairs as quietly as possible. In the kitchen, Jonathan opened one of the cupboards and pulled down an old ice cream tub. When he opened the lid, it was full of sweets and chocolate bars.

"For you, for helping us with our problem," said Jonathan offering the box to the Doctor to take his pick.

"Really, it was nothing, literally," he chuckled to himself as he perused the contents of the box.

"But if you insist," he said unable to resist and delving into the box to take a chocolate bar for himself.

"Thanks ever so much for helping. I don't know what we'd have done without you," whispered Jonathan as he quietly put the box away. Then showing him to the door, they waved goodnight to the Doctor as he sure-footedly made his way through the bushes and disappeared into the darkness.

-7-

DINNER

ONE AFTERNOON AFTER school, Jonathan's mother called to him from her study.

"Jonathan! Jonathan!" she yelled, not bothering to get up off her chair. Racing downstairs to see what she wanted; Jonathan poked his head round the corner of her study to find his mother busy working on her computer.

"What's the matter?" asked Jonathan.

"Here," she said.

"This is an invitation for the Doctor to come and join us for dinner. I'd like you to drop it round to him."

"Okay, do you want me to do it now?" he asked. His mother nodded and Jonathan rushed downstairs to put on his shoes.

The Doctor was busy making himself afternoon tea when Jonathan turned up at the back door of the house.

"Come in, my dear boy!" he said greeting Jonathan excitedly and inviting him into the kitchen.

"Would you like slice of cake?" asked the Doctor. Jonathan politely declined knowing that he was going to have his dinner soon.

"Shame, I've made a lovely sponge," admitted the Doctor shaking his head.

The Doctor's kitchen was nothing like the one in Jonathan's house. It had high ceilings, four sinks, a big walk-in pantry and lots and lots of cupboards that were all painted in a shiny cream-coloured paint.

"Why've you got such a big kitchen when you live on your own?" asked Jonathan puzzled. As the Doctor measured out a heaped spoon of tea leaves to put into the teapot, he explained the reasoning behind it.

"Back in the day they needed a kitchen this size when the house had servants," he told him.

"We had staff that would wait on you hand and foot and do everything for you, from cook your breakfast to iron your shirts. I even had my own nanny as a little boy, but those days are long gone. I much prefer my own company. I can't stand being fussed around," he admitted taking the kettle off the stove as it began to sing.

"So, what brings you round here, eh?"

"I'm here to invite you to dinner," Jonathan told him. The Doctor stopped what he was doing and put the kettle down.

"Dinner?" he repeated as if he had not heard right the first time. Sounding puzzled by the request, he looked over at Jonathan.

"You want to invite ME to dinner?" he enquired as if he could not quite believe it. Jonathan nodded.

"Well, it wasn't my idea really; it was my Mum and Dad's. They said they hadn't met you and would like to invite round to dinner one evening next week."

"Well, I am honoured," remarked the Doctor looking misty eyed for a moment.

"I haven't been invited to dinner in…oh, I can't remember when."

Jonathan then handed him the invite. The Doctor removed the piece of paper from its envelope and perused it at his leisure.

"An evening of social interaction…with humans," the Doctor duly noted.

"That will be novel. I must look my best; we want to make a good impression, don't we? We can't have anyone seeing me in my scruffs now, can we?" he said looking down at his cardigan and examining the holes in it.

Showing Jonathan to the door, they made their way down the steps and across the garden towards the greenhouse, the Doctor carrying with him his tea tray as he went. Holding the greenhouse door open for him, Jonathan followed him inside, into his thinking room.

Sitting down, the Doctor took the weight off his feet while taking a bite of cake.

"Scrumptious! Are you sure I can't tempt you with some?" he asked, delighted with his own home-baked sponge cake.

Shaking his head Jonathan marvelled at the long avenue of marble sculptures when he had a question to ask of the Doctor.

"In a few weeks..." he began.

"...we've got a show and tell at our school and... I was wondering if I could take my biosphere with me to show everyone," the Doctor nearly spat his cake out when he heard this.

"Heavens no, Jonathan!" he replied almost choking on the crumbs. Sitting bolt upright in his chair and taking a sip of tea to clear his throat, the Doctor then gave him the reasoning behind his abrupt response.

"You see, people don't believe in..." pausing as he thought about what he was going to say.

"...and I hate to use the word, but people don't believe in *magic*. To them the world is explained in nice little scientific laws and principles and heavens above if anybody should think differently to them..." said the Doctor shaking his head.

"If you went into school with your biosphere and told them that you had thought it into existence you would be ridiculed. It must be our secret; we can't let the outside world know that we are here. Do you understand?"

Jonathan was unable to hide his disappointment.

"Don't be down," said the Doctor putting his hand on his shoulder and reassuring him.

"I'll figure out a way in which we can do something truly astounding for your show and tell, something that will be just as amazing; just you wait and see," he assured him, which seemed to cheer Jonathan up.

Seeing the time on his watch, Jonathan suddenly realised that he had to be home for his dinner and rushed to the door.

"Don't forget to tell your parents that I will be more than happy to accept their invite!" the Doctor called out after him.

As the Doctor sat there on his own in his greenhouse, he knew he had to do something marvellous to cheer Jonathan up. He hated disappointing people and so all that evening and into the night he sat there thinking. The cogs turned and slowly he conjured up thoughts, which turned into an idea, and that idea formed the outlines of a plan, and that plan became a real working thing. An invention that was bound to put a smile on the faces of both Jonathan and his sister.

The following Saturday evening, there was a knock at the front door of the Bawtry household.

"Jonathan, can you let the Doctor in please?" shouted his father from the kitchen. With his mother upstairs doing her hair and putting the finishing touches to her make-up, Jonathan rushed to the door closely followed by his sister.

There, standing on the doorstep was the Doctor. Instead of his usual worn tweed trousers and thread-bare cardigan, he was wearing a very smart dinner jacket with tails and a black bow tie. Jonathan stood there open-mouthed thinking that the Doctor looked somewhat overdressed for the occasion.

With his black dinner jacket and trousers neatly pressed his shoes shone so much that Jonathan could see his face in them. He also had a large daisy in his buttonhole and his hair was flattened down to his head, while with him he carried a big bunch of flowers in one hand and under his other arm a box of chocolates.

"These are for your mother," said the Doctor holding them out for Jonathan to take as his mother came rushing downstairs, fiddling with one of her earrings.

"Do come in," she urged the Doctor as she struggled to catch her breath, nearly tripping up over her heels.

"These are for you," he said presenting her with a bouquet of flowers and box of chocolates.

"They're from my very own garden," he proudly noted.

"Oh, they're wonderful!" gushed his mother full of praise. With his apron still on, Jonathan's father came through from the kitchen to greet him. With a look of shock on his face, it was clear to see that their father thought the Doctor was a little overdressed too. However, choosing not to say a word, their father kept his thoughts to himself and instead gave the Doctor a hearty shake of the hand.

"Pleased to meet you Dr Fife, I'm Colin," said their father introducing himself.

"Oh, do call me Oban, please," replied the Doctor, being as charming as ever.

"I find the whole Doctor thing a little too formal for my liking," he smiled kindly.

"Well, do come in. There's no need to stand on ceremony in this house," said their father showing him through to the living room.

"Please excuse me, but I'm afraid I'm busy with the cooking. I'm sure my wife and children will keep you entertained," he said, before disappearing back into the kitchen.

As their mother escorted the Doctor into the front room, she enquired what he would like to drink.

"I think I'll have a ginger and soda please."

"Jonathan, can you fetch the Doctor a ginger and soda please? Jonathan obliged and returned, carrying with him a tray with a tumbler full of ginger beer and ice, the closest thing he could find to ginger and soda.

"Here you are," he said offering the drink to the Doctor. Picking the glass up off the tray, the Doctor gave Jonathan a knowing wink that only friends give each other.

"Thank you, Jonathan," he replied raising a glass to toast their company and settling back in his chair.

"I must say, Mrs Bawtry, Liz and Jonathan are a real credit to you," he commented in between taking delicate sips from his glass.

"Oh, call me Carol, please," replied their mother as she put her hand to her chest pretending to be all bashful.

"That's very kind of you to say," she said.

"Tell me, your name, are you of Scottish ancestry?" enquired their mother wishing to know more about their guest.

"My great, great grandfather was Scottish. He came from the west coast, a tiny island called Tamaree. Do you know of it?" enquired the Doctor. Their mother shook her head.

"I'm afraid I've never heard of it."

"No, not many people have," laughed the Doctor as he relaxed into his surroundings.

"It is a beautiful place. I've no idea why he should want to leave, but he came to seek his fortune and that's how I came to be living in such a large house," he explained.

"Do you have any other family?" enquired their mother as Liz and Jonathan sat quietly eating the little crackers with fancy bits on that their father had put out to eat.

"Please, a nibble?" their mother gestured, wrestling the tray away from her children.

"In reply to your question, I'm an only child," answered the Doctor while taking a moment to decide which of the nibbles he would like.

"Oh, I'd love to visit the Scottish Isles; they look such a beautiful place," gushed their mother, trying to make small talk.

"Just as long as ye watch out for the wee midges though," chuckled the Doctor putting on a fake Scottish accent as he played up for his host. It was then that their father stuck his head round the door to let everyone know that dinner was ready.

As the guest of honour, they allowed the Doctor to lead the way.

"I thought we'd start with soup." said their father showing Dr Fife to his seat.

"How delightful!" remarked the Doctor as he shuffled forward in his seat looking somewhat out of place with his dinner jacket and bow tie.

As they settled down to eat, the conversation turned to what it was that the Doctor actually did.

"Jonathan tells me you're a scientist, some sort of inventor?" said their father directing his question at the Doctor. Putting his spoon down and finishing chewing the mouthful of bread, the Doctor spoke, explaining what it was that he did for a living.

"I like to think of myself as not just as a scientist, but as a voyager of the mind. Someone who is free to think beyond what is possible, someone who can see beyond all this…" he said waving his hand around as if indicating to his surroundings.

"I'm the sort of person who wants a better future for everyone," he stated.

"Oh… really?" replied their father taken aback by the Doctor's answer and looking somewhat baffled by his explanation as to what it was, he exactly did.

"Well, I think it's very noble of you, may I say, Oban," interjected their mother.

"It's about time more people thought like you."

"He can make animals disappear too!" added Liz. Jonathan threw his sister a sideways glance as if to say *what did you have to say that for*, while the Doctor gave Jonathan a slightly worried look.

"Oh, really dear?" giggled his mother, looking over at his sister.

"You do have a wild imagination, don't you?" she tittered making light of what she thought to be sheer nonsense. Screwing up her nose in frustration, Liz looked over at her brother. He knew she was telling the truth but couldn't reveal to his parents that the Doctor was more than just a scientist, that he was a spaceman with special powers.

It was as a relief to Jonathan when they finished their starters. Saving him from having to explain what his sister was talking about, he cleared away the bowls; helping bring the rest of the food through. As his dad served out the main course, he engaged the Doctor in further conversation about the nature of his work.

"Tell me what are you working on at the moment?" enquired their father making small talk. Taking a drink from his glass, the Doctor cleared his throat before beginning to speak.

"I have been tinkering with a new machine that will repair the hole in the ozone layer, and it is coming along quite well if I may say so. Also, I have devised a way in which to remove all plastics from our oceans, and recently I have been working on a revolutionary new type of energy," he divulged.

"It will grant everyone in the world access to free unlimited power. It will allow the deserts to bloom, put an end to all pollution and it will allow people to travel around the world freely." Taken aback by the Doctor's claim, their father put down his knife and took a gulp of wine.

"That's pretty amazing stuff if what you're saying is true, Oban," remarked their father looking impressed by the Doctor's claims.

"I suppose the implications would be massive," he said dabbing his forehead with his napkin as if taken aback by the enormity of what he was proposing.

The Doctor, putting his knife and fork down, removed his napkin from his lap and dabbed at the corner of his mouth.

"It would be a huge leap for humanity," he admitted.

"I should say so," gasped their father reaching for another drink.

"But that's not my greatest achievement, I'm working on something far greater than that."

"And please do tell. What is this invention that you're talking about, Oban?" asked their mother, joining in the conversation.

"I'm afraid I can't really say as I haven't got a name for it yet, and I can't even tell you what it does as it's my most secret and revered invention yet,"

"Oh, it does sound exciting, this new invention of yours," gasped their mother putting her hands together in delight.

As Jonathan sat there at the table listening to their conversation, he had a strange feeling that what the Doctor was on about had something to do with the mirrored disc and the light that he saw from his bedroom window at night. However, not wanting to let the cat out of the bag, Jonathan chose to keep his mouth shut.

After they had finished their meal, the children and Dr Fife retired to the living room while Jonathan's parents were busy in the kitchen tidying away and making coffee.

"Pssst…" said the Doctor, leaning forward to make sure he was not overheard.

"I've got something I want to show you if you come round to my house tomorrow," he whispered in a secretive manner. Jonathan leaned in closer, propping himself up on the arm of the chair.

"What is it? Is it something good?" he wanted to know. The Doctor sat back in the chair with his hands together, his fingertips touching.

"It's better than good!" he declared with a big grin on his face.

"What is it?" Liz wanted to know, pleading for him to tell her. The Doctor put his finger to his lips and whispered.

"Tomorrow. Be at my house tomorrow and I will show you," he uttered so as not to be overheard.

Just then their mother walked into the room carrying with her a tray of coffee and chocolate mints.

"May I say Mrs Bawtry, err… I mean Carol, it has been wonderful to have shared such a lovely evening with people as nice as yourself," the Doctor politely remarked.

"That's very kind of you to say, Oban; it's been nice to have you as our guest," she replied setting down the tray on a small coffee table.

"It's very rare that I get out these days," exclaimed the Doctor.

"I think the last time I had interactions with other human beings must have been… Oh some twenty years ago," said the Doctor scratching his head as if trying to remember.

"Oh, I am sorry to hear that," said their mother. The Doctor attempted a half-hearted smile but there was a wistful look on his face, one that said he wished things weren't that way.

"I'm afraid it's my work," he lamented.

"I used to be invited to all sorts of social functions that the scientific community held, but as my work became far more cutting-edge and challenged established thinking, the invites dried up until one day they stopped coming and ever since then I have found myself more and more withdrawn."

"How sad," commented their mother, pouring the coffee.

"It's a shame that such a brilliant man as yourself is overlooked. It sounds from what you are telling me that THEY could learn a lot from you."

The Doctor smiled and thanked Mrs Bawtry for her kind words before carrying on with what he was saying.

"Unfortunately, the scientific world has turned its back on me, and I have now become the laughingstock of the community; my name is now synonymous with hairbrained schemes and crackpot ideas…" he admitted.

"…but my work is far beyond what regular academics can comprehend. I like to think of my work as the science of consciousness," he confessed.

As Liz and Jonathan listened to what the Doctor had to say, they felt sorry for him, sitting there in his dinner jacket with his daisy in his buttonhole. They just wanted to give him a big hug and make him feel better. After all, the Doctor was just trying to make the world a better place and what was wrong with that?

Deep down, Jonathan wished that everybody could see just how amazing the Doctor was, then they might have a different opinion of him. Trying to cheer him up, Jonathan came to the Doctor's aid.

"Oban, why don't you tell Mum about the Fug Munchers?" With a look of shock on her face, his mother turned to her son, aghast.

"There's no need for that sort of talk in here is there, Jonathan Bawtry?" she said scowling at him.

"No Mum, that's what they're called!" It was then that the Doctor stepped in to help explain things a little better.

"What they are in fact, are micro biotic, polymeric, carbon, lipid, semi-conducting metal nanoparticles, but just to make it easier and not such of a mouthful, I call them my Fug Munchers."

"I can certainly see why. It is a bit of a mouthful, isn't it?" commented Mrs Bawtry, looking slightly awkward and rearranging her hair.

"They're brilliant mum; they ate all our rubbish,"

Taken aback by her children's enthusiasm, their mother didn't know what to say. It was then that the Doctor spoke up to explain.

"What they do is recycle all the waste that we humans throw away," It was at that point that their father entered the room.

"Am I missing anything?" he asked as he sat down on the sofa next to his wife and picked up a coffee.

"Apparently, Dr Fife, Oban..." she said correcting herself.

"...is working on some of project to help the environment by using micro biotic, poly what-sits..."

"Polymeric," said the Doctor correcting her.

"...carbon, lipid, semi-conducting metal nanoparticles," he said finishing her sentence for her.

"Yes, that's it," added Mrs Bawtry.

"That's a bit of a mouthful," admitted their father taking a sip of his coffee.

"They're really called Fug Munchers," said Jonathan putting his hand to his mouth and whispering into his father ear.

"Fug Munchers!" coughed his father, laughing at their name. Once he had finished spluttering and clearing his throat, his dad enquired as to what the Fug Munchers did.

"Oban was just saying that the nano lipid wotsit thingies recycle all waste that we throw away," said his wife educating him on the finer points of the Fug Munchers.

"I've got to hand it to you, Oban; you're a clever chap," said their father, applauding him for his efforts.

It was then that Jonathan proceeded to tell his father all about how they had seen the Fug Munchers at work.

"Liz and I went round to watch them, Dad," began Jonathan all fired up with enthusiasm.

"The Doctor let us look at them through a really big microscope. They're hairy little creatures that squiggle and shuffle about a lot..." he explained.

"...and we took a bag of our rubbish with us and dropped it in a big bin and watched them eat their way through it till it all disappeared. And do you know?" Jonathan continued.

"They break all the rubbish down into its individual chemical components and you can re-use it over and over again." Their dad nodded and raised his eyebrows in admiration.

"Tell me Oban, how do you know all this stuff? Is there some magical place in your brain where all this stuff comes pouring out?" their father enquired wanting to know more. The Doctor smiled and took off his glasses to polish.

"I suppose I must admit that it does come from somewhere deep inside, a place that I like to call the secret library. I have worked hard over the years to create a holographic repository for knowledge, where I am able to download information straight to my mind. All the information that has ever been and ever will be is written down on the record, contained within a holographic memory bank, and the best thing about it, it's free to use for those with a generous heart,"

Their father astounded by the Doctors brilliance let out a gasp of amazement. However, the Doctor continued to enlighten them.

"The key to everything is maths really. Everything in the universe has a mathematical formula behind it. Be it the shell of a snail, the honeycomb of a bee, a tree in the field, us sitting here right now talking," he expounded.

"There are millions of calculations going on every second, every possible outcome from this conversation is being worked out through mathematical probability and that's how the universe works…that *and* geometry," he sighed giving a little laugh.

His mother and father exchanged glances, bemused, and perplexed by the Doctors claims but not wanting to appear rude she had an idea.

"I don't know what you think Oban, and excuse me for being forward, but Jonathan struggles ever so with maths. He's a dreamer and always has his head up in the clouds, and I was wondering…" she said getting all flustered.

"…as your such an accomplished inventor and mathematician would it be possible for you to tutor Jonathan, for his maths I mean…?" The Doctor looked taken a back that he should be asked to perform such a favour.

"…no, no, it's alright; it was rather forward of me," apologised Jonathan's mother not wanting to seem too intrusive.

"I should have known you're a busy man." Jonathan put his head in his hands; the last thing he wanted was to have a maths lesson. Trust his mother to ruin his fun.

Returning his glasses to the bridge of his nose, the Doctor took a moment of quiet reflection to think about it.

"I'm afraid I am not what you would call a teacher in the conventional sense, Mrs Bawtry. I prefer to work with a more hands-on approach. I like my subjects to get to know maths by having them take part in experiments where they can see mathematics at work. I am not of the mindset of having someone learn from a textbook."

"Oh no, I never thought you were that sort of person, it's just he struggles ever so to get a grip with maths," she added.

Biting his wafer-thin mint in half, the Doctor took stock of what had been said, and sitting forward in his chair reached for his coffee.

"I have a proposition for you. I will tutor both your children for a nominal fee so long as I am allowed to teach them in a way that I see fit. None of this studying from a textbook nonsense and repeating timetables like a parrot, do you understand?"

"Oh yes, anything you say, Oban," their mother answered, pleased that her children would get private tuition in maths.

"Well, there's no point in wasting anytime," remarked the Doctor placing his cup down on his saucer.

"How about we start their education tomorrow?" Jonathan's mother looked over at their father for confirmation.

"As long as we're not putting you out in anyway,"

"Not at all, my dear Carol," he replied merrily. For the Doctor it was the perfect excuse to have more time with the children. After all it enabled him to show them his many marvellous inventions, including his greatest and most accomplished work of all, the earth-shattering, mind bending, truly one off, disc of light.

-8-

LESSON IN DREAMING

THE FOLLOWING MORNING, Jonathan and his sister went to see the Doctor for their first maths lesson. Having squeezed through gap in the fence, Jonathan and Liz made their way through the grounds of the once magnificent house, chatting as they went.

"I hope the Doctor doesn't make us do sums," Jonathan grumbled, unhappy at the prospect of a maths lesson on a Sunday morning.

"I'm sure he won't. I think he'll have something exciting to show us; he might even show us the light, the invention he keeps secret," said Liz hopefully.

As they walked along marvelling at the secret garden, Liz turned to her brother. "Don't you think it's sad that the Doctor doesn't have anyone to love?" Jonathan shrugged.

"I suppose so," he replied, having not given the subject much thought.

"And didn't you hear last night at the table. He said that none of his friends wanted to see him anymore. I wish there was something we could do to help him out," said Liz as she considered the Doctor's plight.

"Like what?" Jonathan asked.

"Surely, if he can make things disappear with his mind then he can find somebody to love. It can't be that hard, can it?" She asked.

"I don't think it's that easy falling in love. I think it's far more complicated than that. I mean adults are weird and have strange habits," Jonathan replied letting his thoughts be known on the matter.

"You only have to look at Mum and Dad," he said, as though he knew what he was talking about. Deep down Liz knew that there must be something that they could do to help the Doctor, but right now she did not have the answer.

Ringing the front doorbell, Liz pulled the big brass handle and waited for an answer. Somewhere off in the house, they heard the distant chime of bells and after they had waited for what seemed like an extremely long time, they heard the clunk of a key being turned in the lock. Slowly, the door opened and through the narrow gap at the bottom sauntered Ajna, who decided to roll about in the late morning sunshine that was warming up the steps.

The door opened further, and there stood the Doctor wearing a purple silk dressing gown, slippers, socks with sock suspenders and a black velvet hat with a tassel on. Looking a little worse for wear, he leant on a golf putter for support as he engaged the children in conversation.

"Good morning. It's still morning, isn't it?" he asked bleary eyed as he struggled to read the time on his watch.

"I'm afraid I'm not used to such late nights these days," he said with a weary smile.

"We're here for our maths lesson," said Jonathan in a less-than-enthusiastic tone.

"Oh that," said the Doctor recalling what he had promised last night.

"Never mind that, right now I think I need a breath of fresh air to perk me up. I don't suppose either of you fancy a round of golf, do you?" he enquired. Liz pursed her lips as she thought about it.

"Please, indulge a gentleman in the autumn of his years," begged the Doctor as he pleaded with them to follow him.

Making their way up the grand staircase, past the suits of armour and huge paintings that hung from the red velvet walls Liz asked as to why they were climbing the stairs to go play golf.

"I'm not like everyone else, see. My putting green is on the roof!" replied the doctor with a smirk, revelling in his eccentricity.

"You see, due to rising costs I had to dispense with the services of my gardener. Sadly, the garden became overgrown, and I had nowhere to play golf anymore, so I had to move my putting green up onto the roof where it was free of weeds." The two children gave each other an odd stare, aware that the Doctor was definitely not like anyone else they knew.

The stairs climbed higher and higher, and soon they were at the very top of the tower. Finally, the Doctor opened one of the round windows that led out onto the flat expanse of roof.

"See, I'm not as mad as people like to think!" chirped up the Doctor as he shimmied out of the window helping the children out.

"This lovely flat surface makes an ideal place to play golf," he declared as he scrambled to his feet and brushed the dirt from off his knees. Leaning on his putter, the Doctor surveyed his kingdom. It was then that Liz noticed something peculiar about the roof.

"Why have you got bathroom sinks set into the roof of your house? It looks more like crazy golf than a putting green to me."

"I knew you were going to ask that," remarked the Doctor, raising his finger in the air as if he had a perfectly good explanation for it.

"You see, golf holes or holes for golf balls, depending on how you look at it, are hard to come by, and it occurred to me I had all these bathrooms in my house that I was not using, so I might as well use the holes from all the sinks," explained the Doctor.

"However, getting the holes from out of the sinks was harder than I thought so I decided to use the sinks themselves. It was easier than un-screwing a lot of holes!"

"But what do you do when it rains?" enquired Liz, wanting to know how it all worked.

"Ahh… that's the good bit," exclaimed the Doctor.

"You see, when I installed the sinks along with their holes, I made sure I connected it all to the guttering, so any rain just pours off the roof. Admittedly, it's not exactly a professional approach, but it works all the same," said the Doctor tossing a golf ball down on to the ground whilst tightening the belt on his dressing gown.

"Right, who wants to go first?" he enquired as he handed a ball to each of them. The children's hands shot up in the air as they burst with enthusi-asm at the prospect of going first.

"How about we let your sister go first, eh? After all, she is the young-est." Jonathan agreed and set his ball down on the ground while he waited for his sister to take her first shot.

Holding her putter like a hockey stick, she struck the ball so hard that it went bouncing across the roof and hit the stone parapet that ran around the building before finding one of the many holes.

"Hurrah!" cheered Liz, overjoyed that she had got her ball in a hole.

"It's not the right hole," complained her brother.

"You're supposed to get it in the hole with the flag that says number one," he told her, but Liz wasn't bothered that she hadn't got it in the right hole.

"It doesn't matter. I still got it in a hole!"

"Yeah, but not the right one," her brother argued.

While Liz retrieved her ball, Jonathan got ready to take his shot. With a steady hand, he let the club make contact with the ball and watched it trickle towards the hole. Stopping just a few feet short of the flag, he stood back as the Doctor took his turn. While they waited for the Doctor to take his shot, Liz took the opportunity to ask the Doctor a rather personal question.

"Oban, my brother, and I were wondering if you wanted somebody to love?"

Caught off-guard by her question, the Doctor hit the ball awkwardly and it went scuttling off in the opposite direction, disappearing into the guttering.

"Well, I can't say I was expecting that!" he replied taking her directness all in good part.

"We were only wondering…" she said hoping that she hadn't offended the Doctor.

"…but last night you said you had no friends and that you hadn't been out in years. We thought you might be lonely, that's all."

The Doctor smiled patting Liz on the head while letting out a small chuckle to himself.

"You see Liz, my life is not like everyone else's," he said as he stared off into the distance, looking to the city beyond.

"I have been sent here to Earth for the benefit of all sentient beings upon it," he said with a gentle smile on his face.

"I have been reincarnated so many times on different planets that I have forgotten how many lives I have actually lived through," Liz looked up at the Doctor dressed in his purple dressing gown and black velvet cap.

"What's a sentient being?" she asked.

"It is any life form that feels," he explained to her as he stood there with his putter in his hand like a wise old sage with his staff.

"You see you're a sentient being, any animal or insect is a sentient being, trees are sentient beings, even the Earth is one."

"Oh," replied Liz slightly overwhelmed by the huge nature of the world that the Doctor was describing to her.

"My life is given over to the service of all sentient beings. So, in that respect I have a lot of people to love, but it is true that I do feel lonely at times," admitted the Doctor.

"But wouldn't you like somebody to keep you company?" Liz wanted to know.

"My work is very solitary, and I have Ajna for company. But yes, I suppose there are times when I would like to share my life with someone…" he reflected.

"…but that opportunity has never arisen, and so I am left here to carry on my work alone," he sighed.

"At night, after I have finished my work for the day, I come up here and stare up at the stars, then I feel not so alone," he said casting his gaze upwards at the clouds scurrying across the sky.

"But you're a spaceman. Can't any of your family come and visit you to cheer you up?" asked Liz.

"They stop by once in a while with their spaceships. Sometimes I wish I could just step on board and leave the Earth behind and venture into the stars once more, but I have been given this life here on Earth and I know that I belong here," noted the Doctor looking a little down.

"To cheer myself up though…" he continued.

"…I look across the city at night to all the twinkling lights and I think of all the countless millions of lives out there, and how I can make the world a better place for them and all the other sentient beings on this planet," he said with a smile returning to his face.

"That gives me an immense sense of well-being that can never be matched. Nothing comes close to the feeling that you are doing something positive to help humanity," he said with a twinkle in his eye.

As Jonathan listened to the Doctor, he found himself drifting off into one of his many lovely daydreams. Dreaming of blue skies and warm sunshine on his face, he suddenly found the Doctor appear next to him in his dream.

"What are you doing in my dream? This is my dream," he said indignantly with his hands on his hips.

"I know it is, but it looked like such a lovely dream that I couldn't help joining you. I hope you don't mind," said the Doctor, excusing himself.

"How can I see you in my dreams? I didn't know you could do that," Jonathan demanded to know when he suddenly found himself on a mountain top looking down at the world below him.

"It's one of my many abilities," answered the Doctor joining him on top of the snow-covered peak.

"Dreams like yours are precious and should be treasured. They are like shining jewels in the night sky. You see, Jonathan, the secret to this world is being able to share your dreams with other people. You see when everybody's dreaming the same wonderful dream, that's when the world sparkles and comes alive with all sorts of magical things."

Next, they found themselves on a sailing boat in warm, sunny waters bobbing along.

"This boat here that you're on..." said the Doctor, running his hand through the azure blue water as he leant over the side.

"...this is the key to your destiny. It will take you wherever you want to go in life, whatever the weather may bring. Just have faith in your dreams and they will lead you to fantastical places."

For a while, they sailed along together basking in the joy of the serene blue waters and watching the fantastical coloured fish swim by until they were rudely awakened by Jonathan's sister.

"Are we here to play golf or are you two going to stand there all-day dreaming?" she asked interrupting their blissful fantasy.

"Oh... but dreaming is essential," declared Oban, giving a knowing wink to Jonathan.

"The world wouldn't turn if it wasn't for dreams like yours and your brothers," said the Doctor, addressing the pair.

As they got back to their game of golf, the Doctor remembered what it was they had come round to his house for.

"Ahh… yes, I promised your parents that I was going to give you a maths lesson today, didn't I?" recalled the Doctor. Jonathan groaned out aloud.

"Not maths, I hate maths!" he moaned.

Lining up his shot, the Doctor smiled and then gently tapped the ball. With one easy motion, it rolled towards the hole and dropped in with a satisfying "plop."

"Well, don't worry. I don't think the type of learning that I am going to be asking you to do will be the sort you were expecting."

"Why what is it?" asked Jonathan cautiously, trying not to get his hopes up just in case it did involve doing page after page of brain twisting sums.

"Well, if you'd like to follow me then maybe you will find out," replied the Doctor escorting them down off the roof and back into the house.

Closing the window behind them, the Doctor stood there at the very top of the stairs.

"Hang on a minute. I think you might find it a bit more fun if you have one of these," he said issuing them with a silver tea tray each.

"Why what's this for?" Liz wanted to know, inspecting it with a critical eye.

"All will be revealed in a moment, my dear girl," replied the Doctor as he took a run up on the landing and launched himself headfirst down the stairs.

"It's a sledge!" he shouted over his shoulder as he tobogganed down the steps laughing like a child. Jonathan and his sister followed suit and soon were skating down the smooth red carpet as if on snow.

With the tails of his dressing gown flapping wildly and showing off his tartan underpants, the Doctor encouraged the children to go faster. Descending flight after flight of stairs it was just like being on a helter skelter. Coming to a grinding halt in the hallway, the Doctor got to his feet and cheered the children on.

"Fun, eh? I do this when I'm bored and want a rest from inventing," he said with a big grin on his face.

"Can't we do it again?" pleaded Jonathan.

"Why not?" replied the Doctor as they raced up the stairs. Running ahead of him, they were soon at the top while the Doctor was left flagging behind.

Firing down the steps, the children yelled and screamed as if they were on a fairground ride while the Doctor whooped and cheered them on as he followed them down.

After a few more runs down the stairs, the Doctor was left begging the children to stop so he could have a rest.

"Can't we have one more go?" asked Liz excitedly, but Jonathan could see the Doctor was beginning to tire.

"I need a rest; besides I've got something to show you" he gasped breathlessly.

"What I want you to see is outside in my laboratory," he said ushering them through into the kitchen. Fixing them milk and biscuits, he left them sat around the large wooden table while he went and got changed.

Not having been gone long, he returned wearing his usual tweed check trousers, a knitted tie and old cardigan. Partaking in a cup of tea while the children finished off their biscuits, the Doctor then invited them to accompany him out to the garden, taking the well-trodden path to his laboratory.

Encouraging the children to take a seat on some old packing cases, the Doctor bent down and fiddled with an old washing machine that sat in the middle of the floor.

"You remember you told me you had an upcoming show and tell at school? Well…I've been working on something you might both like."

After twiddling a few knobs, flicking a few switches, and connecting a few wires, the Doctor took a step back to present his latest work.

"I give you the Eagle," he said with his arms open wide. Jonathan looked at the washing machine disappointed.

"It's a washing machine," he complained.

"Ah-ha!" chimed the Doctor, raising a finger in the air.

"But I can make it fly! You see when you asked me the other week if you could take your orb to show and tell, I felt terribly disappointed that I had to say no, if there's one thing, I can't stand it's to ruin other people's dreams. So that's when I came up with this…"

"But it's just a washing machine, where's the fun in that?" replied Jonathan.

"You're not thinking inter-dimensionally Jonathan. With this, we can go anywhere!" the Doctor chirped up. Jonathan and his sister looked blankly back at each other.

"We'll never all fit in there," answered Liz looking decidedly uninterested in the Doctor's plans.

"Ahh…but this is only the beginning; I've got bigger plans for this," explained the Doctor.

Rummaging about his tool bench, he attached some jump leads to two metal points that had been welded to the top of the washing machine.

"But why a washing machine? It's boring." Said Jonathan unable to summon up any interest in the washing machine. The Doctor sighed shaking his head in frustration.

"I don't think you understand, Jonathan! We're not going to be using the washing machine for its intended purpose, but from this prototype we will gain the knowledge for inter-galactic travel. That's why I have named it the 'Eagle.'"

"'The Eagle?' It looks more like a heap of old rubbish to me," said Jonathan.

"Oh, ye of little faith!" replied the Doctor as he leapt around the room excitedly.

"I have called it the Eagle after the Apollo Eleven Lunar Lander that landed on the moon. I think you'll find that the small round door of the washing machine makes for a fitting tribute to the original machine.

"But that thing will never get us into space," remarked Jonathan.

"Duly noted," said the Doctor taking off his glasses to polish them and bouncing up and down on his tippy toes with excitement.

"That is why Ajna will be our first test pilot,"

Jonathan and Liz looked at each other aghast, wondering what the Doctor was thinking. Unable to comprehend what he was about to do, they sat there open mouthed.

"I am planning my first test soon," he informed them.

"What, you're putting Ajna in the washing machine? How's that going to work?" asked Liz, looking concerned for the cat's well-being.

Standing up straight with his hands in his pockets, the Doctor looked them firmly in the eye.

"I will be using a principle known as the Biefeld-Brown effect, which allows objects to become weightless and levitate, and I would be honoured if you will join me for its first flight."

"When do you plan on doing this?" asked Jonathan, his curiosity now getting the better of him.

"I'm not sure yet," replied the Doctor pursing his lips as he thought about the matter.

"I've got a few little tweaks left to make and then I will let you know."

"How will we know when you're ready to test it?" asked Liz.

"Mmm… that's a very good point. How about I place an empty milk bottle on top of the fence when I'm ready? That way we can keep it our secret and your parents won't get suspicious," he replied, satisfied that a milk bottle was an acceptable means of communication.

"Just above the gap in the fence?" said Liz just checking.

"That's right, just above the gap in the fence," confirmed the Doctor happy with their plans.

-9-

TEST FLIGHT

THE WEEK PASSED slowly. Each evening Jonathan made his way down the garden to the gap in the fence. Pushing back the flowing limbs of the old willow tree, he peeked behind, hoping that he would find an empty milk bottle sitting there, but nothing. Monday came and went. Tuesday was the same and by Wednesday Jonathan was getting fed up of waiting.

That evening before bed, he stood looking out of his bedroom window. As the lights of the city twinkled like bright shining stars against the night sky, he wondered what the Doctor was up to. Between the trees he could make out the bright spark of a welder's torch flickering away, accompanied by the fizz of metal on metal as the Doctor worked tirelessly into the night.

Thursday came and Jonathan sauntered down the garden not expecting to find anything when he noticed an empty milk bottle sat on top of the fence. Quickly taking it down so his parents wouldn't get suspicious he rushed inside to tell his sister who was upstairs playing in her bedroom.

"Liz, Liz," he whispered keeping his voice down so their mother wouldn't hear.

Closing the bedroom door, he told her that the milk bottle had at last appeared.

"Really?" said Liz sounding excited.

After dinner the children made their way down the garden to see the Doctor. In the warm evening haze of a thousand dancing midges, they found him hard at work outside his greenhouse. Shouting to him the Doctor pushed up the visor on his welding mask giving them a cheery hello.

"Good evening," he said greeting the children with a beaming smile and removing the helmet from his head.

"Nice evening for a test flight, eh? I was just making a few last-minute adjustments to the Eagle," he remarked taking off his heavy leather gloves and turning off the welding machine.

The washing machine was painted in a black and white chequerboard pattern and stencilled on the side in big black letters was the name EAGLE. In the background, there could be heard the faint hum of electricity as it coursed through the wiring of the Eagle at high voltage. Meanwhile the air was charged with static making the hair on the children's arms stand on end. Even the birds were aware of the machine's presence as they tweeted and flitted around the trees in an unusual manner.

Removing his heavy welder's apron and laying it down on a brick wall, the Doctor asked if either of them had a phone with them.

"I do!" answered Liz.

"Well, if you wouldn't mind videoing me, I'd like you to capture this moment for posterity. If you will." asked the Doctor, smoothing down his hair that had become ruffled from wearing the welder's mask.

"Jonathan, can you help me please? We need to tie these chains to the Eagle," he said indicating to four thick, heavy chains that were anchored into the ground with great spikes.

"What are these for?" Jonathan asked.

"For holding the Eagle in place. I don't want it to fly away," replied the Doctor stepping back to admire his creation.

"The Eagle is going to be sucking up some serious juice you know… we'll be using enough electricity to power a whole city for two days.'" he grinned mischievously.

"But won't it be dangerous?" asked Jonathan looking slightly nervous. The Doctor gave a little laugh.

"Not so as we need worry about it," he giggled.

Making sure the chains were anchored firmly in the ground, the Doctor let out a pained sigh as he rose to his feet.

"I'm going to have to give up all this funny business. My body is getting too old for it and can't take it anymore," he winced, rubbing his back as he did so.

Leaving the Eagle to gently hum away to itself, the Doctor showed them into the greenhouse. Taking a slurp from a stone-cold cup of tea, he called them over to see the pet carrier.

"Liz, I would like you to look after Ajna for me. I have prepared him for the very first flight in an anti-gravity device,"

Liz looked inside the pet carrier. Ajna was dressed in a silver space suit made of tin foil and on his head, he was wearing one of the Doctor's scientific glass jars as a space helmet.

"Why's he wearing a spacesuit?" asked Liz.

"Ah...do forgive me, Liz. But I couldn't resist a touch of whimsy. Technically, he doesn't need it as he will be perfectly fine in the Eagle, but to honour those early pioneers of space I had to do it just for my own personal gratification."

Liz bent down and stuck her finger through the slats of the pet carrier. Eager to see her, Ajna tried rubbing himself against Liz's hand, but instead found himself banging his head against the door with his new space helmet.

"Poor old Ajna! Is he going to be alright?"

"Absolutely fine," remarked the Doctor who by now was getting quite excited at the prospect of take-off.

"Here," he said distributing a set of welding goggles to the children as well as two oversized white lab coats.

"The goggles are to protect your eyes from the glare it will be giving off, and the lab coats make the whole thing look more official, don't you think?"

The Doctor paced back and forth along the greenhouse ticking things off on his clipboard.

"Free flow electro-magnetic circuits, check. Three-phase warp conductor, check. Wavelength damper, check."

Standing next to him, Jonathan could see all the complicated calculations that the Doctor had made. At school he found maths really boring, but here he realized that it was something to get excited about. It made things come alive and if this is what you could do with the application of mathematics then he thought maybe he should try a little harder. After all he wished he too could make a washing machine levitate.

"If you could pass Ajna over here, I think we're ready to go," said the Doctor as he took the pet carrier from Liz. Making his way outside, there, stood in the clearing was the washing machine. By now, a light mist had formed around the Eagle as it was beginning to interact with the environment.

Purposefully, the Doctor strode towards the Eagle with Anja in his basket as Liz filmed him with her phone. The Doctor had gone to the considerable length of erecting floodlights, which lit up the whole area, casting an eerie glow upon the trees.

Crouching down, he released the catch on the washing machine door and turned to Liz.

"Are you getting this?" he wanted to know. Liz nodded and kept on filming not wanting to interrupt his train of thought. Letting Ajna out of his basket, he then lifted him up for the camera to see and began to speak as if addressing an audience.

"This evening, we will witness the first demonstration of a manned craft using anti-gravity technology developed by myself, Dr Oban Fife. We will be using my cat, Ajna, as a test subject..." he said lifting him up for the camera to see.

"...and we will be performing a short propulsion test. The subject vehicle, a washing machine, will be powered by a zero-point energy generator that will send power to three electro-magnetic phase dampers. This will allow the device to levitate and thus create its own pocket of gravity, separate to that of the Earth," concluded the Doctor as he placed Ajna into the washing machine.

Sealing Anja in the drum the Doctor closed the door behind him, making sure it was snapped shut. Jonathan and Liz looked on concerned as they could see Ajna's anxious face looking back at them from out of the circular window.

"Are you sure he's going to be alright?" asked Liz dubiously.

"Course he is!" the Doctor replied dismissing Liz's concerns as nothing to worry about.

"He'll be just fine. The worst that can happen is that we have a complete power failure and the whole thing comes crashing to the ground, but don't worry. Cats always have a way of landing on their feet."

"Yes...but he's stuck inside a washing machine," said Liz

"I know, I know, but trust me, this is all going to work fine. I've every confidence in my own invention," he stated confidently, waving his hand as if to say it was nothing to worry about.

The Doctor suggested they retire to a safe distance should they be affected by the electromagnetic field it was giving off. Hiding behind what was left of an old metal water tank, the Doctor suddenly realised he'd forgot something. Running back to the washing machine, he returned dragging a length of cable behind him.

"Oops... I nearly forgot the power control!" he giggled, blushing ever so slightly. He then flicked a switch on the power box and slowly turned up the dial.

There was a sense that something special was about to happen. The birds in the trees had stopped singing apart from a lone blackbird, who knew something incredible was about to happen. Then, the air in the clearing got very still and an audible hum could be heard. As the Doctor turned up the dial, the hum became more intense, and a faint light began to appear around the washing machine.

"Better put your goggles on," he warned, aware that things were about to get interesting. Through the tinted lenses of the goggles, it was hard to see anything, but as the doctor turned the power up, the light from the washing machine became so bright that it was like looking at the sun.

Consumed by a blistering light, they could barely make out the washing machine as it began to slowly rise up off the ground. At first it wobbled ever so gently, and then as the hum grew in pitch, it rose higher into the air, dragging the chains with it. By now, it was impossible to see Ajna as the light was so bright.

The washing machine was now at head height and floating totally unhindered, apart from the chains that tethered it to the ground. Bobbing around, it was a wonderful sight to see. Not content to sit idly by the Doctor increased the power as the Eagle rose higher into the air, becoming level with the treetops.

"Look at it I can't believe it, it's really happening!" exclaimed Jonathan

"Course it's happening, you didn't really think it wasn't going to work, did you?" said the Doctor looking down at him with his welder's mask on.

Slowly he increased and decreased the power so it rose up and down like a weighted pendulum. Jonathan couldn't hide his amusement and began to laugh and point as the washing machine serenely and gracefully hovered in the clearing.

"Can I have a go?" he asked.

"Course you can, just be steady with it. Small corrections that's all it needs," said the Doctor handing over the control box to Jonathan. Ever so carefully, Jonathan turned the dial and watched as it responded to the tiny adjustments he made.

"Liz, have you seen this?" He said to his sister as she turned the camera on him, zooming in with her phone.

"Can we take the chains off?" asked Jonathan.

"Good gracious no! This is a propulsion test, not a systems control test. I have something far more interesting planned for the future than just this," replied the Doctor grinning from behind his mask.

"Seeing as things have gone well, I think it's about time you bring it down now. Better safe than sorry, eh?"

Jonathan powered down the washing machine and the craft slowly descended to the ground. Gently touching down, the capsule hummed and ticked as it came to a rest.

"Right, let's see how Ajna is," said the Doctor rushing over to inspect the machine and retrieve his beloved pet. Popping open the catch on the door, he reached inside.

"How are you, my dear Ajna?" asked the Doctor lifting him up in his arms like a victorious returning hero. Ajna didn't seem particularly phased by the whole incident, just a little stunned.

"Is he alright?" asked Liz.

"He's fine; in fact, he's more than fine. He's the first cat in the world to ride an anti-gravity device," enthused the Doctor, pleased that his test had been a success.

While the Doctor cradled Ajna in his arms, Liz helped remove the helmet from the big furry tomcat.

"There, that's better," observed Liz pleased to see Ajna back on the ground.

On being set down on the grass, the cat showed his displeasure at being cooped up in the washing machine by instantly running off in the opposite direction.

"There's no pleasing some people, is there?" joked the Doctor lightheartedly as he watched his cat skip off to the safety of the greenhouse for a well-deserved lie down.

Scrolling through her phone, Liz announced that she was going to upload the footage to the internet.

"No, no, you can't possibly do that!" insisted the Doctor reaching out to stop her.

"If you do, we'll have every man and his dog from here to Timbuktu turning up and demanding to see the Eagle,"

"I suppose so," agreed Liz sounding somewhat deflated.

"For the time being, we'll have to keep it top secret. If you promise not to say a word about this, I swear I'll have a real treat for the both of you, something that I'm sure you'll enjoy." The Doctor winked.

Collecting their things together and turning off the power to the Eagle, the three of them headed to the greenhouse for a well-deserved celebration. While the kettle boiled for a late-night hot chocolate, Liz shared her video with the Doctor, who sat in his chair watching the spectacle on his laptop.

"Have you seen this?" he marvelled as he sat mesmerised in front of the screen.

"…if everybody had access to this sort of technology then we would all be able to fly free like birds. Just imagine…" he said, shaking his head before putting his laptop down and rooting around for a celebratory packet of biscuits. Finding a half-open pack, the Doctor pushed the biscuits in the direction of the children before getting up and pacing excitedly back and forth in his laboratory.

"Can you imagine a world united, free to come and go as it pleases with no borders and no restrictions… my, that's some kind of dream!" The Doctor then paused mid-sentence as if he had suddenly thought of something.

"You know, it just occurred to me; it's no longer a dream, we have turned our dreams into reality." he exclaimed as he waltzed around his laboratory deliriously happy.

It was hard to get the Doctor to come down off his cloud. So, while the Doctor revelled in his glory, Jonathan got on with making hot chocolate for everyone. Not wishing to forget Ajna, he put some extra cat biscuits in his dish for him. After all he was the first cat in history to travel in an anti-gravity device.

There was no containing the Doctor's excitement. While Jonathan and Liz sat blowing on their hot chocolate, the Doctor was still prancing about the greenhouse, marching up and down between the benches, busy talking to himself.

"When can we do it again?" asked Jonathan, interrupting the Doctor's incoherent mutterings.

"Oh yes, you mean the Eagle," said the Doctor showering Jonathan with a mouthful of biscuit crumbs.

"This is just the start of things. I've something much more impressive planned for the future,"

"Really?" asked Liz who thought that the evening's entertainment had been amazing.

"Really," affirmed the Doctor, biting down triumphantly on his biscuit.

With the onset of darkness, the children knew they would have to go home soon, but it was hard to leave as they watched repeat after repeat of the Eagle's fantastic flight. With heavy hearts, they said goodnight to the Doctor, promising him they would be back tomorrow.

The following day, Jonathan and Liz returned to see the Doctor. They found him in his laboratory; in his wicker chair relaxing and watching last night's escapades on his laptop.

"Last night was brilliant!" exclaimed Liz all excited as she burst in through the door.

"How's Ajna?" she wanted to know.

"Ajna's fine," replied the Doctor nodding to the cat who was seated in the bottom of the window soaking up the sun. Getting up from his chair, he instructed the children to follow him outside.

"I've got something you might want to see," he said, wandering through the waist-high grass and stroking his chin as if looking for something.

"What is it? What is it you're looking for?" asked Jonathan trying to help.

"I'll remember in a minute… wait, wait, it'll come to me," he said raising a finger in the air. Then he suddenly remembered.

"It's over here!" exclaimed the Doctor heading off hurriedly in the direction of the old tennis courts. Picking up a stick he began beating a path through the overgrown bushes.

"It's in here somewhere," he said thrashing about wildly in the brambles with the stick as if he knew what he was looking for. Finding a fallen branch, Jonathan copied the Doctors actions.

"What are we looking for?" asked Jonathan. The Doctor remained tight-lipped.

As they thrashed away at clumps of nettles, Jonathan came across an old car.

"Is this what you're looking for?" he called out. Taking one glance at the rusted Rolls Royce the Doctor dismissed it out of hand.

"I'm looking for something in particular," he shouted back as he continued chopping down the tangle of weeds. Soon, he had found what he had been looking for.

"Here! Look at this beauty!" he shouted breathlessly.

As he stood there patting an old blue car, Jonathan thought that their discovery maybe more akin to treasure, but this looked like some beat-up old wreck of a car.

"This is just what I've been looking for! A nineteen seventy-five Reliant Robin!" declared the Doctor, pulling the remaining brambles and knee-high grass away from the vehicle.

"It's only got three wheels though; isn't one missing?" asked Jonathan. The Doctor shook his head.

"It's exactly how she was meant to be," he smiled as he gave the car an affectionate pat on the roof.

"This here used to be my little runabout. Here, give me a hand to push it out of this grass," he said directing Jonathan to come and help him.

"This is going to be our next project, a flying car. The washing machine was just the start of things," said the Doctor as he put his back into pushing the car out of the long grass.

"A car like this doesn't suddenly fly without the application of mathematics. There's lots of sums I must do in order to get this thing off the ground, and I've spent many hours problem solving first. This car is like the washing machine only bigger!" He said stepping back to admire the old car.

"You know, I could take you to any point in the universe merely using the arrow of time to form our own space time geometry," he said matter-of-factly.

"You mean we can go anywhere?" exclaimed Liz excitedly.

"In theory," remarked the Doctor nodding his head and pursing his lips in a considered manner.

The two children were understandably excited at hearing this news and instantly demanded that they go to the moon.

"Please? Please take us?" they begged of him.

"That way, you might not feel so homesick," remarked Jonathan thinking how a trip into space might cheer him up. The Doctor laughed at their enthusiasm.

"It's not that simple. You see, we need life support systems to go to the moon and I only have one part-made atomic space suit. It would take me another twenty years to create enough thread to make a spacesuit for you each." The children looked glumly down at their feet.

"However, we could go anywhere we want here on Earth. What about a little round the world trip eh, just the three of us?" Straightaway, the children broke out into smiles.

Getting Jonathan to give him a hand to push the car out of the long grass, the two of them soon had if free of the weeds while Liz sat in the driver's seat steering. Slowly the car inched towards the greenhouse.

"That'll do!" shouted the Doctor as the car came to a grinding halt.

"I'll set up a tarpaulin over it so I can work on it outside. It shouldn't take much to get it operating. I'll take the zero-point energy generator out of the washing machine, add some large magnets to the underside of the car and run some cabling around the outside of the vehicle, and hey presto we should have the thing up and running in no time!" he noted as if it didn't sound like a big job.

~ 10 ~

THE TOP ROAD GANG

JONATHAN AND LIZ took their time walking home from school. Sharing ideas about all the amazing places and things that they'd like to see; they made a list of where they would like to go most in the world.

"I'd like to see Niagara Falls," exclaimed Liz with her satchel slung over her shoulder and head buried deep in her coat.

"Well, I'd like to see the Grand Canyon and maybe a whale…and a tiger…and the world's tallest building and the world's biggest apple pie," added Jonathan.

"The world's biggest apple pie?!" questioned his sister.

"Why not? You could eat as much as you want and have as much ice cream as you liked!"

Liz thought about what her brother said and liked the idea of being able to eat as much ice cream and apple pie as you could possibly manage.

Trailing along behind her brother, Liz thought that there must be so many amazing places in the world that they didn't even know about that they really should research it on the internet.

As they walked along the rest of the children who had been accompanying them on their way home were now beginning to thin out. Peeling off one by one, it wasn't long until it was just them and a bunch of stragglers left.

However, Jonathan soon slowed his pace when up ahead, he spied Naza Hav'em and the Top Road Gang. Being the new boy at school, he had received more than his fair share of attention from them in the way of their nasty antics.

Well renowned for making people eat their bogies, putting worms down their underpants as well as holding them down on the ground and trumping on their heads just for fun the Top Road Gang were in short, quite detestable.

"Stop, let's wait here a minute," said Jonathan grabbing his sister by the arm.

"Why, what's wrong?" She asked looking worried.

"You see those kids up ahead. They tried to beat me up at school just because I was new," Liz looked worried for her brother.

"Why don't we cross the road? That way they might not see us."

"They might notice us though if we do. Let's just hang back here," said Jonathan keeping his head down in the hope that they wouldn't be seen, but his plan did not work.

Within seconds, an eagle-eyed Dazzler and Mad dog Mortimer from the gang had spotted Jonathan and shouted to Naza that they were going after him.

"Look there's that posh kid, and he's got his sister with him too!" he yelled as the rest of the gang ran towards them.

Jonathan grabbed his sister and took off running. Going as fast as their legs would carry them, they tried getting away from the gang, but they were soon caught. Grabbing Jonathan by the scruff of the neck, they pulled him to the ground and sat on him, while Furious Phil Fackler and Lanky Tom Longbottom took hold of his sister.

Puffing and panting, Naza Hav'em caught up with them and glared at Jonathan, who was squirming and struggling on the ground.

"Look!" sneered Naza, pointing.

"It's the posh kid who tried to run away from us at school. I was wondering when I was going to see you again," he gloated all pleased with himself.

"Let go of my sister!" shouted Jonathan, kicking and screaming.

"Get him to his feet," glared Naza with his fist clenched.

"I'm going to give him a good bashing; he deserves it! But before I give you a doing over, I'm going to have some fun first. How about a Chinese burn?" taunted Naza.

"Go on, give him a proper stinger!" laughed Dazzler.

"Yeah, make him squeal!" added Mad dog as Naza took hold of Jonathan's arm. Twisting for all he was worth, Naza made Jonathan yelp.

"Let go!" Jonathan squealed.

"You want me to let go? Are you sure?" said Naza as he then took hold of Jonathan by the short hair on the side of his head and pulled.

"Owwwwww!" squealed Jonathan helplessly.

"That was for getting away from us last time!" sneered the bully as he prepared to punch Jonathan in the stomach.

Just as he was about to punch him, Naza was interrupted by a high-pitched scream that nearly made his ears bleed.

"Let my brother go!" shouted Liz at the top of her voice as she desperately tried to break free from the bullies' vice-like grip.

"What's this, you've got your sister fighting your battles for you now?" glowered Naza as his attention was suddenly turned to Liz.

"Give me her rucksack," he demanded.

Yanking her rucksack from her back, Lanky Tom Longbottom handed it over while Furious Phil Fackler held on to her tightly.

"What have we got here?" he said unzipping it and peering inside.

"Nothing, that's mine!" snapped Liz fearlessly.

"Mmm…I'll be the judge of that," he sneered as he took a closer inspection.

He then decided he was going to tip the entire contents of Liz's school bag out onto the ground.

"Stop it!" Liz shouted, but all Naza could do was laugh as he watched her textbooks, pens, pencils, and sandwich box spill onto the pavement. He then decided to throw her things into the middle of the road where they were run over by-passing cars.

"You're nothing but a bully, and you're a terrible excuse for a human being!" She shouted at him.

"I think we need to teach this one a lesson, don't we?" Naza stated, folding his arms behind his back, and awaiting a response from his gang as what to do with her.

"Shall I give her a Chinese burn?" asked Lanky Tom Longbottom seeking permission from Naza to torture their victim. Stroking his chin, Naza thought for a moment.

"Mmm… she is a girl, but why not?" he replied callously. Immediately, Lanky Tom Longbottom took hold of Liz's arm and began to slowly twist it.

"Does it hurt?" he wanted to know as a sick grin played across his face.

"I don't know, does this?" asked Liz who bit down hard on Furious Phil Fackler's arm making him shriek at the top of his voice.

Across the road, an old couple were busy tending their garden when they heard a commotion going on.

"What's going on over there, dear?" asked Margaret of her husband. Looking up Jack, the old man tried to get a better view of what was happening.

"I think it's some children fighting," he growled, displeased by what he was seeing.

"You better go over and do something," his wife urged him. Jack shook his head disapprovingly and set off up the garden path as fast as his elderly legs would carry him.

"Oi you lot!" he shouted waving his fist at them from across the road.

Naza, seeing the old man approaching immediately decided to run away.

"Quick, scarper!" he shouted as the gang split in all directions.

Stopping the traffic with his hand, Jack ran out in front of the passing cars.

"Come here!" he shouted as he waved his fist in the air. Letting go of Jonathan's sister, Lanky Tom Longbottom and Furious Phil Fackler went racing off like a scalded cats while Naza puffing, and panting struggled to keep up.

"I know who you are!" Jack shouted as they disappeared down the road leading into the estate.

Liz stood there in tears while Jonathan lay on the pavement groaning.

"Come here, love," said Jack wrapping his big arm around Liz to comfort her. Having made sure she was alright; Jack went over to see how Jonathan was. Bending down, he saw that the boy had a bloody nose. Reaching into his trouser pocket he pulled out a handkerchief and handed it to Jonathan who had managed to prop himself up on his hands.

"Those blooming thugs!" grimaced Jack as he offered Jonathan a hand to get up.

"I don't know what's wrong with them, eh?" he grumbled, looping his arm through Jonathan's to steady him. It was then that Jack realised who they were.

"Hang on, you're Colin and Carol's lad, aren't you?" he said quizzing the young boy as to his identity. Jonathan nodded.

By this time, Jack's wife had made it across the road and was looking after Liz.

"Are you alright, my dear?" she asked Liz giving her a hug. Margaret could see the two children were upset.

"It's Colin and Carol's kids from down the road," Jack told his wife.

"Why don't we take them over to our house and we can look after them there," Suggested Margaret.

Taking the two children under their wing, Jack stepped out into the middle of the road stopping the traffic. Striding out, he wrapped his big bear-like arm around Jonathan's shoulder while Margaret ushered Liz across the road, picking up her school things as they went.

"Are you alright, my dear?" she asked pushing open the garden gate. Liz managed to raise a smile.

"I hope you gave 'em what for," remarked Jack gruffly looking down at Jonathan.

Ushering them into the front room, Margaret insisted they take a seat on the couch.

"Jack, I'll ring their parents to tell them what's happened." Immediately Jonathan told her that he didn't think there would be anyone home.

"It doesn't matter, I want your parents to know that you're safe and I'm not letting you go home till I know there is someone there to look after you," replied Margaret as she disappeared into the kitchen to get some paper towels for Jonathan to wipe his nose with. Returning with a handful of paper towels Jonathan dabbed at his nose.

While she phoned their parents, Jack stood looking out of the living room window to see if he could see any sign of the bullies.

"Looks like they've gone to me. Next time, if you and your sister have any problems, just come straight over here and I'll sort them out," he said pacing back and forth in the window with his hands behind his back.

"Don't bother knocking, just come straight in," he told them as he was interrupted by his wife.

"I don't think anyone's answering the phone," said Margaret.

"Never mind, I'll try again in a bit and if there's still no one home you can always stay and have tea with us."

Jonathan's nose had stopped bleeding and apart from it feeling a little bit sore he already felt much better.

After getting no reply from their parents Margaret asked if they would like to stay for tea. Gratefully, they accepted the offer.

"Oh, that's wonderful news. It will be nice for Jack and I to have some company for a change."

"Do you like chips?" Both Jonathan and Liz nodded their heads enthusiastically.

Margaret had been gone some time when she came through with a giant plate of chips. Jonathan and Liz looked at each other in astonishment. They had never seen such a huge pile of chips before in their life.

"You can't go wrong with a chippy tea, can you?" she giggled urging the children to tuck in.

"Help yourself. There's plenty of bread to go round," nodding to a mountain of bread and butter on the table.

"And would you like some sauce with that?" she asked. They both nodded.

While Margaret went out to the kitchen to get the sauce, Jack came in and sat down on the sofa. Giving the children a friendly wink, he leant over for a slice of bread, took a great handful of chips, and artfully arranged them on his bread. Then, neatly folding it in two, he raised the sandwich to his mouth and took a bite.

As they sat there chatting, Margaret asked if they were going anywhere nice on holiday. Liz shook her head.

"No, but the Doctor is taking us on around the world trip in his flying car," said Liz.

"A flying car? How sweet," smiled Margaret clearly not believing a word Liz was telling her. Jonathan looked at his sister as if to say not another word, but it was too late. Liz was already telling the elderly couple of all the places that she wanted to go in the world.

"The Doctor…a flying car, you say?" asked Jack, who clearly thought there was something more to it than just idle gossip.

"And just how does that work?" he asked Jonathan.

At first, he was reluctant to say but seeing as Liz had already let the cat out of the bag, he thought he might as well tell him how it operated.

"He showed us an experiment where he got a washing machine to levitate in his garden,"

"Did he now?" asked Jack helping himself to another chip butty.

"He put his cat inside the drum, and we watched it go up and down." Jonathan told him.

"Really?" asked Jack, so taken by the children's story was he that he sat on the edge of his seat listening intently.

"I've heard some pretty wild stories about the Doctor over the years," the old man told the pair.

"All of which to the best of my knowledge are true," he added.

"Some say he can read people's minds and see the future, and some say he can make things disappear in front of you. Some have even gone so far as to say the Doctor can float in mid-air just by using the power of his mind," Jack told them.

The children sat there in disbelief, not sure whether to believe what he was telling them. It was then that Liz piped up.

"He told us that he's a spaceman who's been sent here to help make the planet a better place." Jonathan gave her a dig in the ribs, but it was too late. Liz was already telling the couple of all the amazing things that he had invented.

"He's made these special glass orbs that are like mini worlds in a bottle…," she explained.

"…just in case we make a mess of our planet."

"Is that so?" noted Jack, nodding his head whilst mulling the matter over.

"A spaceman so you say. It doesn't surprise me."

Putting his plate down, Jack then stood up and walked towards the window, staring out of it as if recalling some dim and distant memory.

"I've seen some pretty strange things over the years of living here you know. Things that have been mainly connected with the Doctor," he said pursing his lips and nodding in the direction of the Doctor's house.

"Remember that night I told you about, dear?" he said turning to his wife and looking rather serious.

"It was late one evening and I had been busy working on my model railway. I had come out of the garage for some fresh air, and I was stood in the front garden having a cup of tea, when five spaceships turned up, hovering right over the Doctor's house," he said nodding to the children.

"I remember that love," said his wife recalling the incident.

"At first it was hard to see them as you could see right through them. Then as if they came out from the other side of the light barrier, you could see them properly. They shimmered like holograms and when you looked up at them you could see all the stars through them. It was incredible!"

"That's the Doctor's family!" piped up Liz.

"He said they sometimes come by to visit him," she told them. The old man turned and smiled at the children.

"But that's not the half of it… we've had all sorts of strange things fly over the house, making a beeline for the Doctor's place, you know," he added.

"Tell me, have you two noticed anything strange in the night sky recently?" asked Jack.

Liz and Jonathan both looked at each other wondering what he was on about.

"After midnight when I've finished playing with my trains, and I come out for my cup of tea, I've noticed something rather odd, and it's happening every night," said Jack divulging what he knew.

"There's a strange hum in the air, the house begins to shake, and an almighty flash of light goes shooting up into the sky. Have you seen it?" he asked.

Jonathan was careful not to say anything, not wanting to give away the Doctor's secret.

"The light, it's coming from the Doctor's place, you know. Has he said anything to you about it?" asked Jack eager to know if the children knew anything more. It was obvious to Jonathan that what Jack was talking about was the mirrored disc.

"It's the biggest project he's ever worked on," admitted Jonathan careful not to give away too much.

"He says that it's his life work, his greatest invention yet,"

"I knew it!" Jack muttered as he paced back and forth excitably in front of the window.

"Calm down, dear," Margaret urged him patting the empty sofa for him to come and sit down.

"We don't want you having a heart attack with all the excitement, do we now?" She said. Sitting down on the sofa next to his wife, the old man leant forward wishing to know more of what Jonathan had to tell him.

"He hasn't got a name for it yet, but he says that when he unveils it, it will change the world for the better," Jonathan told him.

Rubbing his hands together in excitement, Jack laughed loudly.

"That old boy, he's a wily old fox, isn't he? I bet it's some amazing new device to help us all out, isn't it?"

As they ate the last of the chips, all Jack could do was chuckle away to himself as he thought about what the Doctor's latest invention could be.

-11-

THE POSITIVE THOUGHT ACCUMULATOR

JONATHAN AND LIZ found the Doctor hard at work in his greenhouse muttering away to himself. With a pencil stuck behind his ear he was poring over his laptop, examining his many plans while surrounded by endless pages of calculations, rubbings out and pencil shavings.

"Hello, you two," he called out suddenly becoming aware of the children's presence. Pushing his glasses up onto his forehead, he rubbed his eyes wearily.

"I was just busy with my work here," he said tipping his head in the direction of his plans and blueprints that had spilt over his desk and onto the floor below him.

"Don't you ever rest?" Asked Liz.

"I find it hard to rest when there is so much to be done here on Earth," he replied.

Then, casting his gaze over at the children, he noticed that Jonathan was looking a little down. Rummaging around in his cardigan pocket, he looked for a sweet.

"What's the matter, eh?" asked the Doctor offering him a toffee. Taking the Doctor up on his offer, Jonathan reluctantly told the Doctor about the incident with Naza and his gang on the way home from school.

"That dastardly child!" remarked the Doctor, snorting down his nose in disgust.

"His gang are the ones that throw stones through my windows. It's about time someone gave him a taste of his own medicine!" fumed the Doctor.

Pacing up and down the greenhouse he thought of how best to deal with this dreadful boy.

"I know, I could invent a treacle gun and we could hose him down from head to toe in the black gooey stuff, or we could dangle him head first in a vat of Fug Munchers and he would be forced to breathe in their terrible stink... or I could put him in my atomic thread extruder and we could stretch him until he popped like a grape," the Doctor deliberated as he weighed up what should be a suitable punishment for the bully.

"I'd like to see him covered in treacle, that would be fun," laughed Liz.

"And what say you Jonathan, a treacle gun eh?" said the Doctor seeking the opinion of the young boy.

"Can't you invent a pant wedging machine that pulls his pants up so tight around his ears that they split?"

"Ahh...I like your style; now you're beginning to think like them," noted the Doctor taking a pencil out from behind his ear and doing a rough sketch on the corner of an old jotter.

"Something like this I presume," he said handing over the drawing.

"That's it," replied Jonathan letting out a giggle.

"Then he'd know what it feels like to be bullied."

Folding up the piece of paper, the Doctor put his drawing to one side just in case it needed to be consulted on at a later date. That's when Liz took the opportunity to ask the Doctor a question that had been on her mind.

"The man over the road says that you can levitate in mid-air just by using the power of your mind,"

The Doctor stopped what he was doing for a second and looked down at the little girl.

"Who is this man that you're talking about?" he enquired with a look of surprise on his face.

"Jack, who lives across the road. The man who saved us from the bullies," she said pointing.

"He sounds like a nice man, not that I've met him mind you, and what is it he's said about me?" enquired the Doctor as he tinkered with a piece of equipment on his bench.

"He says that you can float in mid-air using your mind."

"Whether or not I can float in mid-air is inconsequential. IF, and I'm only saying this …IF I could float in the air using the power of my mind then I would not spend all my time doing so. Especially not when there are so many people in the world that are in need of my help. It would be a great waste of my time to do so."

"But can you?" asked Liz persisting in her questioning.

"You're relentless, aren't you?" he said letting out a long sigh.

"Maybe one day when you're old enough, you can answer that question yourself."

Liz was disappointed that she didn't get an answer from him, but she was sure that floating in mid-air was something the Doctor was capable of.

Patting her fondly on the shoulder, the Doctor went in search of some clean cups leaving her with something to think about.

"Anyway, are you two ready for our little road trip?" he asked tipping Ajna out of his chair as he pushed past him to fill the kettle up.

"We've thought of some places that we'd like to visit," replied Jonathan pulling out a folded-up piece of paper from his pocket.

"Go on then, I'm all ears," said the Doctor running the kettle under the tap and putting it onto boil.

Unfurling the piece of paper, Jonathan began to read aloud all the places that they'd like to visit.

"Niagara Falls, The Grand Canyon and Liz would like to see a kangaroo,"

"A good choice," said the Doctor brushing the cat hairs from the cushion and taking up position in the chair.

"Carry on, carry on," he said encouraging the young boy as he pulled out a box from under the bench for Liz to sit on.

"The Himalayas, The Pyramids, The Leaning Tower of Pisa…" Jonathan continued.

"I'd like to see a blue whale and a tiger if that's possible and Liz would like to go dog sledding in the snow."

"I'm not sure that we'll be able to fit them all in, but we'll give it a try," noted the Doctor letting out a great big yawn as Jonathan continued to read off his list.

"The Great Barrier Reef…and the biggest apple pie in the world made by Mrs Maperson of Wenatchee, Washington State, USA."

"The biggest apple pie in the world?" declared the Doctor.

"Surely that's been eaten by now?"

"Yes, but apparently they still make apple pies and they're supposed to be the best in the world."

Having completed his list, Jonathan sat down on a box taking the weight off his feet while the Doctor poured himself a cup of tea.

"Is there anywhere that you'd like to visit?" Liz asked the Doctor as Ajna leapt up onto her lap for a stroke.

"Mmm…where would I like to go most on Earth?" he said aloud as he stroked his chin thoughtfully.

"You know, there's only one place a chap such as myself would like to go. Up there! So, I could look down on the Earth and behold what a fantastical sight it is," he said, pointing up at the blue sky above his head.

"It has to be somewhere on Earth; you can't choose space, silly," Liz reminded him.

"In that case I don't know, maybe under the sea so I could look at all the pretty fishes perhaps," he answered before sitting back in his chair and dunking his biscuit in a cup of tea.

As they sat there sharing a drink and biscuit together, the Doctor enquired as to the progress of Jonathan's biosphere.

"We haven't had any unexpected leaks recently, have we?"

"No…" replied Jonathan.

"… but we have had to put a blanket over the top of it to stop my parents from being able to see the light that comes from it."

"Ah…talking of your parents," remarked the Doctor taking a sip of tea and reclining in his chair.

"We'll have to come up with a way in which we can get you off school for the day. I could ring your respective schools and pretend to be your father. That way I could tell them that you're sick and that you won't be coming in. How does that sound?"

"But what about our mother? She always knows when someone's lying," replied Jonathan anxiously.

"Don't you worry about that. I've thought of that too. I'll write a letter to your parents saying that were going on a school trip. I thought a trip to the seaside, or the zoo would be an appropriate place for a day out. How does that sound?" Jonathan bit his lip nervously unsure of the Doctor's plan.

"I'll run it up here on my laptop," explained the Doctor trying to put his mind at his ease.

"I can even put the school emblem in the corner and make it look all official, and you can get your mother or father to sign it to say they give you their consent. They won't suspect a thing once I've had my hand in it," noted the Doctor with a sly wink. Dunking another biscuit in his tea, the Doctor sat back in his chair with a smug look on his face.

He then asked if they might be interested in seeing the latest developments he had made to his flying car.

Outside, the late afternoon sun shone down on the tarpaulin that was strung up above the car. With every gust of wind, the nylon sheet billowed and buffeted like a ship in full sail making a terrible racket. Showing them around the car the first thing they noticed was that it no longer had any wheels and was jacked up on axle stands.

"Where have the wheels gone? We're going to need wheels, aren't we?" asked Jonathan bending down to take a better look. The Doctor laughed at him.

"Jonathan, as far as I'm concerned, the wheel has been consigned to the scrapheap of history," scoffed the Doctor flippantly putting his hand on the young boy's shoulder.

"I have replaced the wheels with large magnets from a public address system and along with a high voltage wiring loom I have installed it will propel the car wherever we want to go – we'll never need to venture onto tarmac ever again."

"But wouldn't it be sensible to have some wheels?"

"Sensible!" roared the Doctor.

"Is it sensible that we drive around in horribly polluting cars, clogging up the whole world with our dirty exhaust fumes? That doesn't seem very sensible to me when we can fly free like birds. Look, just hang on a minute. I've got something to show you." The Doctor jumped in the car and flicked a switch on the dashboard.

As he did so Ajna decided to stroll underneath the car making his fur stand on end.

"Ajna, let's have you out from there!" shouted the Doctor beckoning for his favourite pet to come out. After shooing Ajna out from underneath the car, he enquired if they would like a ride. The children nodded, eager to have a ride in the Doctors new flying car.

Holding the car door open for them, the children scrutinised it carefully before agreeing that it looked safe. Folding down the front seat, the children then scrambled into the back. It was then that Jonathan cried out that there was no steering wheel.

"Of course not, why would there be when we can use the power of our mind to navigate our way around?"

From the driver's seat the Doctor explained that the car could read brainwaves. Excited and wanting to know more, the children pulled themselves up on the front seats to have a look.

"How does it work?" asked Jonathan.

"All I have to do is place my hands on these sensors here. Then I just think where I want it to go, it's that easy. Are you ready?"

"Are you sure this is going to work?" asked a worried looking Jonathan.

"Oh, ye of little faith!" laughed Oban dismissing Jonathan's concerns.

"We'll just take it for a quick once round the garden eh, nothing too difficult,"

Upon placing his hands on the pads, the car reacted instantaneously as if connecting with the Doctor's mind. Rising ever so slightly into the air, it trembled like a leaf on a gentle breeze and then instantly leapt five feet into the air and came to a dead stop. With the tarpaulin flapping wildly against the roof of the Reliant Robin the children were thrown from their seats and against the roof of the car, such was the acceleration.

"Sorry about that," apologised the Doctor.

"I've got to get used to the controls again. It's a few lifetimes ago since I last flew one of these things. Right let's have another go," he said laughing.

Reminding him to be a little bit more careful this time, Liz held on tightly while her brother did the same. Gently the car descended back to the ground and concentrating harder the Doctor made the car glide gently forwards, out into the clearing that surrounded the greenhouse.

Making no sound whatsoever, they rose higher into the air as the Doctor exerted the power of his mind over the car. However, the crows nesting in the trees were startled by the appearance of the car and began to squawk loudly.

"Look we can see our house from here!" declared Liz. Seeming pleased with his efforts the Doctor gently brought the car back down to the ground. As he did so, Ajna ran underneath.

"That drated cat!" The Doctor cried from the driver's seat.

"Get out of the way, you daft thing!" he yelled, shooing Anja away with his hand. With a bemused look on his whiskery face, the ginger tom let out a terrible screech as if he had just been trodden on as he ran for cover in the bushes. Hovering on a cushion of air, the car came to rest just above the ground.

"Can we have another go?" asked an exuberant Jonathan.

"All in good time, my dear boy. Good things come to those who wait." declared the Doctor, opening the door with a faint crackle of static.

Back on the ground, Jonathan stood in awe of the would-be spaceship.

"Won't it be amazing when everyone has a flying car," remarked Jonathan, barely able to contain himself.

"Mmm it will…but there will be something far more amazing than that in the future," replied the Doctor.

The Doctor taking his time sat down on an old cast iron grass roller that was rusting away in the long grass. Leaning back with his arms folded, he cast his gaze upwards.

"That up there, that is the future," said the Doctor pointing to the mirrored disc that sat a on top of his greenhouse.

"That my dear boy is the thing that will make people's dreams come true," he said excitedly while patting the old roller for the children to come and join him.

"I'd like to let you in on a little secret. I want to let you know that I have thought of a name for my machine," declared the Doctor. I have decided to call it the *Positive Thought Accumulator*…" he announced.

"…Or **P.T.A** for short." Liz thought about the name for a moment.

"You mean it's called Peter?" she said.

"What do you mean it's called Peter?" The Doctor asked.

"Well, if you say each of the letters individually then it sounds like Peter."

"Pee…Tee…Ahh," she elaborated as she spelled out its name.

"Pee…Tah, you see!"

"Oh, I'd never thought of it that way. How clever!" the Doctor mused, taken aback by Liz's inventiveness.

"But what does it do?" asked Jonathan wanting to know more.

The Doctor let out a long sigh as if all the years of accumulated pressure working on the project had finally been released.

"What doesn't it do is more to the question. I like to think of it as a dream machine where dreams can come true, which should suit you two down to the ground as you're such great dreamers," the children looked at each other astonished.

"What do you mean, it makes *your* dreams come true?" Asked Liz.

"It does precisely *that!*" remarked the Doctor as he tickled Ajna behind the ear.

Instantly, Liz's mind flew to all the amazing things she could think of as well as all the happy thoughts that she could make come true.

"You mean we can do anything we want?" she asked, unable to believe what she was hearing.

"Anything at all." the Doctor replied before continuing to elaborate on the properties of the Positive Thought Accumulator.

"You see what it does is… it takes all these wonderful dreams that people have and mixes them together like water in the ocean. It's all one giant computer programme really," he mused while picking away at the worn twill on his trousers in a studious manner.

"Is that what you've been doing all these years, working on the Positive Thought Accumulator?" asked Jonathan, taken aback by the profoundness of the Doctor's new invention.

"That's right. It is what I was put on this planet for, to make people believe in the power of their own amazing dreams. So, they may realise they can live in a world that's more magical than you can ever imagine, however…" continued the Doctor.

"…the Positive Thought Accumulator is far greater than I am. It is self-aware."

"Is that what the light is at night… people's dreams going out into the world?" asked Jonathan.

"Correct," replied the Doctor, revelling in the machine's greatness while leaning back on the old grass roller and stretching his legs out.

"It's billions and billions of marvellous dreams going out into the world for people to dream," he replied wistfully as he thought about how amazing his invention truly was.

"But what about bad dreams, where do they come from?" asked Jonathan concerned.

"Boggrobblers!" replied the Doctor abruptly.

"Boggrobblers?" questioned Jonathan who thought he hadn't heard right.

"Yes Boggrobblers! Spiteful little creatures that like to get in the works and cause all sorts of havoc," said the Doctor with a pained expression as he explained what they were.

"I do my best to track them down. They like to spoil people's dreams. They lurk in the deepest, darkest bits of the programme and cause horrible nightmares. Do you know how I trap them?" asked the Doctor.

"I tempt them out of their dark little holes with rotten eggs. There's nothing more they like than the stench of a sulphurous egg…" the Doctor elaborated.

"…and then when they are just about to grab the egg, they fall through a trap door I have created in the programme, and they're shredded into millions of tiny little pieces. Rather ingenious of me if you ask me," the Doctor giggled.

"But they're nothing to worry about. They can't harm you," he hastened to add.

"When will we be able to have a go?" asked Liz tugging at the Doctor's sleeve, already with a thousand and one fantastical dreams of her own that she wanted to come true.

"There's a few more tweaks that I'd like to make to the machine, or Peter as you call it, then we should be ready," answered the Doctor.

"I assure you; you'll be the first to see it when I have it fully up and running… mark my words." Rising to his feet, he almost tripped up over Ajna as he went to close the doors on the greenhouse for the night. After a most entertaining evening, he wished the children goodnight, warning them not to say a word to their parents about their upcoming round the world trip.

-12-

AROUND THE WORLD TRIP

THERE WAS A nip in the air that morning as the two children made their way over to the Doctor's house. Setting out earlier than usual for school, Jonathan was wearing his big, thick jacket with a furry hood and Liz, her duffle coat, mittens, and hat. The Doctor having stipulated that they wear something warm for their trip.

Having left the front gate unlocked, the children made their way up the drive not bothering with the front door. Round the back of the house, they found the kitchen lights on, and the windows steamed up – a sure sign that the Doctor was up and about. Giving a knock, Jonathan opened the door and shouted to the Doctor.

"Come in, come in!" he replied from somewhere off in the kitchen. Filing through the pantry and cloakroom they found him busy in his kitchen.

"What a fantastic day we've got ahead of us, eh?" enthused the Doctor as he paced back and forth making sure he had got everything they needed for the trip. On the table were picnic baskets full of goodies.

Clattering around his cupboards whilst searching for what he was looking for, the Doctor engaged the children in conversation.

"How did you like my impression of the school secretary over the phone to your mother yesterday?" he giggled.

"How did you do that?" Jonathan asked, looking completely baffled as to how the Doctor had managed to fool his mother by impersonating the school secretary.

"I thought we were going to be in big trouble."

The Doctor laughed as he put one of his homemade cakes in a plastic box and sealed it tight.

"I had foreseen that your mother was going to ring the school and check-up. Fortunately, I have the ability to see into the future and so was one step ahead of her. You see if she had found out about our little trip we would have been completely scuppered."

"You can see into the future?" gasped Liz, amazed that such a thing was possible.

"Yes, it is one of my many abilities. It is a very useful gift but something I like to keep quiet. I only use the ability when absolutely necessary and the situation demands it," said the Doctor giving a sly wink.

"It must be brilliant to see the future," she added looking astounded.

"Seeing into the future is not all it's cracked up to be," replied the Doctor with a furrowed brow.

"But there must be all sorts of brilliant things you could do?" she said intrigued to know more.

"Ahh…yes there is," the Doctor admitted.

"You have the power to change all sorts of things and make the world a better place, but the downside is that you get to see all the terrible things that humans can do to each other I'm afraid," he said stroking his chin and looking in one of the cupboards as if he had forgotten something.

"Ahh… yes sandwiches!" he said to himself as if he had remembered.

"What were we talking about?" he asked Liz as if losing his train of thought.

"The future," she reminded him.

"Ahh…yes that was it, the future!" recalled the Doctor taking his sandwiches from the fridge and packing them in his cool bag.

"The future is not set you see, anything can happen. Yet there are certain events that, shall we say, leave an imprint on the field of consciousness. One can read them as one of the many possibilities that the future holds…" he continued to elaborate.

"…but the future is like rippling waves on a giant ocean, nothing is permanent. That is why I built the Positive Thought Accumulator. To harness all the good energy and dreams in the world and to make it a better place for everyone. Thinking good thoughts and nice things for people is the key to it all," he said as he rooted around to make sure he had packed his best China for the trip.

"What? It's that easy to make a better future?" questioned Liz not believing it could be as simple as that.

"People like to think that making the world a better place is such a difficult task, when in reality all you have to do is get along with one another," stated the Doctor.

As he surveyed what he had packed, he suddenly remembered something and clutched at his forehead in despair.

"Ajna!" he cried out aloud.

"How could I forget my dear old Ajna?" he said bending down to tickle the fickle tomcat under the chin.

Nipping into the pantry, the Doctor poured out a large saucer of milk and put some biscuits in his bowl before finally running through what was left to do.

"Ahh... that's it, all I have to do now is ring your schools and pretend to be your father and tell them that you are ill and won't be in today," he said giving the children a mischievous grin.

"Are you allowed to do that?" asked Liz.

"I'm a traveller of space and time; I can do whatever I like, within reason of course!" he giggled before disappearing into the hallway.

While the Doctor rang the school, Liz and Jonathan carried the bags out to the car. It wasn't long before the Doctor joined them. Wearing a flat cap, earmuffs, an Inverness cape that went down to his knees, a pair of sheepskin mittens and a pair of tan, knee-high boots, the Doctor was ready for the off.

"So, my young explorers, are we ready?" he asked them as the sun began to filter through the trees. The children nodded as they clambered into the back seat of the car.

"I have made a flight plan that should take in all the sights and have us home in time for supper," he informed them as he settled down into the driver's seat.

Putting his hands on the thought controls, the car gently rose into the air and cleared the trees surrounding the house.

"Wow, what a sight!" declared Liz as she watched the sun rise over the city and catch on all the buildings.

"It really is something, isn't it?" remarked the doctor, squinting through the harsh light of dawn.

With the gravity damper on and the electromagnetic plasma drive engaged, the Doctor pressed the hyperdrive button and the car was suddenly charged with high voltage power that went surging around the car.

"Next stop, the Artic Circle!" he called out over his shoulder as the old Reliant became translucent and reality became fluid. The car then disappeared into a gravity displacement hole of its very own making.

Soon the land was zipping by below them, and they were heading out across the ocean towards the North Pole, their first stop. All around them a multitude of racing colours flashed by, while down below the Earth looked even more magnificent than it normally did.

"Is this what it feels like to fly a spaceship?" Liz asked.

"Pretty much," replied the Doctor casting his memory back several lifetimes ago.

"However, the craft that I used to pilot was far more advanced than this, I hate to say."

With barely time to blink, they had crossed the time convergence threshold and arrived at their destination.

"Ahh, looks like we're here!" he said spotting a small group of Inuit who had set up camp on the far shore of the frozen ocean.

"Didn't you want to go dog sledding?" asked the Doctor. Nodding, Liz pulled herself up on the seat in front to get a better view.

Hovering above a deep bank of snow the Huskies began to bark wildly at the arrival of the strange object that descended from the sky. Everyone from the village came out to see what was going on. Having never seen a flying car before, they rushed over to take a closer look and were most surprised to see the Doctor and two children alight from the strange looking vehicle.

Going over to meet the village elder the Doctor rubbed noses with him; such was the custom in these parts. Unable to speak Inuit the Doctor communicated telepathically, allowing his mind to show the elder that they were very much hoping to go for a sled ride. The village elder nodded and smiled from behind his fur-lined hood. All the while the whole camp looked on in amazement, wondering who the strangers were and if the hovering car was some sort of spacecraft.

Deciding that it would be nice to offer the residents of the village some of his homemade sponge cake, the Doctor opened the boot of the car. Taking out his picnic table, hamper and, his best China, he set it out on the frozen ocean for a tea party. As Jonathan was well trained in table manners, he cut slices of cake for everyone and poured cups of tea, which the Inuit seemed very much delighted by.

The village elder then beckoned for the Doctor to join him on his sled while Jonathan and Liz were shown to another sled belonging to the elder's grandson. The dogs set off at great pace, yelping and pulling on their leashes, such was their excitement.

"How do you like your sled ride?" shouted the Doctor to the children from over on his sled.

"It's fantastic!" Liz shouted back.

As they travelled through the icy landscape, the silence was immense. Taking out their phones and selfie sticks they tried to catch the beauty of the moment. It was then that the Inuit showed them a paw print of a polar bear. Wishing to take a photograph, Jonathan got his sister to put her foot next to the imprint so he could take a photo for everybody at his show and tell. However, as time was pressing the Doctor let the chief know that they should return to camp.

Back at camp, everyone took turns to rub noses, but not before Liz and Jonathan had the opportunity to take a good look inside an igloo. With time running short, the Doctor called to the children.

"Come on you two, we've got a lot of places to tick off before we get you home tonight," he said. Saying goodbye to their new friends they got back in the car and took off.

Flying in the Doctor's car was a strange sensation. It was more like dreaming than anything else. Reality became fluid and didn't react in the same way as it normally did. It felt as if you could put your hand right through the skin of the car and almost scoop time up in your hands; such was the odd sensation.

It wasn't long before Niagara Falls could be seen. Bringing the car to a hover over the falls, they sat above the rim – at the point where the water plunged over the edge and cascaded down onto the rocks below. Jonathan keen to get a memento of his trip insisted that he fill a jam jar full of water from the falls.

"Do we have to?" Said the Doctor sounding a little exasperated.

"Of course we do, I'm collecting things for my show and tell."

Clambering into the front seat, the Doctor edged the car even closer to the falls, so Jonathan could lean out of the window and hold the jam jar under the water. As he did so the Doctor noticed they were starting to attract the unwanted attention of one or two sightseers who had noticed the car and were beginning to point up at them.

"Right, I think it's time to leave," declared the Doctor aware that they had outstayed their welcome. Looking at his watch, he thought it was about time for breakfast.

"How about we call in on Mrs Maperson of Wenatchee for a bite to eat?" Said the Doctor patting his stomach.

Skipping across the whole of the United States in a heartbeat, they were soon circling over Wenatchee on the lookout for the home of the world's largest apple pie.

"It must be there!" shouted Liz from the backseat as she spotted what looked like a large sign in the front garden of a house. The Doctor put the car down in the street outside and without anybody noticing they all got out.

After investigating the sign outside the Doctor found that the café was not open till eleven.

"But it's only nine o'clock. We can't wait that long," grumbled Jonathan.

"Not to worry, I'm sure that when she hears that we've come all the way from England to taste her world-renowned pies, she'll be most agreeable to our arrival," noted the Doctor taking off his mittens. After knocking loudly on the door he removed his earmuffs and cap and flattened down his hair with his hand as he tried to make himself look presentable. While they waited for an answer, they breathed in the sweet, scented air of freshly baked pies.

The door opened and out stepped a warm-faced, rotund lady with an apron on.

"Good morning madam, we were wondering if we could taste some of your wonderful pies," said the Doctor in his best English accent.

"I'm sorry honey but we don't start serving till eleven," she replied.

"Ahh… well," explained the Doctor.

"We have flown all the way here from England in our car, you see, and my little friend here was rather hoping to set eyes on the world's largest pie," said the Doctor presenting the young boy for her to see.

"Aww…shucks honey. Ain't nothing left o' that but the tin. But seeing as you've come all the way from the UK, how about you come in and try one of my pies instead. Follow me an' step inside," she said inviting them in.

Taking off their coats, they sat down at one of the booths and waited for her to serve them.

"Hank!" she shouted to her husband in the back. "We got some folks here from England to see the pie."

From out of the back came a man with a bald head, greying beard, and a tanned complexion.

"So, which one of you has come to see the world's biggest pie eh?" he asked. Jonathan's hand shot up.

"Well sonny, let me show you what's left of it," The old man led them over to the window and pointed.

"See that?" he said nodding to a large metal dish half buried in the garden.

"Well, that's all that remains of the world's largest apple pie: the tin,"

Liz and Jonathan propped themselves up on the window as they tried to get a better view.

"It's smaller than I thought it would be," remarked Jonathan, sounding a little deflated.

"What were you expecting?" asked the Doctor.

"I thought it would be as big as a house," Jonathan answered back.

"Let me tell you sonny, it took some cookin' mind you," came the man's quick reply.

By now, Mrs Maperson thought it was time that her husband returned to the kitchen to get on with his work and after shooing him away, she came to take their order.

"Now what can I get y'all?" she said taking her notepad and pen from her top pocket. While they perused the menu, Mrs Maperson wanted to know how they had travelled there.

"By flying car," replied Jonathan quick as a flash before the Doctor had chance to speak.

"Heck honey, ain't nobody got a flying car!" she said as Jonathan pointed to the old Reliant sat hovering just above the road.

"Well, I never. I s'pose you've all got flying cars in England now, haven't you?"

"Not exactly Madam," the doctor piped up.

"This is an experimental vehicle, a one-off."

"Ahh… I see and is this a vacation you're on?" she asked. The Doctor explained to her that it was an educational field trip that he was taking the children on.

By now Jonathan, had decided what pie he would like and that he'd have rhubarb with cream. Mrs Maperson then asked Liz what she wanted.

"I'll have coconut cream pie, I think." While the Doctor plumped for a traditional apple pie with ice cream. They didn't have to wait long to be served, and the good thing about being so early was that all the pies were fresh out of the oven, and they were still piping hot.

After finishing their pies, they went outside with Mr and Mrs Maperson to have their photo taken in front of the world's largest pie tin. Before they left, Mrs Maperson gave each of them a hug and kiss on the cheek and told them they could come back anytime, and she even gave them a couple of free pies to take away.

As the car rose silently into the air, they waved goodbye to the sweet old couple. The Doctor pointed the car south and they then headed out over the ocean. Below them, fishermen were paying out their lines in their small, brightly painted boats. Like tiny dots upon the azure ocean Jonathan couldn't imagine a more perfect day even in his most amazing dreams.

Heading for Sugarloaf Mountain and the sweltering beach of Copacabana they flew over hundreds of miles of pristine rainforest. It was just like the Doctor said: like one of his biospheres, only better! The Doctor, giddy with excitement, called out to the children.

"It's just like the old days, flying my spaceship around the universe!" he reminisced.

"One minute, I'd be flying around the planet Lahanti in the Tarnakhan Galaxy and next I was racing through the Parphellion star belt with giant nebulae all around me," he gushed excitedly, recalling the memory of several lifetimes ago.

It was mid-day when they reached Australia. Setting the car down under a shady grove of Eucalyptus trees the Doctor took out his picnic basket and set up his foldaway table and chairs, insisting that they put the tablecloth on first before they ate.

"We can't let standards slip, can we?" he remarked laughing at his own eccentricity.

"Sorry, there aren't any kangaroos, Liz. I thought they'd be everywhere. I didn't realise they'd be so hard to find," he said looking out from the shade of the trees at the baking hot rocks protruding from the red earth.

"It doesn't matter. I think it's too hot to go looking for them anyway," she said wafting her hand in front of her face as she tried to cool down.

As they sat there resting in the shade drinking plenty of water and eating their sandwiches, the children showed the Doctor all the photographs and videos they had taken of their morning's activities.

"See, it's better than a day at school, isn't it?" the Doctor mused as he sipped on his ginger and soda. It was then that Jonathan told the Doctor that when he was older, he'd like to build his own flying car. The Doctor applauded Jonathan's vision.

"That's wonderful news!" replied the Doctor who was busy eating his peanut butter and banana sandwich with the crusts cut off.

"And you know what? You've already got the most important thing essential for any inventor."

"What's that?" Jonathan asked intrigued.

"You're a dreamer! Dreamers are by far the best people in the world; they make the future come true, you see," he said, reaching into his pocket and dabbing his forehead with his handkerchief.

It was then that they heard the rustling of leaves and from out behind a bush, a slender man emerged walking towards them. They realised it was that of an Aboriginal man carrying with him a tall thin stick. The Doctor immediately got up from his chair to greet him.

"Hello, would you like to join us in a spot of pie and ice cream?" he asked holding out his hand for the gentleman to shake. The tall thin man introduced himself as Yileen and sat down on a rock, studying them closely.

"I saw you arrive in your spaceship. I've been watching you from over on that rock there," he said pointing.

"Have you travelled far?" he asked, half expecting they'd come from the other side of the galaxy. Liz politely explained that they had come from England. The Aboriginal man thought about it for a second before speaking, still convinced that they were from space.

"I suppose you could go to the stars in that thing if you wanted to though?" he asked, eager to know more.

"Technically, we could but as this is only an experimental vehicle. I wouldn't want to take such a risk on a flight like that," replied the Doctor.

"I've seen spaceships before…but not like this one," Yileen said as he looked the old Reliant over. Taking out one of the pies the Doctor cut him a slice.

It was then that Liz asked Yileen if he knew where they could find any kangaroos. He replied that he did but said they would have to take the spaceship as it was too far to walk.

While they sat around eating, Yileen asked the Doctor how he was able to build a spaceship. The Doctor explained that many lifetimes ago he had been a spaceman on another planet and was able to tap into the collective knowledge of the universe.

"Part of my mission here on Earth is to help humans evolve so they may one day be accepted into the interstellar community. Unfortunately, humans are not the easiest species to work with."

Eating his pie, Yileen mulled over what the Doctor had to say.

"Yeah, humans are big dumb monkeys if you ask me." he laughed agreeing with the Doctor.

After packing the picnic things away, the Doctor invited Yileen to take them to see some kangaroos. It being one of the things on Liz's list. Clambering into the car, Yileen was inquisitive to know how the Doctor flew it as there was no steering wheel, and so the Doctor explained to him that what he did was to think his way to wherever he wanted to go.

"You mean you dream it?" asked Yileen with a big grin on his face as if he knew that was the only way that something like that would work.

The Doctor shuffled over inviting Yileen to take up position in the driver's seat. Placing his hands on the thought pads, Yileen's mind connected with the sophisticated conscious-based computer and within seconds they were racing over the rocky landscape.

Spotting a troop of kangaroos feeding below them he set the car down.

"Is that close enough?" he asked flashing a big toothy grin at the children. Getting out of the car, he instructed the children to wait while he went and cut down a tall stand of grass with his knife.

"Are you sure they wouldn't prefer a biscuit?" asked the Doctor holding out a half-eaten pack of biscuits and waving it in the direction of the kangaroos. Yileen shook his head as if he was crazy!

Returning with a large bundle of grass under his arm, he handed a clump to each child.

"Here we are, this should get them eating out of your hand." As the children stood there, the Doctor encouraged Liz to hand over her phone so he could film her feeding the kangaroos.

"Hold it out towards 'em," Yileen instructed. Slowly, a large mature roo approached the children and, standing tall on his hind legs with his ears pricked up, looked them up and down. Then, twitching his nose the giant kangaroo began to eat the grass from out of Jonathan's hand.

It didn't take long for the rest of the kangaroos to join in. As Jonathan and Liz fed the roos, Yileen cut down some more grass and handed it to them. Even the Doctor joined in with the fun, offering biscuits to the hungry creatures.

Standing in the stifling afternoon heat, things were beginning to get a little too hot for Jonathan and he began to complain he wasn't feeling well. Helping Jonathan back to the car the Doctor made sure he had plenty of cold water to drink and said to Yileen that they better call it a day.

"Any chance you can drop me off at home on your way to which ever star system you're going to next?" asked Yileen still half suspecting they had a trip to the stars planned that they weren't telling him about. The Doctor said it would be no problem and so saying their goodbyes to the group of kangaroos, Liz joined her brother in the car as they took off to take Yileen home.

On approaching his home, Yileen invited them to have something to eat with him, but concerned for Jonathan's condition the Doctor politely declined, wishing to take Jonathan somewhere a little less hot. Waving goodbye to him, the car vanished into thin air right before Yileen's very eyes.

Before you could say "hoojamaflip" they were hovering over the pristine white sands of a beach on the Great Barrier Reef. Changing into his knitted swimming trunks, the Doctor ran down to the ocean clutching his mask and snorkel and dived straight in.

"Come on in, the water's lovely!" he shouted. Not needing any further encouragement, the children rushed down to the beach and were soon cooling off in the refreshing waters of the Pacific Ocean.

"I think you had a touch of sunstroke, my dear boy," remarked the Doctor standing up to his waist in the crystal-clear blue waters and putting his hand to Jonathan's forehead to feel his temperature.

The children, with their goggles on, swam around for hours marvelling at all the amazing fish and pretty-coloured coral before the Doctor called them out. Drying himself off with a towel, the Doctor looked at his watch.

"Gosh, I didn't realise the time; we'd better get you home!" he declared as he hopped around trying to dry his feet off without getting sand on them.

Jumping back in the car, they were soon racing faster than the crossing point of light with only the coefficient of cosmic drag to slow them down.

It was getting dark when they arrived back. As dusk was setting, they spotted Naza Hav'em and the Top Road Gang loitering around on a street corner. Being as unpleasant as possible to one other, they were wiping bogeys on each other, jumping through hedges, and holding a spitting competition to see who could spit the biggest, nastiest greenie the furthest.

"Look! There's Naza Hav'em and his gang," shouted Jonathan pointing out of the window of the car to the group of troublemakers below.

"Mmm…Naza Hav'em. Isn't that the boy who's been bullying you?" asked the Doctor taking the car round again for another look. Jonathan had an uneasy feeling that the Doctor was up to something.

"I think that boy deserves a taste of his own medicine, what do you say?" said the Doctor as he took the car down lower so as it was skimming the rooftops. Emitting no sound whatsoever and giving off a dazzling white light, the car flew silently towards the bullies.

As Naza Hav'em was coughing up the biggest, fattest most disgusting mouthful of spit he had ever produced, he suddenly caught sight of something in the night sky.

"What's that?!" he cried out pointing up at the bright light. Dazzler turned to look.

"It's a spaceship! Run for it!" yelled Dazzler seeing the bright light coming towards them. Terrified he broke into a sprint. Meanwhile, the rest of the gang split. Furious Phil Fackler, Lanky Tom Longbottom and Mad Dog Mortimer ran as fast as their legs would carry them, while the Doctor circled around Naza Hav'em giving him all his attention.

Running as fast as his pudgy legs would carry him, it wasn't long before Naza ran out of breath and the Doctor caught up with him. Blinded by the light that radiated from the car, Naza put his hand up to shield himself from the glare.

"Please don't take me away!" he blubbed as he began to cry like a baby.

The Doctor looked over at Jonathan in the back seat.

"Do you think he's learnt his lesson?" He said with a smile on his face. Jonathan nodded. Seeing Naza huddled in the street crying and having wet his pants, Jonathan took pity on him.

"Naza, it's alright we're not going to hurt you, it's just our flying car," he said leaning out of the car window.

Naza, put his hand to his face to see and looked up to see Jonathan staring down at him. Not able to comprehend what he was seeing he began to cry some more.

"I think our work here is done, don't you?" Said the Doctor with a satisfied smile on his face.

"I don't think you'll have any more problems with him, do you?"

-13-

HOW TO MAKE A
DREAM COME TRUE

I T WAS PLAYTIME at school when Jonathan was busy showing his
new friend Jacob videos on his phone of all the amazing things that they
had seen on their round the world trip. It was then that Jacob noticed something out of the corner of his eye.

"I don't want to worry you…" said Jacob looking worried.

"…but it looks like Naza Hav'em wants to see you," he said as Naza
charged across the playground making a beeline for them. Jonathan froze in
terror, hoping that Naza would not notice him. But he was wrong. Suddenly
he felt the big pudgy hand of Naza pressing down on his shoulder. Turning
around his worst fears were confirmed. There, stood in front of him was
Naza scowling back at him from under his thick set brow. However, there
was something decidedly different about Naza this morning.

"Jonathan, Jonathan," gushed Naza taking hold of him by the hand and
shaking it vigorously.

"The other night I saw you in a spaceship. Had aliens taken you away?"

By now, the rest of the Top Road Gang had run across the playground
and were crowded round Jonathan looking him up and down.

"It wasn't a spaceship," replied Jonathan.

"It was a flying car invented by the Doctor who lives next door to me."

"So, it wasn't aliens then?" asked Naza, still convinced that it was a
spaceship that he'd seen.

"Had you been to the moon?"

"No, we'd just been on around the world trip," Jonathan replied.

"Mmm… around the world trip, but I bet you could go into space with it if you wanted though, couldn't you?"

"I've already told you. It's not a spaceship; it's a flying car," said Jonathan in an effort to put Naza right.

Meanwhile, Jacob was quivering in his boots, wondering if at any moment Naza might take an instant dislike to them and they would find themselves with their underpants wrapped around their ears.

"I was wondering, would you like to be in my gang?" he asked spitting on his hand and holding it out for Jonathan to shake. Jonathan thought about the offer but politely declined.

"What's wrong with my gang?" grunted Naza, sounding insulted as he wiped the dirty great big ball of spit on his shorts. Jacob felt anxious for his friend. Gulping, he wondered what they had got themselves into.

"It's very kind of you to offer Naza, but I don't really want to bully people; it's not nice," said Jonathan bravely. Naza was quite shocked that somebody had said no to him, and it took a minute for him to take it in.

"So, you don't want to join my gang then?" he said.

"No, not really," replied Jonathan

"We could stop bullying people, if that's what you'd like?" said Naza, desperate to be friends with Jonathan.

"Yes, I'd like that, but I still don't want to be in a gang. They do bad things, like putting stink bombs through people's letterboxes, calling people names, pinching people's underwear from the gym as well as telling lies. I don't want to do any of that. Can't we just be friends without having to be in a gang?" Naza took a minute to think about it.

"But if I wasn't to be in a gang anymore, I'd have to give up things like trumping on people's heads, Chinese burns, stealing people's dinner money, tying people's shoelaces together, sticking bubble-gum to chairs, writing rude words on bus stops, putting pepper in my granny's tea, pinching sweets from the shop, making a mess of flowerbeds, chewing bits of paper and firing them at the teachers as well as generally being nasty and mean to people?"

"Yes, you'd have to stop all of that," said Jonathan firmly. Naza took a minute to consider the commitment he was about to make.

"If we give up doing all those bad things, do you think the Doctor would let us have a ride in his flying car?"

"He might, but you've got to do more than just give up bad things you know; you've got to do nice things for people."

"Like what?"

"Picking up litter, helping old people cross the road, planting trees, smiling at dogs, making homes for bees and doing things for people who are less fortunate than you, that sort of thing," Jonathan told him.

"Well, I suppose if that's what it takes to be your friend, I'll do it. But I will miss trumping on people's heads!" said Naza shaking his head at the thought of having to give up his nasty ways.

The bell then rang for the end of playtime and Naza's gang took it in turns to pat Jonathan on the back. Once they had all gone Jacob looked over at his friend.

"I thought we were going to be in trouble then. Well done for standing up to them," said Jacob patting his friend on the back and congratulating him.

"You even said that gangs were rubbish. That took guts." Jacob said. Jonathan didn't know what all the fuss was about, but if it meant the days of Naza Hav'em terrorising people were over then he was glad. Not just for him, but for all the other children at school and for that of his neighbours who had been victims of his wayward antics.

Back home it had been a while since Jonathan had last seen the Doctor, and he couldn't wait to let him know how well his show and tell had gone down at school. Finding him asleep in his greenhouse with Ajna on his knee, Jonathan tugged gently at his sleeve. With biscuit crumbs down the front of his cardigan and his head hung forward, the Doctor came to with a start.

"Wartle valves!" He muttered to himself as he came round.

"Oh, it's you, Jonathan. I was just having a lovely dream, sorry," he said all bleary eyed as he reached for a cold cup of tea beside him.

"I was wondering when I was going to see you. I have some important news to tell you," he said, taking a gulp of tea from his mug and spilling it down his chin.

"Not before I tell you mine!" said Jonathan, desperately wanting to share his news about his show and tell.

"Very well, very well," replied the Doctor wiping the tea from his chin with the back of his hand. Jonathan sat down on an old tea chest opposite him.

"Go on, I'm all ears," said the Doctor listening.

"Guess what? I got three gold stars for my show and tell about our trip!"

"Congratulations!" cheered the Doctor, applauding him.

"And the teacher said it was that good that she wanted me to do it in front of the whole school at assembly."

"Good for you!" smiled the Doctor, leaning forward in his chair and pretending to punch Jonathan on the shoulder.

"Well, I've got some news for you too," he added, sitting back in his chair, and looking pleased with himself.

"I am ready to put the Positive Thought Accumulator through its first proper test, and I'd like you and Liz to be present when I do."

"What, you mean it's finally ready?" gasped Jonathan, excited to hear the great news.

"Let me tell you, it's taken my whole life to get to this point," said the Doctor shooing Ajna off his lap as he eased himself out of his chair and got to his feet. Burying his hands in his cardigan pockets, he invited Jonathan to walk with him as he spoke of what had moved him to build the Positive Thought Accumulator.

"When I was a little boy like you, I couldn't understand why people fought and threatened to destroy the world. To me, it all just seemed like utter madness. I didn't know what I could do to help..." the Doctor reminisced, recounting his youth.

"Then I never forget the time I saw my first ever spaceship. I can remember it now as if it was clear as day. I was nine years old, the same age that you are now," the Doctor added as he stepped into the central rotunda where the Positive Thought Accumulator stood.

"It was one dinnertime at school. I was busy playing with my friends in the playground, and there before my very eyes, breaking through an overcast sky was the most amazing thing a child could ever see. A flying saucer!" said the Doctor raising his hand to the sky as if reliving the moment.

"What did you do?" asked Jonathan fascinated by the story.

"What was there to do. We stood there and watched it."

"Weren't you scared?" The Doctor laughed at the boy's question while pulling at a loose thread that had unravelled itself from his cardigan.

"Even as a young boy I reasoned that if a civilisation had that level of technology, they had the ability to wipe us out in an instant, but they didn't. So, I began to wonder what it was that had allowed them to evolve to a level where they were able to live in peace with one another. That's when things began to get interesting," the Doctor remarked, throwing Jonathan a knowing look.

"Let's take a walk outside," he said, inviting Jonathan to follow him. Stepping out into the late afternoon sunshine, the Doctor continued to tell his story.

"As I got older, I started to notice things about myself that were slightly different from that of other children. I found that I could read people's minds and knew when something bad was going to happen, and so I began to wonder where all this came from. It was then that I discovered that I had once been a spaceman on another planet."

"It must be brilliant being able to read people's minds and know what they're thinking; you could do all sorts with it," said Jonathan. The Doctor looked down at the boy.

"You would think so," he said, smiling back at him fondly.

"But there are some people out there who have terribly selfish minds, and let me tell you Jonathan, a selfish mind is not a pretty thing to look at," the Doctor warned him.

"Anyway, time passed, and the spaceships kept coming. It was then as I got older, I found myself having a few peculiar turns, which were not pleasant I must admit, but I got better and that was when I came up with the idea for the Positive Thought Accumulator. Something that could bring all of humanity together,"

Just then Jonathan spotted Tessa, his cat, wandering about amongst the bushes.

"There's my cat!" declared Jonathan pointing to the black and white cat, who was lying on her back clawing at the air wildly with not a care in the world.

Picking her up with his hand under her tummy, Jonathan gave her a stroke before handing her over to the Doctor.

"My, she is a very friendly cat, isn't she?" Remarked the Doctor.

"You see this is very much a wonderful world, Jonathan…" continued the Doctor as he stroked the cat.

"…and it is my intention to help people to recognise this fact. That is why I developed the Positive Thought Accumulator, to make people happy you see," he said, turning round to look up at the great mirrored disc.

"I never thought this day would come when I would have it up and working. Well, I sort of did, but you can never quite believe it when it happens, you know… when you get the opportunity to make your dreams come true," winked the Doctor.

"And you know what? The more people we can get dreaming the same happy dream, then the better this world shall be," he said holding the cat up on is shoulder as if to include her in what he was saying.

"So, I would be grateful if you and your sister could join me in my first real test of Peter. If you could both bring along a dream with you that would be nice. It doesn't have to be anything fancy, just something that will put a smile on your face. Just make sure you jot it down on a piece of paper, right?" he instructed him as he gave the cat one final stroke before handing it back to Jonathan.

Later that evening at the dinner table Jonathan mentioned the test run of the Doctor's new invention to his parents.

"He calls his new invention Peter you know," said Jonathan informing his parents of the Doctor's new contraption. It was then that Liz interrupted the conversation.

"It was me that came up with that name for it!" She said proudly.

"Peter, that's an odd name for a machine, isn't it?" questioned their mother as if not believing her daughter.

"Its real name is the Positive Thought Accumulator…" Jonathan explained.

"…but it's a bit of a mouthful to say, so Liz decided it should be called Peter after its initials. You see PEE…TEE…AAH. It sounds like Peter when you say it out loud,"

"That's clever," noted their father congratulating his daughter on her inventiveness.

"What does it do?" He asked.

"It's a machine that makes dreams come true," said Jonathan explaining in the best way he could.

"I'm not sure I like the sound of that," said their mother, anxious as always.

Jonathan then explained to them how it worked, or at least, how he thought it worked.

"You take a dream, and the machine makes it real…well, at least that's what the doctor says."

"Seems like a simple principle to me," said their father as he happily tucked into his dinner.

"I'm not sure you should be messing about with other people's dreams," said their mother in a disapproving tone.

"But they're good dreams. The Doctor wouldn't do anything to harm anyone," Jonathan replied defending the Doctor's new invention.

"I know, but you shouldn't go poking round with other people's dreams, they're private," argued his mother. Their father however thought it was a fantastic idea.

"I tell you what, son," he said giving Jonathan a wink.

"I'll give you extra pocket money if you can make my dream come true,"

"Why what's your dream?" asked Liz. Leaning back in his chair, their father then put his hands behind his head and began to speak.

"It goes something like this. Imagine there's a beach, somewhere warm and there's a gentle breeze blowing. There's palm trees," he said smiling as he basked in the radiance of his own dream.

"Oh, palm trees, I'd love to be on beach with palm trees," said Liz already picturing herself there.

"And I'm lying there with my feet in the crystal-clear water, and there's you two there and your mother," he said.

"We're watching the sunset when a pod of dolphins jumps out of the water, how about that? Does that sound like a good dream or what?" he asked his children.

"I like that," replied Liz with a smile on her face.

"And I tell you what," he said turning to Jonathan.

"If you can make my dream come true, I'll give you extra in your pocket money," Jonathan promised his dad that he'd try but wasn't sure how well the Doctor's dream machine worked.

It was a Wednesday of no particular significance when the Doctor decided to run his first proper test of the Positive Thought Accumulator, a day that would go down in history. Rushing home from school, Jonathan and Liz got changed from out of their uniforms and hastily made their way over to the Doctors house, not even stopping for a drink of juice or a biscuit.

They found him busy beavering away in the central rotunda of the greenhouse, wearing a studious expression and hovering around a flashing control panel. With a pencil tucked behind one ear and his glasses perched on the end of his nose, he looked up at them from over his clipboard, distracted from his calculations.

"Is it ready?" asked Liz trying to peek under the dust sheets that shrouded the Positive Thought Accumulator.

"Not yet," replied the Doctor pulling the sheets tight together so she couldn't see.

"I must tell you I've never done a practical test on the Positive Thought Accumulator before, not one that involves the human mind. Up until this point, all my tests have been theoretical and as far as I'm aware it's perfectly... safe," he said, looking a little uncomfortable as if trying to brush the whole matter under the carpet.

"Safe? You don't sound so sure," said Jonathan looking up at the towering machine that was hidden from view by paint splattered dust sheets.

"Technically... it's safe," said the Doctor, as if not quite sure of himself.

"Well, should we be testing it if you don't know whether it's safe or not?" asked Jonathan dubiously.

"I'm sure it will be fine," replied the Doctor waving his hand and dismissing Jonathan's concerns as trivial while busying himself with more calculations.

"FINE?" replied Jonathan picking up on the Doctor's hesitation.

"FINE? Why, what could happen?" he demanded to know. The Doctor looked somewhat uncomfortable at having to answer Jonathan's question.

"Erm…there is always the slight possibility that the Positive Thought Accumulator might…err… fry your brain,"

"Fry my brain!" Jonathan cried out aloud.

"…don't worry, the effects are only temporary and will wear off after a couple of days…or years depending on the nature of your mind."

"Years!" exclaimed Jonathan aghast.

"I don't want to have my brain fried for that long,"

"Don't worry, don't worry. I'm only going to run the machine on half power," the Doctor reassured them, gently patting Jonathan on the arm.

"Now, have you both brought a dream along with you that you would like to come true?" he asked.

Liz said nothing. She had been thinking about this for a while and had spent quite a few nights lying awake contemplating what she wanted her dream to be. She had thought long and hard and had decided that it would be nice if someone else could benefit from her dream. So, she had put all her hopes into the possibility that one day the Doctor might find love. That he could find that one special person to share his life with. However, she was careful to keep this a secret. Having written it down on a piece of paper, she made sure she said nothing to her brother or the Doctor about the contents of her dream.

Jonathan's dream on the other hand was much simpler. What he really wanted was a double thickness peanut butter milkshake just like the ones he had at the seaside with his parents.

The Doctor was bursting with anticipation in his eagerness to show the children his greatest invention yet. Gripping the lapels of his lab coat, he cleared his throat and began to speak.

"…I have dreamt about this day for so long that I have played it out a million times in my head. I have waited all my life to reveal the Positive Thought Accumulator to the world and it is my greatest hope that through the use of my machine people will learn to live together as one, bringing peace and harmony to the world," he uttered with heartfelt conviction as he continued to talk.

"It is my desire that through the dreams the Positive Thought Accumulator brings, it will one day help humans reach the stars," said the Doctor looking hopefully up at the bright blue sky above him.

Asking for their help to remove the dust sheets they gave them a great big tug, and they dropped to the ground with a thud, revealing the Positive Thought Accumulator in all its glory.

"Tah-dah!" announced the Doctor celebrating the unveiling of his new invention. Stretching all the way up to the roof was the machine in all its magnificence, crowned at the top by the mirrored disc.

Supporting the great disc was a central column of polished steel covered with a thin coating of ice. Attached to it were various lengths of pipework that hissed steam as well as insulated coils that crackled and fizzed with electricity and pulleys and belts that did goodness knows what.

Around the base of the machine, arranged in a circular fashion were numerous dials, gauges and valves that controlled the Positive Thought Accumulator. With flashing buttons, screens and whirring computers, the machine was alive as if divine breath had brought the quantum computer to life.

"Here's where you put your dreams in," said the Doctor pointing to a slot on the control panel. Liz looked at the bank of controls.

"What happens to the dreams from there?" she wanted to know.

"They get fed into the main brain of Peter and then the Tickles take over," he told them.

"Tickles? What are Tickles?" Asked Liz.

"I'm glad you asked," replied the Doctor as he set about explaining what they were.

"Tickles, you could say are like tiny little people that live inside the machine, and they read every single dream that comes into them; then they do their best to make them true."

"What… you've got tiny people living inside the machine?" asked Liz confused.

"They're not real people. They're tiny sparks of light that can do all sorts of miraculous things. Even the most impossible of dreams they can make come true," he told them.

The Doctor took a laser pointer from his breast pocket and pointed to the self-aware quantum computer, highlighting the more interesting parts.

"You see, once the Tickles have finished making a dream, it's sent up to the disc via the pipes and valves and out into the night. That's what the light is. It's all the dreams going out into the world," he said explaining how his machine worked.

"Anyway, enough of me talking. Who'd like to go first?" asked the Doctor stepping up to the console.

"I will!" replied Jonathan putting his hand up.

"Good boy, now when I give you the nod, feel free to feed your dream into the slot. Now if you don't mind, can I ask you what exactly is your dream, just so we don't get any unexpected surprises?" enquired the Doctor.

"My dream is that I'd like to have a double thickness peanut butter milkshake just like the ones at the seaside," Jonathan told him.

"Mmm…a good choice indeed!" said the Doctor making agreeable noises and twisting a few knobs on the control panel.

As Jonathan deposited his piece of paper into the slot, the whole control panel lit up in a flurry of lights and beeping. Then from deep inside the machine, there was a loud clunking noise as if something was not quite right and suddenly the pipes began to hiss with steam.

"Oh dear…. oh dear…oh dear, that doesn't sound right," muttered the Doctor, holding his breath.

The Positive Thought Accumulator shook, then gave a violent shudder before expelling a cloud of acrid smoke and spitting out a handful of nuts and bolts from of one of the pipes.

"That's not supposed to happen," remarked the Doctor pushing his glasses up onto his forehead and rubbing his chin while he deliberated on the matter.

"Were you visualising your milkshake correctly?" he asked Jonathan as he tried to rule out the possible causes for the malfunction.

"Course I was it's your machine that's not working right!" Jonathan protested. The Doctor took his stethoscope from out of his pocket and placed it on the side of the Positive Thought Accumulator.

"Jonathan, can you give that Wartle Valve a twiddle for me?"

"What's a Wartle Valve?" asked Jonathan, who didn't have the foggiest idea what he was talking about.

"The Wartle Valve…you know the thinga-ma-jig," he grumbled unable to explain himself properly.

"The thing that's connected to the spring, that turns the wotsit that's attached to the balance rod, that turns the hoojamaflip, which opens and closes the Wartle Valve," fumed the Doctor. Jonathan had no idea what it was the Doctor was referring to and raised his hands in the air exasperated.

"The big round handle there!" said the Doctor as he pointed directly to it.

"Well, why didn't you say the big round handle in the first place. I've no idea what a Wartle Valve is!" complained Jonathan.

"I'm sorry, I'm just a bit flustered here," said the Doctor apologising for his lack of patience.

Jotting down a few things on his notepad and making some further calculations, he twiddled with the dials some more and cracked open a few more valves on the machine.

"This should get the dreams flowing a little better!" he shouted over the din of the machine, while Jonathan eagerly awaited the arrival of his peanut butter milkshake.

"Right, let's see if we can do a little better this time!" exclaimed the Doctor, looking a little more hopeful and pushing one of the many flashing buttons on the control desk in front of him.

This time, instead of the awful clanking noise that the machine had made before there was a pleasing thrum. Flywheels spun, cranks turned, camshafts lifted and from out of the mouth of long, wide pipe appeared a tall glass overflowing with peanut butter milkshake.

"Well, it's not exactly how I would have imagined it, but it will have to do," professed the Doctor looking around for something to clean the mess up with.

"I'm sure with a bit of fine-tuning we'll have Peter running as smooth as you like," Removing the overfilled glass from the conveyor belt he wiped it down with an old tea towel before handing the milkshake to Jonathan to try.

"What's it like?" he asked, curious to know. Jonathan's eyes became wide as he sucked hard on the straw.

"It's gorgeous, just like the ones at the seaside!" he confessed. The Doctor, clapping his hands together, allowed a great big smile to spread across his face.

"At last, my invention works!" he declared skipping around the room in delight and taking hold of Liz by the hand as he encouraged her to join him in a celebration.

"Can you believe it?" he enthused, spinning Liz around the room in a fervour.

"I never thought this day would come when someone other than myself could engage with the Positive Thought Accumulator. It truly is a remarkable day!" he gushed all overcome with emotion.

After everyone had a sip of Jonathan's milkshake and the Doctor had finished leaping about the room in excitement, he asked Liz to step up to the console.

"Do you have your dream with you?" Liz nodded shyly.

"And may I ask what it is?" enquired the Doctor. Liz remained tight-lipped refusing to say a word. With her dream written down on a piece of paper she held it firmly in her grasp, not wishing anyone else to see it.

"Sorry, is there some reason why you don't want to tell me?" enquired the Doctor gazing over the top of his wire-rimmed spectacles. Liz nodded.

"That's alright, you don't have to tell me. It would be rude of me to pry into someone else's dream if they did not wish me to," he said putting his arm around her shoulder. Only Liz knew what the content of her dream was and stepping forward she bent down to put the piece of paper in the slot.

Stood poised to see the results of her dream the Doctor waited in anticipation, but nothing seemed to be happening.

"Are you sure it's working right?" asked Jonathan as he stuck his head into one of the many pipes to see if there was a dream knocking about in there.

"There's nothing happening!" he shouted, his voice echoing around inside the machine.

"Are you quite sure?" asked the Doctor with a puzzled expression on his face.

"I can't believe it; one minute it's working and the next it's not... what's wrong with this thing?" he complained, feeling responsible for letting Liz down.

Liz didn't know how the machine worked. She wasn't sure if dreams turned up straight away or you had to wait a bit for them to come true; either way she didn't want to reveal anything for fear of completely ruining it.

"Maybe, I'll have to run a few tests on Peter to make sure no Boggrobblers have got in the works," sighed the Doctor shaking his head and running his hand through his hair in despair.

"Just when I thought I'd got Peter up and running, this goes and happens," he grumbled as if resigning himself to failure. Liz then stepped up to his side and took hold of him by the hand.

"Maybe the dream just hasn't come true yet," she said trying to put his mind at rest.

"Maybe it's not Peter; maybe the dream's still out there floating around waiting for someone to dream it," said Liz trying to ease his worried mind.

"You're probably right," he conceded.

"I should probably wait, but in the meantime, I'll make sure Peter's running properly," said the Doctor taking off his lab coat and hanging it on the doorknob as if a sign of failure.

"What I'll do, is tonight I'll take everything apart and have a good look at it all, then we can give it another go of making your dream come true," he said trying to raise the enthusiasm for what he considered to be a crushing blow. Liz seeing his frustration gave him a hug hoping it would make him feel better.

"Don't worry, I'm sure everything will turn out fine," she reassured him as she stared into his deep, dark brown eyes.

That evening after the children had gone home, the Doctor took the Positive Thought Accumulator apart. Bit by bit he scoured miles of cabling, optic fibre, holographic connectors, circuit boards and wiring looms, searching tirelessly for a reason why Liz's dream had not come true. Examining connections and checking endless Wartle Valves, the Doctor could not find anything wrong with the machine and was left scratching his head. However, he was tenacious and was not for giving up. Staying up all night he beavered away into the small hours until he found himself falling asleep surrounded by half-drunk cups of tea, biscuits, and the plans to Positive Thought Accumulator. If there was a Boggrobbler in the works, he was going to find it!

-14-

Miss Bagshaw

SOME DAYS LATER the Doctor was busy having his breakfast. As usual, there was nothing he enjoyed more than a nice cup of tea, a slice of toast with marmalade and to sit there in silence watching the sky-blue magnificence of his mind. That was until the doorbell rang.

"Who on earth could that be?" he spluttered looking up and directing his comments towards Ajna who was happily lapping up his first saucer of milk of the day. Engrossed in his breakfast Ajna was far too preoccupied to acknowledge his human companion, and so left the Doctor to see who it was at the door.

Despite being a spaceman with the ability to see into the future, Oban was totally stumped as to who it was ringing his bell at this time on a morning. Getting to his feet, he brushed the toast crumbs from his robe and made himself presentable, pulling his dressing gown together and tightening the belt around his waist.

As he made his way through the hallway, the thought occurred to him just as to how anybody had managed to ring the bell; after all, the gates were locked to stop people getting in. The bell then rang again, this time with a more impatient tone.

"I'm coming, I'm coming!" he shouted as he quickened his pace. Undoing the many locks and pulling back the bolts, the Doctor was surprised to find a well-dressed lady standing at the door wearing a hat and coat and carrying with her a large leather bag.

"You certainly don't make it easy for visitors to come and see you, do you Dr Fife?" said the lady brushing the twigs and leaves from her coat that she had picked up from clambering over the gate. The Doctor was taken aback that the lady should know his name. "And you are…?" he enquired politely, expecting an answer of her.

"Miss Bagshaw," replied the lady shaking his hand firmly as she stepped through the door uninvited, her heels clattering loudly on the wooden floor.

With rosy, red cheeks, flame red hair and a very business-like attitude, the lady surveyed the cavernous hallway.

"My, my, I can see this is going to require some work," she commented. Meanwhile the doctor was struggling to understand what on earth the lady was doing there in the first place.

"My dear Miss…?" he said, trying to grasp at her name, having already forgotten it.

"Bagshaw!" prompted the lady, shaking her head and tutting disapprovingly.

"Yes, well, my dear Miss Bagshaw, I don't know how you know my name and I don't know what you're doing here, but may I ask you to leave," the lady gave an irritated sigh.

"Are you or are you not Dr Oban Fife?" she asked demanding an answer of him. The Doctor stammered as he tried to comprehend just how the lady knew him.

"Yes!" he spluttered. "That's as maybe, but what are you doing in my home?"

Setting her bag down on the floor she rummaged around in the pocket of her checked jacket, then pulling out a card she handed it to him.

"There," she said presenting him with the card. Adjusting the glasses on the end of his nose, he studied the card carefully. It read…

CLEANER REQUIRED
HOURS NEGOTIABLE
APPLY WITHIN. DR. OBAN FIFE
SUNSHINE VILLA

"Well as you can see Doctor, I'm not here to waste your time and if you don't mind hurrying along, maybe we can get down to the business of the interview?"

The Doctor was flabbergasted. He had no idea as to how this message had been written. He was quite certain that he didn't write it and was pretty sure no one else had. So how was it possible that he was standing in his own hallway with a lady who said he required a cleaner.

"May I ask where you found this card?" enquired the Doctor pressing his finger to his lips in intrigue. The lady sighed and shook her head.

"If you must know, it was in the local supermarket on the pinboard that said, 'help required.'"

"Oh…oh," he replied scratching his head in a bemused fashion.

"Dear Dr Fife are we going to proceed with this interview or are we not?" asked the impatient Miss Bagshaw.

"Yes…yes," acknowledged a confused-looking Doctor holding up the card and reading it for a second time, not quite believing it was real. Showing her through to the hallway, he closed the door behind her and pointed her in the direction of his living quarters.

As Miss Bagshaw made her way through the dimly lit hallway, she couldn't help but comment on the size of Dr Fife's problem.

"My, my, you do have rather a capacious property here, do you not?"

"Mmm…yes capacious," muttered the Doctor holding the card up to the lamp to check if it was real.

"That means big, Dr Fife, you have a big problem here on your hands. This house will take a lot of cleaning," she stated as the Doctor followed on behind in a confused manner, still perusing the card he had been given.

Miss Bagshaw was not quite as tall as the Doctor and was of a rather sturdy build, one that said she was not afraid of hard work.

"I deduce from your family name and your curtains that you're of Scottish descent?" noted Miss Bagshaw who had spied the Tartan curtains.

"Yes, yes," replied the Doctor brushing aside her passing comment, more concerned as to what it was that this lady was doing there.

"About this card, however. I think there's been a mix-up," he confessed trying his best to get himself out of the predicament that he was in.

"You see, I never wrote this card and I never put it up in the supermarket for all to see…" he explained running his hand through his hair in an exasperated manner.

"…and I for one do not require a cleaner," the Doctor stated emphatically. Miss Bagshaw looked Dr Fife up and down in a less-than-satisfied manner, then ran her finger along the top of one of the radiator covers.

"So, you don't require a cleaner, eh?" she said raising her finger in the air to show him the dust that she had just picked up.

"Well, it seems to me that you couldn't be more in need of a cleaner if you ask me," stated a rather zealous Miss Bagshaw. The Doctor looked at the dust on her hand.

"That may be your view of the matter, but I am of the opinion that everything here is just fine," replied the Doctor countering her argument.

"I really don't think that out here in the hallway is the place to be discussing such matters, do you?" she said firmly addressing the Doctor in a forthright manner.

"Now that I am here, I think it would be far more suitable if we get on with the interview, do you not agree?" she said inviting the Doctor to lead the way.

Upon being shown into his living quarters, Miss Bagshaw was immediately displeased to see a bed tucked away in the corner of the library.

"No, no, no, this will not do!" she exclaimed taking him to task on the matter.

"A library is no place for sleeping. For a good night's sleep, you need a still mind and all these books must conjure up all sorts of wild imaginings," she said voicing her displeasure. The Doctor made a hurried apology and, pretending that the bed wasn't there, showed her to the red leather sofa that was situated by the fireplace.

"No, thank you," she said with a hint of kindly impertinence.

"I shall be needing your writing desk; you see, it is I that shall be interviewing you! Do you understand?" The Doctor stood there looking bemused.

"Why should you be interviewing me of all people, when I never asked for a cleaner in the first place?"

"Oh, but you did Dr Fife, you just don't know it. You see, I am not just any old cleaner," she explained.

"How shall I put it, I'm a special kind of cleaner, one that has been sent here to look after you. Do you understand?" said Miss Bagshaw, searching for a response from the robed gentleman.

"What do you mean you've been sent here?" questioned the Doctor trying to understand what Miss Bagshaw was on about.

"The disc, my dear Dr Fife!" she replied with nod of the head to the garden outside.

"You mean the Positive Thought Accumulator sent you?" stammered the Doctor.

"Precisely!"

"But how do you know about the Positive Thought Accumulator?" he asked looking somewhat baffled by the whole matter.

"It is in my job as your cleaner to know certain things,"

"But you're not my cleaner yet," he argued.

"That as maybe, but this interview Dr Fife is a mere formality in proceedings," she answered sounding a little frustrated by the Doctor's lack of cooperation.

Overcome at having his own home invaded by a strange lady, the Doctor became unsteady on his feet and needed a sit down.

"Oh…I think I need a rest," he exclaimed, reaching into his pocket for a handkerchief and dabbing his forehead.

"I mean how is it you seem to know all these things about me?" he wanted to know.

"I've told you Doctor, I'm not your average cleaner, the disc has sent me," she replied taking him by the arm to steady him.

"Now, I can see that this is all getting a bit too much for you. May I suggest you sit down, and we'll get on with the interview?" said Miss Bagshaw ushering him over to the couch.

Doing as he was told, the Doctor felt overcome by a strangeness that he could not quite place.

"I'm afraid I'm feeling all out of sorts." said the Doctor looking a little pale.

"That's alright, we'll get on with the interview while you remain seated,"

In response to Miss Bagshaw's overwhelming directness, all poor old Oban could do was limply wave his handkerchief in reply.

"Whatever you say," he sighed, resigning himself to the fact that she seemed to be very much in charge of things.

Miss Bagshaw was not the sort of lady to hang around, and getting straight to the point, she placed her bag down on the floor, took off her jacket and pulled out a chair from behind the doctor's writing desk.

By now, Ajna had finished his breakfast and came wandering in from the kitchen. Strutting around the library and rubbing himself on any available chair leg Miss Bagshaw spotted him out of the corner of her eye.

"Ahh, I do so appreciate cats," she exclaimed picking Ajna up in an ungainly manner to make a closer inspection of him.

"But I do find that dogs are much more on our wavelength, do you not agree?" Ajna looked rather disgruntled at being handled like a regular cat, dangling in the air with his paws strung out below him in an unceremonious manner.

"Ajna's very intelligent; don't let his cat-like disguise fool you," replied the Doctor standing up for his feline companion.

"Beside his full title is the Emeritus Professor Ajna, if you please."

"Mmm…a bit of a mouthful" remarked Miss Bagshaw.

"I shall not be calling him by that; I think plain old Ajna will suffice. But we're not here to discuss your pet's likes and dislikes Dr Fife. I'm here to discuss you," she said matter-of-factly, setting the cat back down on the floor.

The Doctor thought this was a very strange setup for obtaining a new cleaner. Usually, it would be him interviewing her, but here it seemed as if things were the other way round.

Taking a seat, Miss Bagshaw reached into her bag and pulled out a thick dossier placing it on the desk in front of her. Then searching for her glasses she proceeded with the interview. The Doctor looked at Ajna and gave him a knowing wink.

"It's alright lad, you stick with me, and you'll be fine," he said patting Ajna affectionately on the head.

"Now you might find these questions a little personal Dr Fife, but do be assured they are most necessary," she said shuffling her papers and tapping them on the desk.

"Shall we begin?" she asked leaning forward as if about to give him a stern grilling. The Doctor as if spent of any fight nodded that they should proceed.

"When you were four, did you once tell your mother before bed you had cleaned your teeth when you hadn't; is that true?" asked Miss Bagshaw looking directly at him. The Doctor thought for a moment. Casting his memory back, he realised she was correct. It had been the night when there had been the Persimion meteorite shower. Not wanting to miss out on the dazzling event, he had fibbed to his mother that he had cleaned his teeth when in fact he had not.

"That's correct," answered the Doctor. Miss Bagshaw then moved on to her next question.

"When you were seven and three quarters, did you steal the mummy's golden head piece from its case and run round the house chasing your friends with it whilst wearing it on your head?" The Doctor let out a titter all to himself as he recalled the incident.

"Yes, I did," replied the Doctor with a fond smile on his lips. Miss Bagshaw then looked very sternly at the Doctor.

"Now this next question, I want you to think very hard about," she said as she peered over the top of her spectacles. Aware of the great weight that Miss Bagshaw seemed to be putting on this question, the Doctor sat bolt upright, his back hard against the sofa.

"Did you ever as a child…and I repeat this…did you ever as a child wee in the swimming pool and not tell anyone?" she asked in an accusatory manner. The Doctor looked shame faced.

"I'm afraid I must admit I did," said an apologetic Dr Fife. The lady then looked down at her papers.

"Don't worry Dr Fife, there are no right or wrong answers; all we need is the truth," she said trying to reassure him.

"Can I also ask, at your eighth birthday party, did you spill an ice cream float on your mother's best tablecloth and not own up to doing it?" the Doctor laughed heartily on hearing the question.

"Yes, I did!" he chortled.

"Also, when you were fourteen, did you purposely leave your clarinet on the school bus in the hope that you would never have to play it ever again if it were lost?" the Doctor sighed.

"I'm afraid so," he answered.

"And one final question…when you're alone on an evening and you put your music on, do you dance around the room with Ajna in your arms?" The Doctor looked down at his feet.

"I'm afraid I do," he admitted as if guilty of some crime.

Miss Bagshaw removed her glasses and looked at him with a steely gaze.

"There is nothing to be ashamed of, Doctor. Many of the best people in the world have peculiar quirks. Dancing around the room with your cat is quite way down on the list of bizarre habits and odd traits that people have, that I can tell you."

Shuffling her papers and putting them back in her dossier, Miss Bagshaw removed her glasses and looked squarely at the Doctor.

"Now that we've got all that nasty business out of the way, let's get down to the brass tacks of the matter, shall we?" she said with an unyielding expression of determination written upon her face.

"I expect you up and dressed by eight a.m. sharp, none of this wandering round the house in your dressing gown malarky…" she said pointing a finger to the Doctor's present attire. Oban thought that her regime was a little harsh, but not wanting to interrupt her he thought it wiser if he kept his mouth shut.

"…at which point," she continued.

"I will provide you with a wholesome breakfast of porridge or eggs served to your liking, a pot of tea and toast with a preserve of your choice…" she stated whilst busy taking notes.

"…and after that I will begin with my duties of cleaning, at which point you will be free to spend your day working on your many inventions. Is that clear, Doctor?"

Oban didn't know what to say; he was still bamboozled as to how he had ended up with a cleaner in the first place. All the poor old Doctor could do was stammer and thank Miss Bagshaw for coming. Struggling to his feet, he shook her hand and asked her when he should expect her.

"First thing in the morning, eight o'clock sharp…" she told him.

"…and if you could Dr Fife, would you remove those dreadful chains from around the gates. A lady should not be seen having to climb over them; it is very unflattering and unbecoming if you ask me," she said making her displeasure known.

"Yes, of course. I'll see to it right away," the Doctor replied, nodding his head in acknowledgement as he saw her to the door.

"Good, good," affirmed Miss Bagshaw as she put her jacket on and picked up her bag.

"Remember, eight o'clock sharp!" she reminded him.

After having seen Miss Bagshaw to the gates, the Doctor then retired to the library where he collapsed in a heap on the sofa, wondering what had just happened to him.

"Phew, what was all that about, Ajna?" he asked his cat, while mopping his brow with his handkerchief.

"I have never in my life been so overwhelmed by a person. That Miss Bagshaw certainly is a force of nature, is she not?" asked the Doctor seeking an answer from his feline companion. Keeping his opinions to himself,

Ajna decided to leap onto the Doctor's lap and settle down on his silk dressing gown, padding around with his paws while he made himself comfy.

"But the thing is Ajna..." the Doctor asked in a bemused fashion.

"...she said that the Positive Thought Accumulator had sent her. How can that be? I, for one, have certainly not requested the presence of a cleaner and as for Liz and Jonathan, well Jonathan got his milkshake and I am sure that Liz would not have specified a cleaner for me in her dream," he sighed.

"Maybe, I haven't quite got the Positive Thought Accumulator working right? Maybe the Tickles are having an off day?" he remarked shaking his head and looking for consolation from Ajna.

"What do you think eh lad?" Asked the Doctor of his ginger companion, but all Ajna was interested in was licking his paws and smoothing down the fur on his chest, leaving the Doctor to contemplate the future for himself.

After recovering from the shock, Oban realised that Miss Bagshaw would be back the following morning. Not wishing to be in her bad books, he spent the rest of the day removing his bed from the library and taking it back upstairs where it belonged.

That night, after a day of endlessly clambering up and down the stairs, he found himself back in his old childhood bedroom. A four-poster affair, the bed came with heavy curtains and ornately carved bedposts while from the dark wood-panelled walls hung medieval tapestries. The Doctor sighed as he lay in bed. It had been many years since he had last slept in this old room and while he was lying there trying to get accustomed to his old bed, he couldn't help but feel that something was about to change in his life.

-15-

AN ODD FEELING

THE FOLLOWING MORNING, bleary-eyed, Oban staggered out of bed and looked through his wardrobe. Picking out a smart waistcoat and a natty pair of trousers that he had not worn in a long time, he hoped that his impeccable dress might curry favour with Miss Bagshaw. After making sure his shoes were polished and his bow tie was on straight, he waited in the hallway for her arrival.

Not a minute before or a minute after eight, there was a knock on the door and without delay Oban rushed to open it. There in front of him stood Miss Bagshaw looking a vision of loveliness.

"Good morning, Dr Fife," she beamed with a happy smile.

"What a lovely morning to be alive!" she exclaimed, turning to view the sprawling gardens that surrounded the property.

Wearing a narrow-brimmed hat with a with a posy of lavender pinned to it, she stepped inside as the Doctor showed her in. Removing her hat, she hung it on the stuffed bear that stood in the hallway.

"I must say Doctor, your taste is rather eclectic." she commented while taking off her coat and perusing the life-size bear. It was then that Miss Bagshaw spied an out-of-place shrunken head sitting on the hallway table.

"Now I'm sure there's a place for that..." pointing to the gruesome article.

"... and I am a firm believer that there is a place for everything and everything in its place. It's a mantra of mine," she said.

Making her way through the hallway to the kitchen, she noted the marked difference in the Doctors appearance.

"I must say, I am pleased by your smart turnout." she said with a curious smile of admiration. The Doctor blushed as he pretended to smooth out the non-existent creases in his waistcoat.

"This old thing, I found it in my wardrobe," he added, trying to downplay the effort he had made to look presentable for Miss Bagshaw.

"Well, may I say it suits you," she commented flashing him a smile noteworthy of praise.

"Now what can I get you for breakfast?"

As he followed her into the kitchen, Miss Bagshaw turned around as though something was wrong.

"What are you doing, Doctor? No, no, no, no, no, no," she said taking him by the shoulders and spinning him around.

"As the gentleman of the house, you will be having your breakfast in the banqueting hall from now on, do I make myself clear?" said Miss Bagshaw ushering him out of the kitchen and taking charge.

Escorting him into the cavernous dining room, she sat him down at one of the many chairs that ran the length of the banqueting table. Then removing the dust sheets from the furniture, she gave them a good shake before opening the shutters on the windows.

"There, that's better," she commented as light permeated the house for the first time in many a long year.

Regaling him with a list of what was on offer for breakfast, she then removed the dust cloth that covered the long banqueting table. With the dust tickling his nose, the Doctor let out a great sneeze.

"Bless you, my dear Doctor," said Miss Bagshaw who promptly produced a neatly folded tissue from the pocket of her skirt.

Oban looked upon Miss Bagshaw with the kind eyes of a lonely man. It was quite strange to have the company of someone else in his house. The walls of Sunshine Villa had been quiet for such a long time that he had resigned himself to living the life of a quiet recluse, but now he looked upon this friendly intrusion as a blessing in disguise.

"May I say Miss Bagshaw, it is with welcome relief that I greet your arrival. But it still baffles me as to how that note requiring help came about."

"I shouldn't worry about that," replied Miss Bagshaw revealing the long-hidden paintings and marble busts from underneath the dust covers.

"You don't question why the sun shines do you? So why should you question my arrival?" The Doctor ran his finger along the edge of the table feeling at the squarely carved corners as he considered what Miss Bagshaw had to say.

"You are quite right, maybe I should treat it as one of life's strange little mysteries that defies logic and accept it as that," noted the Doctor as if deep in thought. Leaving him to ponder his odd predicament, Miss Bagshaw went to fix him his breakfast.

While Oban sat there all alone in the huge dining room, he couldn't help but see the funny side of his own circumstances. All these years he had been working for the benefit of everyone else, busying himself with his inventions and labouring to bring the Positive Thought Accumulator to the world, and in the process had neglected his own well-being. Letting out a giggle, he looked down at the rather smart waistcoat and dapper trousers that he was wearing and realised that Miss Bagshaw was already having a positive effect on him. With a slightly giddy butterflies-in-the-stomach feeling, the Doctor wondered what this feeling was. He couldn't be sure, but he knew that he was starting to harbour a certain affection for the kind yet rather forthright Miss Bagshaw.

Each day Miss Bagshaw would arrive at his house at eight on the dot and proceed to make him breakfast. Afterwards the Doctor would retire to his laboratory where he would make further adjustments to the Positive Thought Accumulator and his other inventions. While doing so, Miss Bagshaw set about tidying up and cleaning the house from top to bottom.

With the windows open and the curtains drawn back, she got down to work, removing all the years of accumulated dust by giving everything a good polish. She hoovered the carpets, beat the tapestries that hung from the walls as well as getting rid of all the old newspapers and letters that lay around the place. Soon the house was resembling its former glory.

At lunchtimes, the Doctor would return from his work in the laboratory. There he would find a sandwich left on the kitchen table for him, made by Miss Bagshaw. Alongside it there would be a note to say how much she had enjoyed their conversations over breakfast and that she looked forward to seeing him again in the morning. Dr Fife was getting used to having the company of Miss Bagshaw around and was beginning to like it.

Several weeks had passed since Liz and Jonathan last visited the Doctor; knocking loudly on the back door, they disturbed the Doctor who was busy having afternoon tea with Ajna in the library.

"Hello, you two!" he said with cake in hand as he greeted them.

"Come in, come in!" he gushed, eager to show them in. As they stepped through the door, Liz couldn't help but note how smart he looked.

"What are you wearing?" she asked, observing his smartly pressed pin-stripe trousers, matching waist coat and starched white shirt with cufflinks.

"What's wrong with your cardigan with the holes in and your old tweed trousers?"

"Ahh those old things. I thought it was time I had a change and made a bit of effort at last," Liz raised a suspicious eyebrow.

"What! What's wrong?" replied the Doctor catching sight of her accusing look.

"Can't a man not be allowed to take pride in himself once in a while?" said the Doctor defending his actions.

"But if you must know the reason for my newfound appearance, is that I have a new cleaner."

"I didn't know you needed a cleaner!" remarked Jonathan with surprise.

"Neither did I, but apparently, I do?" laughed the Doctor.

Suddenly a thought shot through Liz's mind. Was it pure chance that the Doctor had a new cleaner or had her dream been granted by the Positive Thought Accumulator?

"Is she a lady?" Liz asked curiously as they made their way through to the library. The Doctor nodded. This got Liz thinking.

She hadn't specifically asked for a cleaner, just someone whom he might fall in love with. However, it seemed more than just a coincidence that this lady had turned up. Perhaps *she* was responsible after all for the arrival of this lady. Suddenly, her brother let out a yelp of surprise.

"Where's your bed gone?" he asked pointing to the spot where it used to be.

"I've had to move it upstairs. Miss Bagshaw said it wasn't right to have my bed in the library," he replied, looking slightly embarrassed about the matter.

Preferring not to answer any more questions, Oban tried distracting the children by taking them to see how clean the house was.

"Wow! It looks much brighter," exclaimed Liz upon seeing the gleaming new hallway.

"And it sparkles!" cried Jonathan casting his eye over the polished floors and the gilded picture frames that hung from the wood-panelled walls.

"…and all the old newspapers and junk has gone too," he added.

"Well, what do you think?" asked the Doctor as he stood there proudly, his thumbs tucked into the loops of his waistcoat.

"I'm afraid none of it is of my doing though; I have Miss Bagshaw to thank for that," he noted, cocking his head at the mere mention of her name.

"Miss Bagshaw, her name is like music to my ears," said the Doctor fondly, lost for a moment in his own happy thoughts.

Liz could tell that the Doctor was enchanted by his new cleaner. Choosing to keep her secret all to herself she let the Doctor continue with his praise of Miss Bagshaw.

"It's funny," said the Doctor scratching his head and looking a little bemused.

"But when Miss Bagshaw turned up at my door, she gave me this," said the Doctor rummaging around in his waistcoat pocket and pulling out a card, which he then presented to Jonathan to read.

"Here, what do you make of that?" Jonathan held the card in both hands and began to read aloud.

"It says: Cleaner required, hours negotiable, apply within Dr Oban Fife, Sunshine Villa."

"And do you know what the funny thing is?" asked the Doctor.

"I've no idea how on earth that card came to be on the pinboard of the local supermarket,"

Liz gulped. She knew exactly where the card had come from. There was only one possible explanation for it. The Positive Thought Accumulator!

Choosing not to say a word, Liz remained tight-lipped as the Doctor continued to deliberate on the matter.

"And do you know what else?" he said shaking his head as if he couldn't make head nor tail of it. "She proceeded to tell me something even more remarkable. She told me that the Positive Thought Accumulator had sent her! I mean how can that be?"

Suddenly all became clear. It was obvious to Liz that the test run of the Positive Thought Accumulator had been a resounding success. Her dream for the Doctor to find someone to fall in love with had materialised. So, it was true if you wished hard enough your dreams really did come true!

"Look…," said the Doctor.

"…I'm planning another test run of Peter next week, and Liz, as it would seem your dream did not materialise, I want you to have another go. This time make sure you bring your most fantastical dreams with you." She wished that she could tell him that the test had been a roaring success but knew that if she said anything she could possibly alter the future. Not wanting to spoil the Doctor's happiness, she kept her thoughts to herself.

Distracted by Ajna the Doctor picked him the up off the floor, and with him resting on his shoulder proceeded to tell them what he had been up to.

"I've taken the Positive Thought Accumulator apart piece by piece and have made sure that all the Tickles are behaving as they should. I have also stripped it right back and have checked that all the circuits, chips and Wartle valves are working properly. This time I'm confident of a better outcome," Oban assured them.

Liz was amazed at the impact that Miss. Bagshaw had on the house and on the Doctor and couldn't help but comment on what a magnificent job she had done. The Doctor then invited them through to the dining room.

"This is where I have my breakfast now," he informed them.

"Miss Bagshaw sees to it that I have a boiled egg or bowl of porridge on a morning before I start my day,"

After showing them how clean and tidy the house was, he escorted them to the door but before they left, he suggested they come round again to give the Positive Thought Accumulator another try, insisting that the outcome this time would be much better.

"What about Tuesday, how does that sound?" he asked.

"Tuesday sounds fine," replied Jonathan as he followed his sister down the back steps of the property. Calling after them the Doctor shouted.

"Remember, bring your best dreams; the world needs a brighter future for everyone!"

It was a wet, grey morning when the Doctor was engaged in extracting some of his finest Fug Munchers from a steaming broth of partially digested rubbish. With an intolerable stink and the sky overcast with drizzle, he was suddenly taken with the idea of giving Miss Bagshaw a present. Something by which he could show her a token of his affection. But what should it be? Thinking long and hard an idea came to him. What better way was there of showing his appreciation than a bin-full of his most advanced environmentally friendly Fug Munchers.

With his white lab coat on and wearing a pair of rubber gloves that went all the way up his arm, Oban was gainfully employed peering down his microscope, trying to hoover up some of the hairy little blighters with a pipette.

"Get here you dratted things!" he cursed as he chased them round a glass petri dish.

Distracted from his endeavours for just a second, he thought he heard tapping on the glass. Taking a moment out from his ragged hunt of the nano-sized pip squeaks, the Doctor looked up stunned. Blinking and with his glasses pushed up on his forehead, he struggled to locate where the tapping was coming from. Then spinning around on his stool, he was surprised to see Miss Bagshaw stood in the rain, with a cup of tea in one hand and a slice of cake in the other.

Sliding off his stool and rushing to get the door, he waved her to come round to the side.

"Come in my dear thing, you must be soaked," he gushed as he opened the door to let her in. Ducking underneath the Doctor's arm, she scurried inside presenting him with tea and cake.

"Here, I brought these for you; I thought you might be hungry," she said with a slightly embarrassed smile. As he took them from her, she informed him that she had made the cake at home. Lifting the plate to eye level and sliding his glasses down onto the bridge of his nose he examined it carefully.

"Well, Miss Bagshaw, it looks a rather fine carrot cake, if you don't mind me saying so." Encouraging him to try a piece, Miss Bagshaw offered him a cake fork. Taking a rather generous slice, he consumed it eagerly as he made appreciative sounds.

"Excellent!" he mumbled with his mouth full before taking a gulp of tea.

"Very good, very good indeed," he said heaping praise on her. While the Doctor applaud her efforts, Miss Bagshaw looked around at the exotic and interesting bits of scientific equipment in his lab.

"Oh, a microscope!" exclaimed Miss Bagshaw standing on her tippy toes trying to look down it.

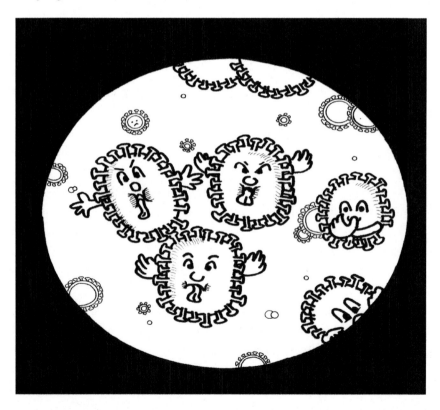

"Here, allow me," said the Doctor coming to her assistance and sliding the stool over to her so she could sit on it. Squinting and peering down the microscope, Miss Bagshaw let out a squeal of displeasure.

"I say Dr Fife what are those horrible things that I can see pulling faces and blowing raspberries at me?"

"Fug Munchers," replied the Doctor.

"I beg your pardon?" she said sitting bolt upright as if the Doctor had just insulted her.

"No, no," he said realising that Miss Bagshaw had misunderstood what he was saying.

"That's what those tiny little creatures are, they're Fug Munchers." Miss Bagshaw recoiled in horror at the very name.

"They're going to revolutionise how we deal with our waste," he told her excitedly.

"What? These rude, impertinent little beasts?" questioned Miss Bagshaw looking somewhat dubious.

"I know they can be quite rude and disgusting, but I have taught them how to break down the many types of waste that we humans throw away. They chomp away on it until it's reduced to its individual chemical components, that way everything can be recycled."

"Really? Those rude, horrid little creatures?" she asked.

"They're not that rude once you get to know them; they're just a bit cheeky," said the Doctor as she peered down the microscope to study them some more.

"My, they are feisty little creatures, aren't they?" she commented as she watched them dart about this way and that.

"I was just in the process of trying to catch some when you interrupted me," admitted the Doctor.

"Oh, I am sorry, I didn't mean to get in the way of your work," she apologised. "It's the last thing I intended."

"If truth be told," he confessed. "I was trying to catch some as a present for you."

Miss Bagshaw looked up from the microscope. "You were trying to catch some for me?" she gushed, raising her hand to her chest as if flattered by the kind gesture.

"I thought you might be able to use them round the house to help with the cleaning," he added, but Miss Bagshaw was not really listening to what the Doctor had to say. She was more taken with the idea that he wanted to give her a gift.

"I don't know what to say, Oban."

"It's nothing," he replied trying not to make a big deal of it.

"Just think of it as a token of my appreciation for all the hard work that you've put in around the house."

"How very kind," she said, touched by the gift as she gazed at him affectionately.

For a moment the Doctor was lost in her eyes and found himself dreaming happy thoughts when he suddenly was overcome by the vagaries of his profound shyness.

"Dear me, my tea will be getting cold!" he exclaimed making a feeble excuse for his awkwardness. Pretending to busy himself, Oban tucked into his carrot cake while Miss Bagshaw tried not to make the moment any more awkward than it already was. With the moment passed, he asked her if she would like to see the rest of his laboratory.

"Oh yes, that would be lovely," remarked Miss Bagshaw slipping down from the stool and fiddling with her hair to make sure her bun was still in place.

"Since I began working for you, I've been dying to know what it is you get up to all day out here on your own," she said intrigued to know more.

Treating her like a visiting dignitary, Dr Fife led the way through the tangle of junk. Tidying away boxes and various plans that lay about the place, he showed her one of his many revolutionary ideas.

"See this," said the Doctor pointing to an odd-looking device.

"This is a zero-point energy generator," he stated with an enthusiastic nod. Bending down to look at the piece of equipment, Miss Bagshaw enquired as to what it was it did. No bigger than a briefcase and with a series of concentric metal rings and cathodes inside, the Doctor explained how it worked.

"It makes free energy!" he declared excitedly pushing his glasses back on his head.

"What...?" she stammered breathlessly as she tried to take in the enormity of what the Doctor was saying.

"You see just by harnessing the flow of electrons we can make electricity, so there'll be no need for dirty big power plants in the future," he declared.

"Oh Oban, how wonderful!" she gushed.

"And that's not the half of it," the Doctor added.

"Just one of these on its own could power a whole city."

In celebration of his great idea Miss Bagshaw huddled closer to the Doctor, squeezing him by the arm.

"Oh Oban, you are amazing," she said smiling and looking him in the eye. Basking in the glow of her admiration, Oban then went on to tell her the best bit.

"It is my aim is that even the poorest, most out of the way remote places will have one of these to help with their power needs…" he said, tapping the top of the zero-point energy generator as if to emphasise what he was saying.

"…and the good thing is, that you don't need to hook it up to anything. You just switch it on and away it goes!" he said giving her a wink of satisfaction.

"Oh Oban, how admirable of you. You're a real humanitarian!" she said with pride and affection.

"Let me show you some of my other inventions," he said pointing out of the window to his flying car that was covered in tarpaulin.

"That's just something I knocked up for the amusement of the children next door," he humbly admitted.

"You've got a flying car!" said Miss Bagshaw, sounding astonished.

"Maybe you could take me on a trip in it some time?" she said blushing.

"Of course, of course, it goes without saying," replied the Doctor more than happy to accept her invitation as he continued to show her round his laboratory.

Noting all the strange bits of scientific equipment and glassware that had liquids of all different colours bubbling away inside, Miss Bagshaw asked what it was all for. The Doctor smiled.

"This is my research. I have created everything from free-flowing wireless electricity to cloud computing, where information is stored holographically in the ether for everyone to download to their mind," he said as if it was nothing.

"That's marvellous!" she said applauding the Doctor for his efforts.

"That's nothing. Let me show you my greatest invention," he said with an encouraging wink. Leading her through into the large glass atrium at the centre of the greenhouse he held up his hand to behold his greatest work.

"I have spent my entire life devoted to this. The Positive Thought Accumulator," he declared.

Raising her gaze Miss Bagshaw followed the maze of twisted pipework, belts, pulleys and wiring that surrounded the machine, right up to the mirrored disc that sat on top of the giant quantum computer. Letting out a silent gasp as she beheld its magnificence.

"Do you know I have dreamt about your machine all my life?" she said sharing her innermost feelings. The Doctor looked at her with a surprised expression on his face.

"Funny, but so have I," he exclaimed, smiling in bewilderment.

"That's where my idea for Positive Thought Accumulator came from… a dream," he said. The two looked at each other and then looked back at the machine.

"Maybe it's your machine that brought us together…" declared Miss Bagshaw.

"… for when I first saw your notice in the supermarket, I just knew that I had to apply. I couldn't help but feel drawn to it, as if the disc was talking to me," she confessed.

The Doctor shook his head in disbelief, knowing that it was more than the random act of chance at work.

"As you say, maybe it is something far greater than the fickle chance of fate that has brought us together. After all, I would be a fool to deny that something greater than my own ability is at work here," he said alluding to the greatness of his own invention. Standing back to take in the towering edifice that was the Positive Thought Accumulator, Miss Bagshaw asked what it was that it did.

"It makes dreams come true," remarked the Doctor as he looked up at the complex beauty of the machine. Touching him gently on the arm, Miss Bagshaw spoke.

"I say, a dream machine – what a fantastic invention!" she declared breathlessly.

"Tell me Doctor, what is your dream?" she asked, her hands clasped together, excited by the very idea of a dream machine. The Doctor let out a long sigh and ran his hand through his hair as if what he was about to express was the culmination of his life work.

"What is my dream?" he laughed shaking his head as if it was obvious for all to see. Pulling up an old wicker chair the Doctor sat down, seemingly spent of energy.

"Do you know how long I have been waiting for someone to ask me that question," he sighed, overcome with emotion from the many long years of labour that he had put into the building of the Positive Thought Accumulator.

"What is my dream?" he chuckled to himself.

"Shall I tell you my dream Miss Bagshaw, shall I? It's a simple one," he said running his hand through his hair once more.

"I dream of a world where humanity can live as one. Where peace and love abound, and people are kind to each other. Is that too much to ask for?" he said looking up at Miss Bagshaw with tired eyes.

"That's a beautiful dream," she said stepping towards him and putting her hand on his shoulder.

"I'd like to share in your dream too," she said. Her hopes and dreams directed towards the great mirrored disc that sat on top of the Positive Thought Accumulator.

-16-

TRIP OF A LIFETIME

I T WAS LUNCHTIME at school, and Jonathan was dangling from some railings busy day dreaming when Naza tried getting his attention.

"Jonathan, Jonathan!" he yelled from across the playground as he ran over to see him.

"Hi, Naza, what's up?" said Jonathan jumping down from the railings.

Although Naza had given up bullying, Jonathan was still wary of him. He still remembered a time when Naza flicked people's ears, threw shoes into trees and stuck chewing gum in people's hair.

"I was just wondering if there's any chance of me having a ride in your neighbour's flying car?"

Jonathan had to think fast. He wasn't sure it was something that anybody could have a go in. Besides, he didn't think the Doctor would let a bully like Naza have a ride.

"The Doctor's working on something better than a flying car!" he blurted out, trying to put him off.

Immediately, the smile left Naza's face and Jonathan could see he was beginning to look less than impressed.

"What's better than a flying car?" he asked as a scowl crept across his face.

"A dream machine." Jonathan told him in the hope that it would diffuse the situation.

"A dream machine! There's no such thing as a dream machine," he argued.

"There is too and the Doctor's made one," Jonathan stated adamantly.

"It's called the Positive Thought Accumulator, and it's massive," Jonathan said trying to show Naza how big it was by standing on his tippy toes and stretching. Naza looked at him dubiously.

"Well, what does it do?" he demanded to know folding his arms and looking decidedly unimpressed.

"It makes dreams come true," shrugged Jonathan thinking it was obvious.

"It makes dreams come true? Nobody has their dreams come true," Naza argued as Dazzler turned up.

"Have you heard what space boy is telling us?" he sneered.

"He says that crackpot Doctor of his has made a machine that can make dreams come true!"

"Ha ha!" laughed Dazzler.

"A machine that makes dreams come true; there's no such thing!" he sniggered, pouring scorn on the idea.

"There is so, and I've seen it!" replied Jonathan. Dazzler looked at him in disbelief.

"I'm telling you the truth, honest!" stated Jonathan with his arms folded, and a serious expression etched upon on his face.

Now Naza had rarely seen such a display of sincerity in all his life, not since his days of bullying when he had someone in a headlock, and that got him thinking maybe Jonathan was telling the truth.

"Really, does it make your dreams come true?" he asked with a raised eyebrow.

"Course it does, otherwise it wouldn't be called a dream machine, would it?"

Naza had to admit that Jonathan did have a point. Jonathan then told him how he had wished for a super thick peanut butter milkshake and the Positive Thought Accumulator had made it come true.

"Are you sure you're not having me on?" Naza wanted to know.

"No of course not. The machine is huge. It's got all sorts of pipes and pulleys on it and a giant mirror on top,"

"It all sounds like nonsense to me," Naza said with an air of suspicion. Jonathan hated to be called a liar and was going to prove to Naza that he was telling the truth.

"Okay I'll tell you what; I'll take you to see it!" exclaimed an infuriated Jonathan.

"Alright," replied Naza taking him up on the offer and with that Jonathan stomped off furiously.

Tuesday came around quickly. After school, Jonathan and his sister arrived home to find an empty house and a note from their dad saying that their dinner was in the fridge and that their mother had a parents' evening to attend.

"Great!" exclaimed Jonathan waving the note in front of his sister's face.

"If we have dinner now, it will give us plenty of time round at the Doctor's." Liz studied the note that her brother handed to her.

"Dad says we have to put our dinner in the microwave as usual," she said reading what it had to say.

"Alright, let's get changed out of our uniforms and I'll put dinner on," said Jonathan taking charge.

Seated around the kitchen table, the two of them tucked into their meal while listening to the radio.

"It's a shame that your dream didn't come true," said Jonathan consoling his sister.

"Mmm…" mumbled Liz with her head down as if she had something to hide. Unable to conceal her guilt any longer she decided it was time she came clean about her dream.

"If I tell you something, you have to promise not to say anything…" she said hesitantly.

Jonathan looked over at her with a puzzled expression.

"Why, what have you done?"

"I haven't done anything, but you've got to swear on it," she insisted.

"Well, if you haven't done anything wrong, why are you making me swear on it?"

"I just am!" said an exasperated Liz.

"Alright, I swear on it," he sighed.

Satisfied that her brother was not about to blab, Liz told him her secret.

"You know the new cleaner that the Doctor's got? Well, I think she might be something to do with my dream."

"Don't be ridiculous. You can't just magic up a cleaner up from out of nowhere," he laughed unconvinced.

"Yes, I know, but I never told you what my dream was, did I?" argued Liz.

"Alright, what was your dream?" he asked putting his knife and fork down and taking a drink.

"Well… in my dream, I asked that Dr Fife find someone that he might fall in love with and… I've got a feeling that *someone* might be the cleaner," she admitted. Jonathan, who had gone back to eating his dinner, thought about what his sister had to say.

"Do you really think so? Mind you, he does seem rather taken by her," he added as he mulled over what his sister had to say.

"I mean he does kind of go all gooey every time you mention her name," he said agreeing with his sister.

"See, that's why I think this Miss Bagshaw is the lady he's supposed to fall in love with, but you've got to swear that you won't say anything otherwise it will spoil it all," Liz pleaded.

"Alright, alright, I promise not to say anything," pledged Jonathan who was more interested in his dinner than who the Doctor may or may not fall in love with.

After helping her brother with the washing up, Liz made sure the cat was fed before going to see the Doctor.

"What time do you think Mum will be back?" she asked.

"Late, these parents' evenings always go on a while," replied Jonathan knowledgeably.

"I'll text her just to say that we will be round at the Doctor's and not to worry."

Locking the door behind them they made their way down the garden and squeezed through the gap in the fence. With the sun low in the sky, they followed the winding path that led to the Doctor's ramshackle greenhouse. It was then that they heard a strange sound come drifting through the trees.

"Ommmmmm…" went the odd noise as if filled with an energy all of its very own.

"What's that?" asked Liz nervously biting her lip. A deep throbbing, bass-like resonance could be heard making their entire bodies tingle from head to toe. Putting his hand on his sister's shoulder, Jonathan reassured her.

"It's alright. It's the Positive Thought Accumulator," he whispered, having heard the sound before.

Cautiously they approached the greenhouse where Liz and Jonathan were struck by something strange. From inside the central rotunda, they could see a pale blue, glow being emitted, like that of electricity flickering away. Then, becoming aware of a rather odd sensation, their hair stood on end. Jonathan laughed at his sister. Having the longest hair, she looked the funniest. Giggling to herself, Liz felt it with her hands.

"It feels all tingly," she said trying to flatten it down. But it was impossible, every time she tried to straighten out her hair, it stood on end again. Jonathan then beckoned her to follow him.

The Doctor was nowhere to be seen, and outside the light was now beginning to fade. With encouragement from her brother, Liz stepped over the threshold of the door where they were momentarily startled by Ajna, who, clearly spooked by something, was running at great speed in the opposite direction.

"Meooww!" he squealed as he shot through their legs in a hurry heading for the door. His fur, like that of the children's hair, all stuck up on end.

"Are you sure we should go in?" asked Liz warily.

"Course, why not?" shrugged Jonathan who was intent on not missing out on the test.

A pale blue light cast a gentle glow across the floor and over the Doctor's scientific equipment. The children made their way past the tangle of instruments and measuring devices, which crackled with life. Every so often a spark of electricity would peel off the equipment making strange fizzing noises as it searched for somewhere to ground itself. Frightened to touch anything for the fear of being electrocuted, Liz and Jonathan kept their hands to themselves as they inched their way along between the benches. Then, they caught the sound of faint chatter from somewhere off in the greenhouse.

"Doctor... Dr Fife, are you there?" Jonathan called out nervously as they made their way into the central rotunda.

When they stepped inside the room was alight with the glow of electricity. With their backs to the wall, the children watched as rippling sheets of electricity coursed up and down the giant quantum computer in great waves as if charged with a will of its own.

It was then that they found the Doctor in his thinking room leant up against one of the marble statues, talking to a lady they'd never seen before.

"Hello, Dr Fife," said Jonathan cautiously from around the corner of the door, not wanting to intrude on the Doctor's privacy.

"Jonathan...Liz, come in, come in!" he said throwing open his arms and ushering them in.

"I'd like you to meet Miss Bagshaw, my new...err... cleaner," he stammered, struggling to find the right words to introduce the rosy-cheeked lady.

Liz looked at her. She was well turned out and although she was old, she was clearly not as old as the Doctor. Wearing a checked skirt, a matching waistcoat, and a pressed white blouse, she stepped forward to greet the children.

"Pleased to meet you," she said giving the children a kind smile and offering them her hand to shake.

"Hello, Jonathan," she said with a little bow of the head.

"And you must be Liz," she said bending down to shake hands with her. Liz and Jonathan didn't know what to make of her. She seemed like a nice lady from what they could make out, but it was hard to tell from first impressions.

"The Doctor has told me so much about you two," said Miss Bagshaw trying to put them at ease and not make them feel too nervous about meeting a stranger.

"He was just recounting your little round the world trip in his flying car," she said as she reached down into her skirt pocket as if looking for something.

"Would you care for a sweet? What's your favourite?" she asked the children.

"Chocolate mint," replied Liz.

Miss Bagshaw looked at the handful of sweets that she had dug out of her pocket.

"I'm sorry, but I don't seem to have any of those with me; if you bear with me for just one moment, I'll see what I can do." Cupping the sweets in her hand, Miss Bagshaw closed her eyes and then gently unfurled the palm of her hand. Liz looked on astonished.

The sweet wrappers seemed to flutter as if caught by a magical breeze, then flicking through all the colours of the rainbow they all at once turned green. Liz gasped in amazement.

"There we are a chocolate mint just for you. I knew I'd find one somewhere," said Miss Bagshaw holding out her hand.

"How did you do that?" Liz wanted to know, her mouth open wide.

"I like to think of it as magic," she said with a knowing wink. The Doctor, who up until this point had been happy just to listen to their conversation, spoke up.

"I'm sorry to interrupt you, Miss Bagshaw," said the Doctor apologetically.

"But here we like to call it what it is. The term 'magic' is no longer relevant. As I have told the children before, what we are actually talking about is higher-level consciousness. None of this mumbo jumbo, if you pardon my expression," he said letting his feelings be known on the matter.

"Oh, I am sorry. You're quite right. It's about time all this myth and fuzziness about magic was dispelled," she said turning to offer Jonathan a sweet.

"After all, it's just a helping hand that makes good things happen," she declared. It was then that the Doctor piped up.

"I hope you don't mind…" he said hopping awkwardly about the place.

"…but I've invited Miss Bagshaw along for the test of the Positive Thought Accumulator," he said placing his hand gently on her elbow as if presenting her for the approval of the children.

Jonathan and Liz could see nothing wrong with inviting Miss Bagshaw; after all, anyone who could magic up a handful of sweets in a multitude of flavours was alright by them.

The Doctor then brought up something that he needed to get off his chest.

"I'm sorry Liz…" said the Doctor regretfully shaking his head.

"…but I'm afraid the first test run of Peter did not prove altogether satisfactory. Whatever your dream was, I think we lost it somewhere along the way. However, I think this time I can provide a satisfactory outcome to your dream," he said looking apologetic.

She wished she could tell him that her dream had come true but didn't want to risk ruining things.

Jonathan's attention was then drawn to what the Doctor was wearing on his feet. Seeing him clattering about the laboratory in a pair of white and tan golf shoes, he wondered what the Doctor had planned.

It had not gone unnoticed by the children that since the arrival of Miss Bagshaw there had been a marked change in the Doctor's dress sense. No longer did he smell of biscuits, brass keys, old jotters, and pencil shavings but of aftershave, soap and washing powder. Jonathan presumed that this was something to do with Miss Bagshaw presence.

"What are those?" Liz asked pointing to the rather short trousers the Doctor was wearing.

"Ahh… these are my plus fours; do you like them?" Sporting knee-high socks, a natty red sweater, a pink bow tie and a rather plush checked cap with a pig red pom-pom on top, the Doctor gave a little twirl to show off his golf attire.

"What are they for?" asked Liz who had never seen somebody wearing such an odd-looking outfit before.

"I thought I'd indulge myself…" declared the Doctor.

"… while I was busy with some last-minute calculations it occurred to me. I've worked hard all my life, so why not have a little fun of my own? So, I've decided to play the last hole of my favourite golf course!"

Turning his back on the children, the Doctor then began rummaging around amongst some old cardboard boxes. Lifting them up and tossing them to one side, the Doctor meanwhile carried on his conversation.

"Have you brought some good dreams with you?" he asked them from over his shoulder. Both Liz and Jonathan nodded.

"Good, good, that's what I like to hear," he replied as he dumped boxes full of old notepads and research papers on the floor.

"Can I help you?" asked the ever-efficient Miss Bagshaw stepping forward to offer a helping hand.

"No, no, it's quite alright," stated the Doctor as loose sheets of paper cascaded wildly on to the floor while he rummaged furiously amongst the boxes.

"I know what I'm looking for," he said determined that he would find what he was after. Then after more frenzied activity, he let out a loud cry.

"Bingo!" he shouted as he pulled out a bag of golf clubs from behind the pile of stacked up boxes.

Throwing the golf bag over his shoulder and neatly rearranging his cap, the Doctor ushered them through to the central rotunda, where the Positive Thought Accumulator was lit up like a giant Christmas tree, fizzing away to itself.

"This way if you please," he said escorting them over to the control panel.

"Wow!" noted Jonathan taken aback by the power surging through the machine.

"The Positive Thought Accumulator seems a lot brighter this evening."

"That's because we're running on full power," replied the Doctor tilting his head back to watch the electricity flicker and wick its way to the very top of the machine.

"After the last test run was not the success that I hoped for, I have made a few design changes to Peter. I have changed out the old Wartle valves for more powerful ones and while I had a spare moment, I designed a way of recycling all the positive energy that's floating around in the world."

"How ingenious! How on earth have you managed that?" asked Miss Bagshaw intrigued to know more; her hands clasped together with excitement.

"It's very complicated," remarked the Doctor trying not to get too involved with the ins and outs of how the Positive Thought Accumulator worked.

"Well, I would like to know," enquired an adoring Miss Bagshaw wishing to take an interest in his work.

Setting his golf clubs down against the control panel, he pushed his cap back and scratched his head.

"Well..." he began as he explained how the thing worked.

"The mirrored disc that sits atop of this machine sends out projected light energy in the form of dreams. It can also collect the very same energy, but in order to do so it has to go through a very complicated process," the Doctor elaborated as he looked over at Miss Bagshaw to see if she was keeping up with him.

"You see the energy that you give out is stored here in the machine in the form of a holographic memory bank, where trillions upon trillions of dreams lie waiting to be dreamt," he said, indicating to the bowels of the great machine.

"It's the Tickles embedded in the software that write the dreams," the Doctor explained as they listened intently.

Miss Bagshaw, looking slightly confused, raised her hand.

"May I ask what are Tickles?" It was at this point Liz turned round to answer Miss Bagshaw's question.

"They're like tiny people that live inside the machine, and they make people's dreams come true," Liz told her.

"Well done!" said the Doctor congratulating her.

"You can see them here at work," he said beckoning for them to join him over by the control desk.

"From here, I can monitor all the dreams going out into the world for people to dream."

There in front of them on a large monitor was projected a black and white checkerboard similar to that of a chess board but differing slightly in the fact that there were no black squares in the middle.

"Here if you look carefully, you can see the Tickles busy at work helping people with their dreams," noted the Doctor pushing his spectacles up onto the bridge of his nose while directing them to look at the blinking squares on the screen.

"You see, the Tickles' main objective is to make nice dreams for people so they can lead happy and fulfilling lives."

"My, that is impressive, Doctor!" gushed Miss Bagshaw, her hand clasped to her chest full of admiration for him.

It was then that Jonathan pulled out a piece of paper from his pocket and handed it to the Doctor.

"Here you are," he said letting the Doctor see.

"These are some of the new dreams that I have written," announced Jonathan, proud of himself.

"Marvellous, marvellous!" chirped up the Doctor congratulating him. Unfurling the piece of paper, the Doctor ran his finger along it as he muttered away quietly to himself.

"Mmm…mmm…very good…yes flying elephants, I like that bit… a swimming pool full of custard, a talking grasshopper, and a flying bike, all very interesting," he said tracing the words with his finger.

It was then Liz's turn to hand over her dreams that she had written. Taking hold of the folded-up piece of paper, the Doctor took his time to peruse her dreams.

"Mmm…high tea with a family of bears?" he said making agreeable noises as he looked over the top of his glasses with delight.

"By any chance would any of them be wearing a hat with a propeller or be able to talk and ride a tiny bike?" enquired the Doctor wishing to know more. Liz shrugged.

"I suppose so. If it makes the dream better," she replied. Giving her a knowing wink, he scribbled something down on her piece of paper.

"I've always thought that if you're going to have a dream, you might as well make it a good one. So, if you are going to invite a family of bears around for high tea, why not have them wearing silly hats and riding tiny bikes?"

Next, he turned his attention to that of Miss Bagshaw who was stood in the corner quietly listening to the children's dreams.

"And what about you my dear Miss Bagshaw… what dream do you have?" enquired the Doctor holding out his hand and drawing her closer to him.

"I'm afraid I don't have a dream that I can share," she said blushing ever so slightly.

"Oh, don't be silly," replied the Doctor.

"Everyone has a dream," he said teasing her as she tried pulling away from his hand.

"I'm afraid I'd like to keep my dream private," she said blushing some more and declining to give the Doctor an answer. Aware that he was making her feel uncomfortable he let go of her hand, apologising for his lack of sensitivity.

"My dear Miss Bagshaw do please forgive me for the indelicate way in which I have trampled on your feelings. I am afraid I am rather clumsy when it comes to matters of a personal nature," he confessed as he bowed his head and took a step backwards.

The children could sense an awkward atmosphere in the greenhouse. It was clear to them that the Doctor and Miss Bagshaw had feelings for each other. With an uneasy silence in the room Jonathan gave the Doctor a gentle nudge, prompting him to get on with the test.

Stammering and looking slightly flushed, the Doctor took the hint to get on with things.

"Err…yes…of course, where was I?" he said, getting down to business.

"I think you'll find this test somewhat more interactive than the last one as I have installed a reality converter," he declared, tapping the side of the console with pride.

"What's one of those?" asked Jonathan, eager to learn more.

"See this," said the Doctor, indicating to a piano keyboard that was attached to the bottom of the console.

"This enables me to change reality and make the biggest of dreams come true," he enthused.

"I'm not talking about the itsy-bitsy ones like making milkshakes – anybody can do that. I'm talking about the really big ones, the dreams that can make lots of people smile." Miss Bagshaw raised her hand.

"Excuse me Doctor, but how exactly does it work?" she asked, wishing to know more.

Tearing himself away from the console for just a moment, he kept his explanation brief.

"What I do is play a series of notes, ones that correspond with the same frequency as this reality and using quantum non-locality it allows us to frequency shift our reality to that of a higher one. Does that make sense?"

"No, not really," replied Miss Bagshaw shaking her head. Taking off his cap and smoothing down his hair, he sought the best way to explain his theory.

"In simple terms, what we do is make this reality that we know as real into a fluid thing where we can then superimpose our dreams onto the basic framework that underpins all of reality. Is that any clearer?" Nodding and pretending to know what he was on about, Miss Bagshaw didn't really have the foggiest idea what he was talking about. He could have been talking gobbledygook for all she cared, but she smiled all the same.

"Now it will get a little loud for a few minutes and things might get a little strange, well quite strange actually, but don't be alarmed," warned the Doctor.

"Are you ready for the trip of your lifetime?" he grinned as he got on with the job in hand.

$-17-$

SOMETHING ALTOGETHER DIFFERENT

A HARMONIOUS TUNE CAME out of the Positive Thought Accumulator, like that of a gentle breeze washing over them. As the Doctor turned up the dials on the control panel it grew louder and louder – to a point where everybody began to feel wobbly inside.

While he played his keyboard, something strange began to happen. The walls and floor of the greenhouse began to melt. Like wax dripping from a candle, they disappeared into thin air. Jonathan had also noticed that the floor had become spongy like a trampoline.

"Look at me!" he shouted to his sister as he jumped up and down making waves in the very fabric of reality.

"What's happening, what's going on?" screamed Miss Bagshaw, grabbing hold of the children.

"Don't worry, I've done this before," said the Doctor raising his hands in the air as if trying to reassure everyone.

Clutching the children, Miss Bagshaw looked on in fright while Jonathan continued to bounce up and down on what was left of a rapidly disappearing reality.

"I'm not sure I like this," she yelled unable to hide the panic in her voice.

Everything fell silent as what was left of reality was being eaten up by an encroaching black nothingness. Alarmed, Miss Bagshaw let out a scream as she fought to remain on the one and only piece of remaining floor.

"You know you can let go of it," said the Doctor who was now floating around freely having a whale of a time.

"What is this?" Miss Bagshaw cried out, unnerved, and clutching onto the children for all she was worth.

"It's what dreams are made of!" he chuckled as he carried out all sorts of acrobatics like an astronaut in space.

"Oban, help me!" she cried out.

Stirring up a cascade of beautiful rainbows and stars in his wake, the Doctor launched himself towards her with all the grace of a ballet dancer.

"It's just like swimming. All you have to do is let go and relax," he explained as he took Miss Bagshaw by the arm and encouraged the children to dive in. Jonathan was first to take the plunge.

Diving into what looked like water, Jonathan suddenly found himself surrounded by a multitude of sparkling rainbows that shimmered like a mirage in a desert. Kicking and splashing about in the nothingness, more and more rainbows appeared, like ripples on a pond.

He was soon joined by his sister. However, Miss Bagshaw still took some convincing.

"Doctor, this is most peculiar if I do say so," she remarked as she anxiously leant forward into the nothingness. Succumbing to the Doctor's gentle persuasion, Miss Bagshaw let out a fretful squeal as she finally summoned up the courage to leap into a beautiful world of rainbows and stars.

Once her panic had subsided, Miss Bagshaw doggy paddled until she was able to find her feet in the sparkling nothingness.

"I'm afraid I'm not a natural to this," she readily confessed.

"Don't worry, we'll soon have things sorted," said the Doctor taking her by the arm and guiding her through the inordinate tiny pools of glistening rainbows that surrounded them.

"Jonathan, can you recall one of your dreams that you wrote down?" he asked.

"Which one?"

"Any, take your pick," the Doctor replied.

From out of nowhere the sun appeared and a radiant fan of peacock feathers spread out across the blue sky like rays of light shooting out from the suns heart. As reality began to solidify once more, all four of them found themselves stood on top of white chalky cliffs looking out over the ocean.

"Oh, that's much better," said Miss Bagshaw relieved to be on firm ground once more, while still clinging tightly to the Doctor's arm. Glad to know that she was feeling much better, he set his golf clubs down next to him and drawing in a deep breath took in the view.

"Mmm…smell that, I love the smell of the ocean," he said, revelling in the salty air carried in on the breeze.

"There's nothing like a sea view to raise the spirits," he marvelled encouraging Liz and Jonathan to follow suit and draw in great lungful's of air.

"Doesn't that make you feel alive?" he said as Miss Bagshaw began to relax and release her grip on the Doctor's arm.

It was a beautiful summer's day. A warm breeze was blowing in off the ocean and out in the distance yachts were bobbing about in the water.

"What do you think of it?" asked the Doctor, nodding towards the ocean.

"It's marvellous," replied Miss Bagshaw, with a bright countenance.

"Not bad for a computer programme, is it?" remarked the Doctor nonchalantly. It took a minute for what he said to sink in.

"What do you mean it's a computer programme?" said Jonathan puzzled.

"I wrote this!" he said indicating with a nod of the head to all that they could see before them.

"What do you mean you wrote this?" said Miss Bagshaw unconvinced by what he was saying.

"The ocean, it's a holographic computer programme that I wrote for the Positive Thought Accumulator so that people can share their dreams with each other." Miss Bagshaw took a step back in disbelief.

"No, you're having us on aren't you, Oban?" she exclaimed raising her hand to her chest and gasping, unable to believe that somebody could make something so beautiful. The Doctor looked at her soberly.

"You're not joking, are you?" she said as the expression on her face changed from mild confusion to complete bewilderment when she realised that he was being most sincere. Struggling to find the words to express herself, she took a moment to compose herself.

"You mean what we're looking at is a computer programme?" she remarked with incredulity while pointing to the sea.

"Yes, that's right. Lines and lines of code," replied the Doctor coolly with his hands in his pockets as he kicked at the ground beneath him.

Liz who seemed to be taking it much better than Miss Bagshaw had a question that she wanted to ask.

"But how come it looks like the sea?" she wanted to know. Taking a step forward, the Doctor got down on one knee and put his arm around her shoulder, pointing to the ocean.

"You see, if I just left the dreams as lines and lines of programming, nobody would be able to understand what they were; nobody would know how to communicate their dreams with other people. It would all just look like gobble-de-gook," he said with a tender smile as he explained to her the best way he could.

"You see, what the ocean does is allow people to share their dreams together. Every good dream starts with the ocean."

"Is that how we will be making our dreams come true?" asked Liz.

"That's exactly how we'll be doing it," he replied giving her a reassuring hug as they looked out at the beautiful blue ocean together.

Letting out a little sigh, the Doctor staggered to his feet and brushed the grass from off his knees as Miss Bagshaw rushed over to his side.

"I must say Oban, how do you come up with the ideas for such things? You're quite clearly a genius," she said adoringly.

"I wouldn't go that far," smiled the Doctor forgetting himself and putting his arm around her.

"Here's something you might find interesting though," he said directing his comments towards that of the children.

"Do you know what inspired me to write this programme?" he asked, nodding to that of the ocean. Liz and Jonathan hadn't a clue.

"Shall I tell you?" he said, excited to recall the events that had brought him to such a manifest discovery.

"It was one Sunday afternoon when I was busy in my laboratory. I'm afraid I had rather over-faced myself at lunch and was not feeling quite as sprightly as normal. You know that feeling you get after you've had a big meal…" he said patting his stomach and implying that the children would know what he was talking about.

"… unfortunately, I was not paying as much attention as I would have liked when I knocked over a beaker of water onto one of my oscilloscopes," admitted the Doctor, shaking his head as he relived the moment.

"The water went everywhere and that's when it gave me a rather nasty electric shock. You should have seen it; I went flying across the room and landed in a heap. Then, while I was lying on the floor I began to dream of the ocean and that gave me a flash of inspiration. It was the motivation for my ocean programme," said the Doctor excitedly.

"You see I wanted to write something that everyone could be part of. Where I could convey a sense of endless possibilities and infinitely different outcomes for people to dream, and so I thought the ocean would be a suitable choice to convey such immense limitlessness. What do you think, huh?"

"How insightful!" remarked Miss Bagshaw applauding him.

"So that's how you came to write your computer programme?" asked Jonathan unable to believe that such an ordinary thing as a spilt beaker of water could inspire an act of genius.

"Anyway, enough of me talking… who fancies a little walk?" he asked looking around for volunteers as he took his lab coat off and folded it away in his golf bag.

At that moment the children spotted a figure in the distance.

"It's Grandpa!" exclaimed the children jumping up and down excitedly.

Waving, their grandfather made his way up the hill towards them pushing a tandem bicycle with him.

"Hello, you two," he called out, his shirt sleeves rolled up and puffing away breathlessly. Racing down the hill, the children threw their arms around him and gave him a great big hug.

"Grandpa!" shouted Liz pleased to see him.

"Well, this is a surprise, isn't it?" he said red-faced with exertion.

"I didn't think I'd be going for a bicycle ride on a flying tandem today," he remarked, taking a minute to catch his breath.

After everything the Doctor had told her about his computer programme, Liz looked awkwardly at her grandpa.

"Are you my real, grandpa?" she asked, looking confused.

"Why do you ask that, my love?" said the rosy-faced old man, trying to keep his hair under control as it flapped about in the wind.

"Well, this is a dream and dreams aren't real, are they?" she said.

"Dreams are as real as you make them. Go on, pinch my arm," he said holding out his arm and encouraging her to give it a squeeze. Liz shook her head, reluctant to do as she was told.

"Go on!" he said holding out his arm.

Tentatively, she nipped the skin on his bare arm.

"Owww!" squealed their grandpa giving a little jump.

"See, I am real."

Happy to know her grandpa was as real as real could be, she gave a smile of satisfaction as she asked what he was doing here.

"I'm here to go on a cycle ride with your brother; apparently, he asked if we could go sit on a cloud and take in the view."

"But why have you brought a bike with you?"

"It's a dream; we can do anything we like…and if you want a flying bike, you can have a flying bike. What about you, what are you up to?" he asked.

"I'm going to have a picnic with Dr Fife and some bears. There not just ordinary bears though," piped up Liz.

"Dr Fife say they can talk and ride bikes," she informed him. Their grandpa looked surprised.

"A talking bear? Now that's not something you come across every day, is it?" he said sounding impressed.

Striding down the path towards them, Dr Fife let out a cheery "hello" as he took his cap off to wave at him. With his golf clubs slung over his shoulder, Oban took their grandfather's hand and gave it a hearty shake.

"Pleased to meet you, sir. Dr Oban Fife at your service!"

"Tom Bawtry," replied the old man shaking his hand.

"Now tell me if I'm wrong but those hands feel like the hands of an engineer if I'm not mistaken," said the Doctor, feeling the rough, calloused skin of their grandfather's hands and recognising the short-sighted gaze of a man who had spent his life pouring over plans and schematic drawings.

"Correct, but a retired one!" their grandfather replied, amazed that any-one could tell.

"Well, it's always nice to meet a like-minded fellow," exclaimed the Doctor taking his golf clubs from his shoulder and setting them down by his side.

"Why? Are you an engineer too?" asked their grandfather. The Doctor, with his hands in his pockets, gave a candid reply.

"I like to think of myself as bit of a part-time tinkerer," he said modestly.

"I think you're rather underselling yourself, Oban," remarked Miss Bagshaw who was keen to let it be known that the Doctor was more than just some weekend hobbyist when it came to the application of amazing inventions.

"That's right!" said Liz.

"He's built a dream machine that brought us here!" she added, praising the Doctor's abilities.

"A dream machine, eh? That sounds impressive!" said their grandfather looking perplexed and scratching the side of his head.

"Tell me, just how do you go about building one of those? It must be some job," he asked, wishing to know more.

"With great difficulty," professed the Doctor making a joke of it as he played down his own abilities.

"If I have to change one more Wartle valve in my life, I'll scream," he remarked.

"Wartle Valves eh? I know what you mean," sighed their grandfather who knew how infuriating a Wartle Valve could be.

Concluding their conversation on matters of a serious nature their grandfather then insisted that he better take his grandson on the trip they had planned.

"I'll have him back in no time. I don't want you getting in trouble for bringing them home late," he promised the Doctor as they got going.

"Don't worry Tom, take your time. You're forgetting that time has no relevance when it comes dreams," said the Doctor.

Waving to Jonathan and his grandfather, Liz, the Doctor, and Miss Bagshaw watched as the tandem began to pick up speed and slowly rise into the air. Overcome with excitement, the three companions cheered the pair on as they pedalled faster and faster rising higher and higher into the air.

"I wish I could have gone with them," said Liz looking down in the mouth.

"But don't you want to join myself and Miss Bagshaw for a picnic with some bears?" asked the Doctor inquisitively.

"I suppose so," remarked Liz glumly. Trying to console her, Miss Bagshaw put her arm around her and went over to a bench that overlooked the sea.

"Why don't we sit here while we wait for the bears to turn up, eh?"

It wasn't long before Liz spotted three tiny bikes with bears making their way along the path in their direction.

"Hullo there?" said a very large bear who was riding a bike and waving his hat at them in a very friendly manner. Following close behind on a tricycle was a very tiny bear, wearing a cap with a propeller on, and bringing up the rear was another large bear wearing a wide-brimmed straw hat with a flower on. The three bears came to a halt opposite the bench. Getting off his bike and putting down the stand, the giant bear approached them walking upright as all talking bears do.

"Which one of you is Luz?" he asked in a deep snuffly voice as he twitched his nose back and forth giving them a good sniff. Liz put her hand up.

"That's me," she replied nervously, getting up off the bench. Rummaging around in his fur, the bear brought out a piece of paper that looked remarkably like the letter which she had written her dream on.

"It says here that you wish to partake of high tea with a family of talking bears, is that right?" Liz replied with a timid nod of the head. The bear then held out his huge paw for Liz to shake.

"Wull, here we are," he said taking off his hat and giving a bow.

Sensing that Liz was scared of shaking hands with an eight-foot bear, Miss Bagshaw thought she might help by taking the lead. Shaking hands with the bear, she introduced herself.

"How do you do? My name is Miss Bagshaw, this is Liz and this is Dr Fife."

"Luz, Muss. Bagshaw and the Doctor," noted the very large bear.

"My name is Pingleton and this is my wife, Launceston, and our son, Little Bear."

"Awww... how sweet!" replied Miss Bagshaw.

Noticing that the Doctor was wearing some rather unusual attire, Pingleton made a closer inspection of him.

"Ahh...whut is this you are wearing?" asked the bear looking him up and down.

"This, this is my golfing attire," replied the Doctor.

"You look vury silly," noted the bear turning around and wandering back to get his picnic hamper that was attached to the front of his bike.

Meanwhile, Little Bear had dismounted from his tricycle and had taken an interest in Liz. Scurrying over to her on all fours, she didn't know what to do as she had never encountered a baby bear before in her life. Remaining absolutely still, she stood rooted to the spot while he sniffed her up and down.

"Hullo, I'm Little Bear," said the tiny bear.

"Errmm...I'm Liz," she stammered unsure of what to make of the baby bear.

"Would you like to play?" he asked. Little Bear got down on the ground and began to roll around as if he was having the most wonderful time, scratting up tufts of grass with his claws.

Noticing that Liz wasn't joining in, he stopped what he was doing.

"Why aren't you playing?" he asked. Liz didn't know what to say as she had never seen this sort of playing before.

"Why don't you join him?" said Miss Bagshaw encouraging Liz to follow suit.

"What? Roll about on the grass?"

"Why not? Little Bear seems to be enjoying it," thinking it might be fun if Liz joined in.

Lying down on her back she rolled about in the grass waving her arms and legs about, copying what Little Bear was doing. It had never occurred to her that rolling around in grass could be so much fun. As Liz rolled about, she was surprised to hear Little Bear laughing. She had never heard a bear laugh before and it went something like this.

"Huh…huh, huh…huh…huh, huh…huh."

Soon she found that she was having more fun than she thought. As she rolled about on the grass, Little Bear bumped into her, tickling her with his claws making her laugh some more. He then rolled on top of her as he played a game of tussle as all junior bears do when growing up.

"Huh…huh, huh," laughed Little Bear as he pinned her down on the ground. Then getting over-excitable, Little Bear showed his teeth and Liz let out a scream.

"What have I told you about scaring people with your teeth?" said his mother scolding him for his excitable behaviour as she led him away by the paw. Sitting upright and sweeping back her hair from in front of her face, Liz brushed the grass off herself.

"Are you alright?" asked Miss Bagshaw coming to her aid.

"I was a little frightened. I've never seen teeth that big before," she admitted.

Making him sit down on the ground and behave himself, Launceston Bear opened the picnic basket. Settling down on the blanket, they were joined by Dr Fife who was interested to see what bears ate for lunch.

"I say what have you got there in the basket, old chap?" he asked Pingleton who was setting out the cups and saucers.

"We huv sandwiches with chocolate spread, then there's chocolate muffins, chocolate chip cookies h'and to finish with have h'a chocolate sponge cake. We also have Lemons because Launceston loves nothing better than h'a fresh tasting lemon after h'all that chocolatyness."

Launceston Bear then handed out the plates and passed around the sandwiches.

"Chocolate spread sandwiches!" said Miss Bagshaw trying to hide her disgust.

"Are there any other fillings?" she asked hopefully. The Doctor gently placed his hand on Miss Bagshaw's arm and whispered.

"It seems that bears are awfully fond of chocolate," he said giving her a sly wink. Miss Bagshaw then asked the bears if they would like to see some magic.

"Don't you mean higher-level consciousness?" said Liz correcting her.

"That I do, thank you Liz," replied Miss Bagshaw getting herself comfortable.

"Mr Pingleton and Mrs Launceston, would you care for a peanut butter and banana sandwich?" she asked, knowing that they were the Doctor's favourite. Pingleton ruffled his nose.

"H'is that crunchy Peanut Butter or smooth?" he enquired, being a bear of discerning tastes.

"The choice is yours; I can rustle up either." Launceston put her paw to her chin while she decided.

"I think I'll h'uv smooth please."

"Smooth it is," said Miss Bagshaw waving her hand over the sandwich. Meanwhile, the Doctor tapped Pingleton on the arm.

"You'll like this bit, you'll see," he said. With a quick flurry of her hand, Miss Bagshaw produced a smooth peanut butter and banana sandwich for Pingleton to try. Pulling the two slices of bread apart, Pingleton was amazed to find that he no longer had a chocolate spread sandwich, but it had turned into a peanut butter and banana sandwich. Giving it a tentative lick with his tongue, he announced that it was good to eat.

"H'it h'is luverly," he said handing it around for his wife and son have a try. Making sure there were enough sandwiches to go round, Miss Bagshaw got busy magicking up more sandwiches.

Pingleton then asked if anyone would care for some lemonade. Liz politely put her hand up while Little Bear sat transfixed by Miss Bagshaw's antics. He had never seen magic before.

Pulling out a bag of fresh lemons from his picnic basket, Pingleton placed a glass down in front of him and with a look of determination crushed the lemon between his paws. The juice ran out of the lemon filling up the glass beneath him. Repeating the process a few more times, he soon had a full glass and adding a spoonful of sugar gave it a stir.

"There you h'ar," said Pingleton presenting Liz with a glass of fresh lemonade. Tentatively Liz took a sip and a smile spread across her face.

"Pingleton makes very nice lemonade," she declared.

While they were busy tucking into their sandwiches, the Doctor stretched out on the picnic blanket taking in the view.

"It's a lovely day, don't you agree?" he said, taking time out to look at the ocean.

"Just look at that," he remarked quietly satisfied with himself.

"Trillions of dreams just waiting to be dreamed," he uttered as if barely able to conceive the enormity and beauty of his own creation.

"I like this dream, thank you Oban," said Liz who was content to sit on the blanket and munch on her sandwiches.

"It's my pleasure," he replied tipping his head back and smiling as if he did not have a care in the world.

"Y'us it's very nice dream," agreed Pingleton.

Once everyone had finished their sandwiches, Launceston handed around the chocolate cookies and muffins, which the Doctor, Liz and Miss Bagshaw politely declined but they were more than happy to indulge themselves in a nice slice of chocolate cake that was being passed around.

As bees buzzed around lazily in the grass, Liz couldn't have thought of a nicer day. Little Bear had enjoyed it so much that he had fallen asleep on the blanket along with the Doctor, who was busy cat napping, his cap pulled low over his face.

"He always has an afternoon nap," noted Little Bear's mother as she tried to wipe the chocolate from his face with a napkin. Making funny little noises to himself, Liz wondered what Little Bear was dreaming of.

"Probably having his paw in a giant barrel of honey," remarked the Doctor sleepily, raising his head ever so slightly from his afternoon snooze to answer.

Watching the bear dream away happily, Liz thought of all the dreams out there bobbing around on the ocean waiting to be dreamed and wished that everyone in the world could have a happy dream.

"Miss Bagshaw?" asked Liz quizzically as she plucked at daisies that were growing in the grass.

"You know earlier when you didn't want to tell anyone your dream. Well can I ask, is it a nice dream?"

Miss Bagshaw looked over at the Doctor to make sure he was still sleeping and then looked back at her tipping her a wink.

"I think you know more about my dream than I do," she whispered. Liz realised she had been rumbled. It was clear that Miss Bagshaw knew what she had asked the Positive Thought Accumulator for.

"It's alright," said Miss Bagshaw gently placing her hand on her arm to reassure her.

"It was a very nice of you to do something like that for the Doctor."

"I didn't know that you knew about my dream."

"It wasn't just your dream; it was my dream too," she confessed, urging Liz not to say word.

It was then that the Doctor came round from his cat nap, pushing his cap back on his head he awoke rubbing his eyes.

"Sorry, have I missed anything interesting?" he asked rolling over on his side and looking blankly over at them.

"No nothing at all, we were only talking," replied Miss Bagshaw saying nothing about her dream.

"Oh well, as long as everybody has had a nice time, eh?" he muttered.

It was time for the bears to leave as they had a long way to cycle back, so getting to his feet Pingleton set about packing the picnic things away.

"Here, I've got something for Little Bear," said Liz who had been busy making a daisy chain while everyone had been talking and snoozing. Placing it over his head, Little Bear wore it proudly round his neck.

"Thank you, Luz," he said as he gave her his paw in thanks. He was most pleased to have been given such a lovely gift that he went off to show his parents.

"Do you think I'll ever get to see the bears again?" asked Liz. The Doctor who was busy arranging the cap on his head gave Liz an affectionate smile.

"'Course you will."

"Do you think so?"

"I'm sure of it. After all I should know, I built the Positive Thought Accumulator!"

They waved as they watched the bears cycle off into the distance. After they had seen them off the Doctor, giddy with excitement went to play the last hole of his favourite golf course while waiting for Jonathan and his grandfather to return from their trip on a flying bike.

-18-

THE POSITIVE
THOUGHT CLUB

THE DOCTOR, HAVING worked extremely hard on the Positive Thought Accumulator, had rather overdone things and was feeling out of sorts. In need of recuperation, he had taken to his bed for a well-deserved rest to recover from his recent exertions when he was roused by a knock on the door.

"Come," said the Doctor as he lay there propped up on his pillows in his silk pyjamas. The door opened and in walked Miss Bagshaw carrying with her a tray full of the Doctor's favourite things. Porridge with a touch of syrup, a full rack of toast, butter in little swirls and a pot of raspberry jam.

"My, Miss Bagshaw, you've really out done yourself!" exclaimed the Doctor, impressed by the spread she had laid on for him. Sitting bolt up-right in bed and keeping absolutely still, Miss Bagshaw set the tray down on top of him.

"How are you feeling?" she enquired, putting her hand to his forehead to feel his temperature.

"Tired!" he replied, with his hair stuck up all over the place.

"You do really over do things if I may say so, Oban. Isn't it about time you took things a little easier?" Said Miss Bagshaw as she unfurled a starched white napkin and tucked it into his pyjama top.

"It's all very well saying take it easy, but who else is going to do my work of saving the world?" he remarked with a casual shrug. Miss Bagshaw gave a disapproving tut.

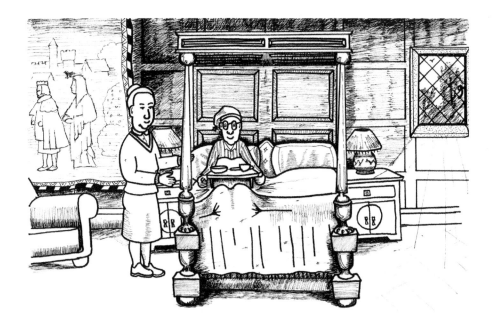

"Yes, but if you tire yourself out like this, you won't be well enough to do your work," she replied.

Looking through his wardrobe, she asked if he would be getting out of bed today. The Doctor took a minute to ponder the matter.

"I might have a mooch down the greenhouse this afternoon if I'm feeling up to things," he answered, holding his bowl of porridge under his chin so as not to spill any on his pyjamas.

"What do you think of these?" asked Miss Bagshaw holding up a pair of salmon pink corduroy trousers and a mustard-coloured cardigan for him to peruse. Looking at what she was holding up he gave his seal of approval.

"I've been thinking. I'm not as young as I used to be, and my time here on this planet is getting less, and the children next door are extremely bright, are they not?" remarked the Doctor finishing his bowl of porridge and buttering a slice of now cold toast.

"Now there's no need for any of that silly talk…" she replied telling him off as she lay his clothes out on the chair for him.

"But maybe it's time I teach them how the Positive thought Accumulator works, so they can keep my work going after I'm gone."

"Are they not a little young to be learning about the Positive Thought Accumulator? I mean it seems awfully complicated to me."

"It's never too soon to be learning about the nature of dreams, my dear Miss Bagshaw. It's what makes the world turn – dreams! I'm going to see to it that I give those children the full breadth of my knowledge before I pop my clogs!" remarked the Doctor busy smothering his toast in jam.

As he munched away, the topic of conversation turned to that of a more personal nature.

"Tell me, we've known each other for a while now, haven't we?" asked the Doctor of Miss Bagshaw.

"And I'm the sort of man that believes that friendship starts with first names. Do you not agree? I mean you know my name, but I do not know yours and I hate to keep calling you Miss Bagshaw all the time; it all sounds terribly formal if you ask me,"

Blushing, she nervously revealed her name to him.

"It's Evelyne,"

"Evelyne!" gasped the Doctor, suddenly taken aback upon hearing her name for the first time.

"What a beautiful name you have, my dear Evelyne," he said reaching out to take hold of her hand. Hesitantly, she let the Doctor's hand encircle hers.

"Do you want to know my full name?" he asked trying to break the ice.

"It's terrible!" he said laughing at the thought of his own name.

"Go on, tell me," said Miss Bagshaw eager to know.

"You promise not to laugh?"

"I can't promise that," she replied, keen to hear what his middle name was. Pushing himself up on his pillows and careful not to disturb his break-fast tray, the Doctor cleared his throat.

"It is Oban Pitlochry Partick Fife." Miss Bagshaw let out a little giggle, covering her mouth with her hand.

"It's not that bad," she said trying to make the Doctor feel better.

Bursting into another fit of giggles, she tried her best to compose herself as he repeated his name once again for the benefit of Miss Bagshaw's amusement.

"I have something I would like to ask of you, Evelyne," he said on a more serious note. Managing to compose herself and stifle her fit of giggles, she enquired what it was.

"I would like to ask if you would join me for dinner sometime,"

"Dinner? Are you asking me out on a date, Dr Fife?" replied Miss Bagshaw sounding quite surprised that the Doctor should ask her of all people.

"And if you don't mind, I would like to cook for you."

Miss Bagshaw pulled her hand away as if taken back by the whole matter. Thinking he had overstepped the mark he immediately apologised.

"I didn't mean to offend you," he said getting the wrong end of the stick.

"You haven't offended me at all. I'm quite flattered actually. Why I'd loved to," she said accepting his offer.

With an awkwardness in the air, the Doctor finished his breakfast and allowed Miss Bagshaw to relieve him of his tray. Backing out of the room, Miss Bagshaw gave a shy smile as she closed the door behind her. Outside in the corridor, she gave a click of her heels and a silent squeal of delight, spending the rest of the day with a head full of happy thoughts.

Meanwhile, the Doctor allowed himself a little time to bask in the momentary glory of Miss Bagshaw accepting his offer of dinner. Relaxing, he waited till she was out of earshot before letting out a little cheer all to himself.

"Evelyne, Evelyne…" he said uttering her name over and over again.

After lying in bed for another hour or so and dreaming the most wonderful dreams, he decided it was time to get up.

It was several days later when Jonathan came to call on the Doctor. Ajna was curled up asleep in the bottom of the greenhouse window when Jonathan found the Doctor busy at work, knitting. With light flooding in from above, he could be seen bent over, studiously working on one of his highly sophisticated garments of the future.

"Haven't you finished that yet?" asked Jonathan, leaning over the Doctor's shoulder and examining his atomic onesie.

With a set of head loop magnifying glasses perched on his head, the

Doctor took a minute out from the exacting work to look up at him, his eyes like that of a goggle-faced goldfish peering at him through the lens of the glasses.

"Jonathan, my boy! What you don't seem to understand is that the thread is so minute that it cannot be seen with the naked eye. Do you know there are over fifteen billion threads in this one tiny patch alone?" he said pointing to an area of cloth no bigger than his thumbnail. Jonathan bent down to see what the Doctor was looking at.

"Here, put these on," insisted the Doctor who was more than happy to take time out from the painstaking work of weaving the microscopic fabric to lend him his head loop. Sitting down in the Doctor's chair, Jonathan looked at the two large knitting needles that he had been using to weave the fabric.

"Those are for my benefit. If you look closely at the ends of the knitting needles, you can see a set of tiny crocodile grips that I have attached to hold the thread with." Half closing his eyes, Jonathan squinted and found that on each one of the needles the Doctor had attached a set of microscopic crocodile grips so infinitesimally small that Jonathan could barely see them, even with the magnifying glasses.

"They're tiny!" he declared, amazed that the Doctor had managed to engineer something so small.

"They have to be otherwise I wouldn't be able to hold the thread with my big fat fingers."

Jonathan looked up at the Doctor, almost blinding him with the light built into the head loop.

"Don't look at me, look at what you're doing," Oban protested shielding his eyes from the dazzling light.

While Jonathan got busy weaving the sub-atomic thread, he enquired as to how the Doctor was keeping.

"I've been better," he replied, arching his back and stretching out his aching muscles.

"You know all this excitement of making the world a better place can get the upper hand these days. I find I'm not quite the spring chicken I once was," he confessed.

"Which brings me on to what I wanted to talk to you about…" said the Doctor slowly pacing back and forth on the black and white checkerboard floor.

"…I'm getting on in years and I'm not going to be around forever. So, I was wondering if one day you and your sister may want to take over the running of… you know, the Positive Thought Accumulator," said the Doctor sticking his finger in his ear and idly rummaging around for earwax.

Jonathan stopped what he was doing and looked directly at the Doctor, blinding him for the second time in as many minutes.

"Take those infernal things off when you're looking at me," demanded the Doctor holding his hands up in front of his face so as not to be blinded. Overwhelmed by what the Doctor was proposing, Jonathan removed the magnifying loop from his head.

"You want me…me… to look after the Positive Thought Accumulator?" I can't possibly do that; I don't know the first thing of how it works," Stammered Jonathan.

"Don't worry, I'm not talking about now. I'm talking about sometime in the future when my body no longer co-operates with me. Besides you're one of life's natural dreamers; it will come easy to you. I'll make sure you're furnished with the necessary knowledge for when that time comes," said the Doctor putting his hand on the boy's shoulder to reassure him.

"Look, there are many great minds that have faced far greater odds and overcome them; just take a look at this lot here," said the Doctor extending his arm in the direction of the marble statues. Trying to inspire him to greatness, the Doctor continued with his little speech.

"I believe you and your sister have it in you to help the world see the amazingness that is the Positive Thought Accumulator."

"Do you really think so?" replied Jonathan unsure of himself.

"Course I do besides, Peter is practically semi-autonomous. It requires virtually no maintenance from me once it's up and running, but I will teach you the inner workings of the quantum computer, so you have a thorough grasp of how the machine operates," he said looking around the place as if his concentration was being drawn elsewhere.

"But I tell you what, how about a nice slice of cake first and then we can have a look inside Peter, eh?" said the Doctor flicking the kettle on and taking a seat.

While they were waiting for the kettle to boil, the Doctor wanted to show him another of his inventions that he had been working on. Rummaging around down the side of his chair amongst old newspapers and discarded plans of unfinished work, he pulled out a small, octagonal box.

"See this. It's a holographic star map of the entire universe."

"Really?" replied Jonathan examining the object and looking less than impressed.

"I was bored one afternoon and in need of something to do, when I found myself busy having a conversation with Gene," said the Doctor pointing to the photograph of the astronaut on the wall behind him.

"It was then that I thought about humans returning to space. Not in rockets but using my anti- gravity device, and I knew then that they'd need a road map for deep space."

"Tea?" enquired the Doctor getting to his feet as the kettle came to a rolling boil. Jonathan nodded politely while the Doctor poured the hot water into the two cracked mugs that sat on the draining board.

"How does it work?" Jonathan wanted to know giving it a shake.

"I'll show you, but we won't really get the best results in here as the suns too bright. We'll have to go to my potting shed to see it working better,"

The Doctor led the way through the greenhouse. Pressing the latch down on the wooden door he navigated the few steps down into the dimly lit room. Clearing some space on his work bench and setting the box down, he motioned for Jonathan to close the door. Then, turning on the power a holographic representation of a Milky Way instantly shot out of the box and flickered into life.

"Wow!" exclaimed Jonathan transfixed by the gas clouds of the spiral galaxy swirling around above his head.

"It's almost as good as my biosphere!" he declared, lavishing praise upon the Doctor.

"Tell me Jonathan, where would you like to go in the universe?" Jonathan didn't know the name of any galaxies so shrugged blankly.

"How about Osephius, my home planet?" suggested the Doctor with a smile on his face. Swiping away at the virtual inventory he found what he was looking for.

"Here we are. This was once my home planet many lifetimes ago,"
Jonathan stared up at the blue glowing orb that circled above him.

"Will you go back there one day?" He asked out of curiosity.

With his hands in his pockets and rocking gently back and forth on the balls of his feet, the Doctor gazed at the glowing ball of light before letting out a long sigh.

"Maybe," he said, sounding unsure of himself.

"But there are many other lives to live and billions of other planets out there that might be in need of my help. Maybe I'll just have a rest next time around," he confessed.

"I've got to say, all this Earth living makes me quite tired. You humans are quite an aggressive species," Sensing the Doctor's longing to be back home, Jonathan tried to make him laugh.

"How do you get a baby alien to sleep?" he asked.

"I don't know, how do you get a baby alien to sleep?"

"You rocket!" answered Jonathan, feeling rather proud of his joke.

Letting out an uncontrollable laugh, a great big smile leapt across the Doctor's face as he chuckled away to himself. Trying to regain his composure, the Doctor couldn't help but correct Jonathan.

"Technically you'd require an anti-gravity device not a rocket, but I'm not going to split hairs over such a matter," he said wagging his finger and chuckling away to himself. After a bit more giggling the Doctor suddenly remembered something.

"Gosh, our tea must be getting cold now?" he said switching off the power to the star map. Making their way up the steps that led out of the potting shed Jonathan closed the door behind them.

Back in his thinking room, the Doctor put his hand to the mugs and sensing they were cold, poured them down the sink while putting the kettle on to boil again.

"I've an idea," chirped up Jonathan eager to tell the Doctor what he had been thinking about.

"I know that the Tickles help write the dreams… but I was thinking," said Jonathan hesitantly. However, the Doctor seemed distracted by what was inside the cake tin. Lifting the lid, he looked inside.

"Ahh… carrot cake. Miss Bagshaw knows I have a soft spot for it!" exclaimed the Doctor, while attempting to coax out of Jonathan what he had to say with an encouraging wave of the hand.

"Go on, I'm listening," insisted the Doctor as he rummaged around for a knife to cut the cake with.

"I thought we might start the Positive Thought Club. We could help write dreams, you know good dreams," said Jonathan trying to convince the Doctor of the idea's worth.

Jonathan had been thinking about this for a while, ever since everybody at school had found out about his trip in a flying car.

"Mmm…" noted the Doctor letting out a sound of satisfaction as he ran his finger along the back of the knife and licked the icing clean.

"I'm not sure I like the idea of a club; the world has enough clubs," noted the Doctor, looking over the top of his glasses in a dubious manner.

"Cake?" he said holding out a plate and trying to tempt Jonathan with a huge slice of carrot cake.

Accepting his kind offer, Jonathan took possession of a cake fork while the Doctor set a mug of tea down next to him. Sitting down in his chair, the Doctor took the weight off his feet.

"You see Jonathan, I built the Positive Thought Accumulator for everyone, not just the few. Life is about is about sharing, togetherness, and that's why you can see I am reluctant to start such a thing," he confessed while delicately balancing a piece of cake on his fork and admiring it.

"Well, why don't we let it be open to everyone, then anyone could join? It would be for people wanting to dream the best dreams for everyone," said Jonathan defending his idea.

"Mmm…I like that. Dreaming the best dreams for everyone, now that's kind of catchy. But there can't be any rules!" stated the Doctor adamantly, pointing his fork at Jonathan.

"Or perhaps just one and that is as well as your own dream, you have to bring a dream along with you that will help benefit the whole world. You know I'm not normally one for rules, but in this case, I think the Earth needs all the help it can get," he said, stuffing a forkful of cake in his mouth and continuing to talk with his mouth full.

"We are free thinkers Jonathan; we must be allowed to dream!" he muttered, spitting cake crumbs all over his cardigan. After careful consideration of the matter the Doctor gave his opinion.

"I think we should give your idea for the Positive Thought Club a try. Besides we need as many good dreams as we can get,"

"I could put up a poster at school to get people interested?" suggested Jonathan.

"Why not!" declared the Doctor happy that the club was open to anyone with a dream.

"Let's see if there are any fresh young minds out there that want to make a better world," he said, giving the go-ahead for Jonathan's new plan.

Having finished his cake, the Doctor put his plate down on the floor making a loud clack on the tiles, waking up Ajna who had been asleep on the window ledge. Letting out an extremely large yawn and stretching out his entire body the cat nearly fell off his perch.

"Sorry about that lad," he apologised, as Ajna teetered on the window ledge before leaping down onto the floor and sauntering over to see the Doctor.

"I'm afraid there's nothing left for you," he said begging forgiveness from his feline companion for his lack of thoughtfulness. However, this did not put Ajna off hoovering up the last of the crumbs off the Doctor's plate. While Jonathan stroked the cat, the Doctor suggested they have a look inside the Positive Thought Accumulator.

Making their way to the centre of the greenhouse, the Doctor took a minute to look up at the amazing machine.

"It's hard to believe that's one man's life's work, isn't it?" he said with his hands in his pockets, looking up at the mirrored disc.

"Did you always know you were going to build this?" asked Jonathan. The Doctor let out a laugh all to himself.

"I suppose I always knew that someday I would," he said confiding in the young boy. Then with a nod of the head, he encouraged Jonathan to follow him.

"Come, you might find this interesting," he said approaching the main control desk.

The Positive Thought Accumulator was an imposing machine to behold. Hissing and creaking, the whole structure was covered in ice from top to bottom as every vent and opening gushed with gas and vapour in an attempt to cool down.

"Why's it covered in ice?" asked Jonathan looking a little wary. The Doctor remarked it was nothing unusual.

"You see Jonathan, being a super-computer, it generates a lot of heat. Even though its memory banks are holographic, light itself creates an immense amount of energy and needs cooling down. You see all these tubes and ducts…" the Doctor pointed out.

"…they all contain liquid coolant and the belts, gears, and pulleys; they all run cooling fans," he explained.

The Doctor approached a steel doorway that was located on the side of the Positive Thought Accumulator's megastructure. Like that of a ship's door, it had a large circular handle in the centre, which the Doctor, taking a handkerchief from his pocket, turned in a clockwise direction.

"What's with the handkerchief?" asked Jonathan out of curiosity.

"It's so I don't get cold burns. This thing runs at absolute zero…but to you and me that's minus two-hundred and seventy-three Celsius,"

"Brrr…that's cold,"

"You're telling me!" said the Doctor careful not to let any part of his exposed skin come into contact with the structure. Kicking the door open with his foot, he turned and gave Jonathan a knowing smile.

"What you are about to witness in here is beyond all space and time," he said excitedly stepping over the lip of the bulkhead and into the heart of the machine.

"Now don't touch anything. Otherwise, you will find yourself stuck to it!" warned the Doctor, being as it was so cold.

The first thing that struck Jonathan as he stepped inside the machine was that it was much bigger on the inside than it seemed from the outside. Inside it was huge, filled with miles and miles of cabling, flashing lights and all sorts of odd bits of equipment that he had never seen before. One peculiar feature of the super-computer was that it seemed to go on forever, tapering away into oblivion. Jonathan had to step outside again just to check his mind wasn't playing tricks on him.

"Why's it so much bigger in here than it looks from the outside?"

"Ha! That's the thing about magic; you must put aside everything you know about reality and be prepared to be amazed," laughed the Doctor.

Inside, everything was dimly lit, but he could make out a huge eight-spoked wheel like structure high above his head, which pulsated rhythmically with light.

"What's that?" asked Jonathan, pointing to the wheel.

"That's where all the dreams are woven together before being sent out to the world,"

As Jonathan stood there staring up at the cathedral-like structure, he noticed a faint light high above him that seemed to be descending towards him, swirling in multi-coloured spiralling patterns. He wanted to know what it was.

"That's the Tickles, they're coming to see you," the Doctor informed him as the spherical balls of light grew brighter.

Soon they had surrounded Jonathan and were floating there, flashing a multitude of amazing colours. Jonathan tried to reach out and touch them, but the Tickles immediately responded by backing away. Playful in nature they swirled around him fizzing with light and jostling each other as they tried to get a better look at him. Then something amazing happened. Jonathan rose into the air.

"Help!" he cried, but the Doctor shouted for Jonathan not to worry.

"They only want to get to know you. They can be a bit playful at times; they mean you no harm," he said trying to reassure him as they carried him higher and higher into the cavernous interior. Soon, they had carried him so high inside the machine that the Doctor looked like a tiny speck below.

All around were glowing balls of light, of many different colours they nudged one another for a better position as they queued up to investigate Jonathan further. Like glass paperweights they all had different patterns inside making each one unique and distinct. As the lights bobbed around inspecting him closely, he heard a voice in his head.

"Will you be our friend?" they asked without a single word being uttered. It was all very strange. Jonathan wasn't sure if he was hearing things, until the thought repeated itself. Unable to quite believe it he realised they were communicating with him using his mind. It was unlike anything he'd experienced before; the Tickles were putting thoughts directly into his head.

"Who are you?" asked Jonathan using his new-found telepathic ability to ask his question.

"We are Tickles, we give light to your dreams, we help operate the Positive Thought Accumulator and we'd like you to help us."

Jonathan was unsure of what they wanted from him.

"How can I help? I'm only a little boy," he replied, but the dancing balls of light reassured him.

"You have the right sort of dreams that we're looking for," came the words flashing up inside his head like a billboard.

Then in a myriad of swirling patterns, they grouped together and showed him all his best memories, like playing with his sister at the seaside, helping his dad in the garden, camping out in the woods with his friends. It was like one giant slideshow! Jonathan didn't know how they were doing it and demanded to know how they could read his mind.

"You are connected to the Positive Thought Accumulator and that's how we have the ability to see your best dreams," they told him letting the thought flow through his mind.

"Your mind is an interesting one and your dreams are happily infectious. We want to give you the opportunity to let your dreams grow," they told him as they buzzed around, their lights flashing and pulsating as they laughed and tittered like children. Overwhelmed Jonathan tried to make sense of what they wanted of him.

"All you have to do is share your dreams with the world," was the collective reply.

"That's it? Share my dreams. Are you sure that's all I've got to do?" he asked as the Tickles shimmered all around giving off an effervescent light.

"That's all," was the reply as they hovered round him with the occasional one zipping off before returning to the exact same spot.

"Alright I'll do it, but first you've got to put me back down on the ground!"

Descending towards the ground, the lights flashed and buzzed with excitement, changing colour and brightness and in his head, he could hear their elated chatter as they talked feverishly amongst themselves.

The Doctor held out his hand to help steady him as the Tickles delivered the young boy safely back to the Doctor's care.

"How was your trip?" enquired an intrigued Doctor, eager to hear what the boy had to say.

"The Tickles want me to share my dreams with the world," replied Jonathan, looking unsteady on his feet.

"I thought they might. That's all the Tickles have been talking about recently – Jonathan this and Liz that, it's been non-stop you know!" admitted the Doctor shaking his head having had his fill of their idle chatter.

Jonathan had so much to tell him that he was bursting at the seams to divulge all the new things he'd found out.

"Do you know you what? You don't even have to speak; the Tickles can read your mind!" Jonathan told him. The Doctor gave a knowing smile.

"Pretty amazing isn't it, who'd have thought, eh?" he answered as if he already knew what the Tickles, we're capable of.

The Doctor decided that Jonathan had probably had enough fun for one day and showed him towards the heavy steel door of the quantum computer.

"How were the Tickles able to lift me up into the air?" Jonathan wanted to know as he stepped over the raised lip of the door and back into the central rotunda of the greenhouse.

"You know I'm not a big fan of the word 'magic'? But I hate to say, it was magic," admitted the Doctor reluctantly.

"Magic?" replied Jonathan, amazed that the Doctor should be bandying about such a word.

"Yes, magic," said the Doctor waving his hand around dismissively as if trying to downplay the importance of the word.

"You see, when it comes to the Positive Thought Accumulator, things can behave a little differently," confessed the Doctor shedding light on the matter.

"… what you thought was a dream can suddenly become real and what you thought was real can become a dream, and that's when the interesting stuff starts to happen."

"Like what?" asked Jonathan.

"Oh, you'll find out in good time," replied the Doctor taking his handkerchief from his pocket once more to close the heavy steel door of the quantum computer.

Turning up the dials on the console, the Positive Thought Accumulator sprang to life as electricity rippled up the exterior and the gears and belts whirred into motion.

"Well, I hope you and the Positive Thought Club have some good dreams up your sleeve, because we're going to need them," said the Doctor as he stood back and watched the machine burst into life once more. Jonathan looked over at the Doctor; he knew he wasn't going to let him or the Tickles down.

-19-

WELCOME TO MY MIND

THE DOCTOR HAD been waiting all week in anticipation of his date with Miss Bagshaw. So much so that he'd hardly been able to sleep a wink. Spending his nights awake, he made best use of his time by deliberating on more earth-shattering inventions while Ajna slept soundly at the foot of his bed. The cat barely stirring except for when the Doctor threw back the covers to pace up and down, ruminating on his ideas and talking aloud to himself.

Occasionally Oban he would take a break from thinking. Wandering downstairs in his dressing gown and slippers, he would make himself a warm milky cocoa and take it back to bed while he thought of new ways in which to make the world a better place. When all that thought and deliberation had got too much for him, he would take a break and search through his wardrobe in order to find something suitable to wear for his date with Miss Bagshaw.

Preoccupied and unable to settle the Doctor spent the week tinkering in his laboratory. Frustrated by a fidgety mind, he was inspecting a Wartle valve for Boggrobblers when he was struck by an idea.

"I know what to give her as a present!" he thought, downing tools, and making a beeline for the potting shed. Ajna who was rarely concerned with the Doctor's plight took a minute out from preening himself to look up in surprise. His ears on end and whiskers proud, he wondered what it was his aged companion was up to.

The Doctor made his way down the steps of the potting shed casting his eyes upon the biospheres lined up on the shelf. Gently glowing away, he pondered which one he should give her as a present. For Oban there was only one. His Boreal Forest biosphere. Lifting it down from the shelf, he gently placed it on the bench, gazing at it in wonder.

"She will be pleased with this," he said to himself as he searched for something to wrap it with.

Rustling underneath his bench, he found a sheet of blue carbon paper that he used for copying his plans, thinking this would make ideal wrapping paper. On it were drawn circles in a series of entwined patterns. For whenever the Doctor came up with an idea, he always thought in circles such was the nature of his thinking.

Taking a ball of green garden twine, he measured out three good arm lengths and cut it with a knife. Then gently setting the glass bowl down on top of the paper, he wrapped it up tying a bow at the very top.

"There, that should do," he thought, satisfied with his work. Taking it back to the house, he set it down on the table in the hallway ready to give to Miss Bagshaw when she called that evening.

Having been so preoccupied with what to give her as a present, he hadn't given much thought as to what he was going to cook for that evening's meal. Rustling through his cupboards, he threw together whatever he could find into a shopping bag. It wasn't really the dining experience he'd planned, but then again, the Doctor had something rather altogether different in mind for their date.

Before her arrival he went upstairs to have a bath and get changed. Having made himself presentable, the Doctor looked in the bedroom mirror whilst making conversation with Ajna who sat on the bed wondering what the old fool was up to.

"Well Ajna, wish me luck, old boy," he said making sure there was not a hair out of place.

"A date, I say this will be a novelty," he said, trying to keep the worst of his jitters under control.

Nervously, he awaited the arrival of Miss Bagshaw. Pacing up and down in the library, he glanced up at the ornate gold clock that sat on top of the mantelpiece, checking the time with every other step. Having almost worn a hole in the rug he jumped when he heard the doorbell ring. The brass bell jangled back and forth on its spring as he dashed out into the hall-way, nearly tripping up over his own feet such was his haste. However, be-fore opening it, he had one last check of himself in the mirror to make sure that he was looking his best. Then taking a deep breath he opened the door.

"Why Evelyne, what a pleasure it is to have you as my guest this eve-ning," he said with a courteous bow.

Miss Bagshaw looked a delight. Wearing a small purple satin hat set at a jaunty angle and a long blue overcoat to keep out the worst of autumnal weather, she looked radiant. However, she was taken aback by what the Doctor was wearing. Looking like he was about to spend the afternoon digging in the garden, the Doctor had on a big thick roll neck sweater, a blue fisherman's cap, a pair of worn corduroy trousers and a pair of wel-lington boots. She was inclined to say something but decided against it as she was sure the Doctor would have a good reason for wearing such unusual attire.

Inviting her in, he closed the door and showed her over to the reception table where his biosphere was sat waiting for her, all wrapped up.

"This is for you," he said.

"Why Oban you shouldn't have," remarked Miss Bagshaw taking off her gloves and clasping her hands together in sheer delight. As the light from the globe diffused through the thin wrapping paper, she was immediately taken by the pattern traced onto it.

"Why Oban, what heavenly design have you created here?" she asked sensing it was something that came from the Doctor's own hand. Trying to be modest, the Doctor downplayed the true nature of his genius.

"This is where all my ideas come from," he nodded, taking off his cap and holding it in both hands whilst looking shy and bashful about the matter.

"Well, it's amazing," noted Miss Bagshaw bending down to take a closer look.

"Your present's inside," the Doctor pointed out, but Miss Bagshaw was so taken by the pattern of the overlapping circles that she was reluctant to unwrap it.

"I don't want to spoil it," she said, her hand on her chest as she gasped at the intricate nature of the design drawn onto the wrapping paper.

"I can save it for you if you like?" he said leaning over her shoulder.

"Oh, that would be nice."

Carefully, she pulled at the twine allowing the paper to unfurl and expose the globe beneath.

"Oh Oban, is this for me?" she gasped with delight, not having seen one of the Doctor's biospheres before.

"It's my favourite," he said lifting it from off the paper and placing it down in a position from where she could see better. Bending down to take a closer look, she enquired as to how it was, he made them.

"Oh, a little bit of this and a little bit of that," noted the Doctor casually, as he began to explain the purpose of his miniature worlds.

"I've been working on these for quite some years," he said pursing his lips together as he admired his own work. He then explained how his biospheres were an insurance policy against humans.

"An insurance policy?"

"I'm afraid you know as well as I do Evelyne that humans are not inclined to look after the world in which we live," said a sorrowful Doctor, blinking wildly as he looked over the top of his glasses.

"So, as you can see, I have been creating my miniature worlds, which mimic every kind of climatic and environmental habitat known to man. All you have to do is take the lid off and watch it grow. This one is my particular favourite," he said with his arm outstretched as if presenting it to Miss Bagshaw for her perusal.

As the shimmering lights of the Aurora Borealis gently flickered away, Miss Bagshaw couldn't believe her eyes.

"Is this what you get up to in your spare time?" she asked.

"It truly is a miracle, is it not?" he said as they watched a blizzard blow in and cover the thin matchstick-like trees in a thick covering of snow. Studying the orb closer, Miss Bagshaw let out a shriek of delight.

"Why Oban, there are animals in it!" she squawked with excitement. To show her appreciation, Miss Bagshaw gave Oban a kiss on the cheek.

"What a wonderful gentleman you are," she declared as the Doctor blushed with embarrassment.

Realising that time was getting on, he escorted her through to the kitchen where on the table was a large shopping basket with a picnic blanket sticking out of the top.

"If you'd like to follow me," said the Doctor rummaging in one of his drawers for a torch.

"I think you might like where we're going," he said grabbing the shopping bag and showing Miss Bagshaw to the back door. Flicking on the torch, Dr Fife held out his hand and guided her down the steps in the dark.

"Where are we going?" Miss Bagshaw wanted to know, unsure of where the Doctor was taking her.

"To my laboratory," he confessed as he shone the torch on the ground in front of them.

Leading the way through the overgrown bushes, he held on tight to Miss Bagshaw's hand.

"Oh Oban, is this really necessary?" she asked, unable to see where she was going.

"Trust me," he said putting his weight against the glass door of the greenhouse and pushing it open.

"Thank goodness!" declared Miss Bagshaw squeezing through the gap in the door and clinging to her hat. At the far end of the greenhouse the faint light of the Positive Thought Accumulator could be seen, gently humming away to itself as the lights blinked rhythmically on and off.

Making their way through the greenhouse in the dark, they did their best not to trip up. Once in the central rotunda, the Doctor placed his shopping bag down on the floor and began powering up the Positive Thought Accumulator. Slowly, the quantum computer sprang into life as lights flashed, gears turned, and drive belts whirred into motion.

"Oban just where are you're taking me?" asked Miss Bagshaw nervously.

"If you bear with me a minute Evelyne, all will be revealed," he said, trying to reassure her. Then, picking up his shopping bag, he took Miss Bagshaw firmly by the hand while the machine began to play a little tune.

"I'm not going to be floating around the place like last time, am I?" she asked. The Doctor smiled and shook his head.

"I promise there will be nothing of the sort," he said taking a step forward and instructing her to close her eyes while popping his dream into the slot. Miss Bagshaw didn't know what to expect. With a firm grip on her hand, the Doctor closed his eyes and thought beautiful thoughts.

Standing there together with their eyes shut tight, reality was beginning to deconstruct and take on a new form. Peeking with one eye open, the Doctor watched as his dream began to take shape.

"It's alright!" he declared. "You can open your eyes now."

Miss Bagshaw wasn't sure what to expect and was somewhat reluctant to open her eyes.

"You're quite alright," he said comforting her. Slowly opening one eye then the other, she was greeted with the most wonderful sight she had ever seen.

"Why Oban!" she gasped.

In front of her, the ocean stretched as far as the eye could see. With the sun beating down on the serene turquoise waters, a small single-masted dingy bobbed up and down at the water's edge.

"Where are we?" she asked with a beaming smile on her face. The Doctor, ever the joker, answered her with his own unique humour.

"My mind dear, my mind! Where else did you think we would be?"

"I know that silly," she said, hitting him playfully on the arm.

"But what is this place?"

As he made his way down off the soft spongy grass of the headland and onto the beach, he took Miss Bagshaw by the hand, guiding her over the rocks and onto the brilliant white sands of this heavenly place.

"This, my dear Evelyne, is a memory from my childhood. When my parents weren't busy running off around the world chasing antiquities, occasionally, we would come to this place where my great, great grandfather grew up."

Letting out a happy sigh, Miss Bagshaw couldn't help but sing the praises of the small Scottish Isle.

"Why would you ever want to leave?" she remarked putting her hand to her face to shield her eyes from the sun. Stepping down off the rocks, Miss Bagshaw struggled to walk on the sand in her shoes.

"Here," said the Doctor suggesting she take them off while lending her his arm to lean on.

After a bit of awkward struggling, he took her shoes from her, putting them on top of his shopping bag. Then, making their way down the beach towards the dinghy, Miss Bagshaw let out a gasp of surprise.

"Brrrr...the water's cold!" she said dancing around on the damp sand.

The Doctor pushed the dinghy off the sand and into water, the hull scraping along the bottom until it floated freely on the turquoise waters. Then with the sea almost up to the top of his wellies, he invited her to join him. Wading through the water with her skirt pulled up high, he offered her a helping hand as she made an ungainly entry into the boat. Flustered and grabbing at her hat, she found a place at the front of the boat, where she sat in a crumpled fashion. Jumping in, he dropped the centre board and took hold of the tiller, setting a course for his own little bit of paradise.

"Where are we going?" asked Miss Bagshaw, facing into the wind, her cheeks all rosy as she turned her collar up to the breeze that blew in off the ocean. The Doctor pointed to a place off in the distance.

"Just up the coast, there is a place where my family comes from," he said raising his face to the sun and letting himself feel as free as the ocean winds that filled his sails.

As the small single-masted dinghy rose and fell on the gentle swell of the ocean, Miss Bagshaw let her hand trail in the water.

"Wouldn't it be nice to live here Oban, far away from the world?"

The Doctor, with his blue fisherman's cap on, chose to say nothing, instead he acknowledged her comments with a peaceful and serene smile.

It didn't take long for them to reach their destination and tacking against the wind, he pointed the little boat towards the shore. It was hard to imagine anywhere more beautiful. Sheltered on both sides by a rocky headland, a bar of pristine white sand ran down to the crystal-clear waters to form a small cove with a cottage sat nestled at the very top.

Thickly built with whitewashed walls, two chimneys poked up at either end while the roof of the property was covered in thatch tied down by stones.

"Oh Oban, it's lovely!" exclaimed Miss Bagshaw as the Doctor pulled the centreboard up and let the dinghy run aground. Tying the boat off on a rusted iron ring embedded in a rock, he helped her from the dinghy. Barefooted, she made her way up the beach while the black-backed gulls rode the wave of rising air that was being pushed up over the headland.

"So, what are we eating?" asked Miss Bagshaw coyly as she held the hem of her coat to aid her progress over the sand.

"You'll have to wait, it's a surprise," replied the Doctor setting his shopping bag down and unfurling the picnic blanket. Miss Bagshaw sat down heavily on the blanket while she watched him prepare the meal.

"If you'll excuse me just a minute, I'm just going to collect some driftwood for our bar-be-que,"

"A bar-be-que!" she exclaimed delighted by the idea. "How lovely."

Although the sun shone brightly and it was the height of summer, there was still a cool breeze that blew in off the ocean. Miss Bagshaw sat curled up as she watched the Doctor potter around the beach collecting driftwood. Keen to contribute, she scooped out a shallow pit in the sand in which to lay the fire.

"Ahh…I see you've been busy," he remarked on his return. Dumping the wood down next to the hollow, he dropped to his knees and began arranging the wood in preparation for the fire.

"If you give me a minute, I should have this fire going and you'll be able to warm up, but in the meantime there's flask of tea in that bag over there." He said pointing to it.

"No, I'm quite alright," said Miss Bagshaw moving a little closer. Taking out a box of matches he struck one, holding it close to the kindling.

It didn't take long for the fire to catch and as soon as the flames had died down, he asked Miss Bagshaw to pass him his bag. Taking out a metal shelf that he had brought from his oven at home, he placed it over the red-hot embers and began chopping sweet peppers. Offering a hand, Miss Bagshaw placed the corn on the cobs and asparagus around the edge of the bar-be-que, while choosing to wait till later to put the veggie burgers on. Rooting around in his bag, the Doctor dug out a bottle of extra virgin olive oil to pour on.

"Why you thought of everything!" exclaimed Miss Bagshaw impressed with the Doctor.

"And a little salt and pepper to taste, eh?" he remarked smugly, amazed by his own brilliance.

While they waited for everything to cook, Miss Bagshaw asked him about his childhood at the cottage.

"Oh…it was wonderful," noted the Doctor, her question rekindling fond memories of the past.

"In the morning my granny would make a great big pan of porridge, and we would all sit around the hearth warming ourselves by the fire. Then after breakfast, I would spend the morning rock pooling or building sandcastles with my parents, or we would just sit around relaxing. Then in the afternoon, my grandpa and I would go sailing in that very same dinghy there," he said pointing to the little boat marooned on the beach.

"We'd be gone hours and he would point out all the other tiny islands around here and tell me their names; it was him who taught me how to sail," he reminisced casting his gaze out towards the ocean.

"It must have been idyllic," she replied, rubbing her hands together and holding them close to the fire.

As evening approached, the shadows became longer, and the Doctor took another blanket from his bag to place over Miss Bagshaw shoulders.

"Thank you," she replied, pulling the tartan throw tight around her. The Doctor, poking at the fire with a stick, turned the food once more before announcing dinner was ready.

Apart from the gentle lapping of the waves and the gulls circling overhead, there was no other sound as they tucked into their meal. Then, Miss Bagshaw spoke.

"It's hard to imagine that this is all a dream," she said.

The Doctor looked up at her wiping his hands on a napkin.

"It's quite amazing, isn't it? To think that this is all a computer-generated hologram that I created," he said reaching for another sweet pepper while offering the plate to Miss Bagshaw. Tucking in, she couldn't help but be caught by the sheer beauty of the place.

"I could spend my whole life here," she remarked staring wistfully at the gently lapping ocean.

"So could I. Tell me Evelyne, do you ever dream of the ocean?" asked the Doctor.

"Now and again," she replied as she tucked into her grilled pepper. With a wilting asparagus perched on the end of his fork, the Doctor began to talk about his aspirations.

"This is the whole reason why I built the Positive Thought Accumulator. So that one day everybody will dream of the ocean and be connected to one another," he told her as he continued to illustrate his point.

"You see when everybody is dreaming of the ocean, that's when the real magic happens."

"I thought you didn't like the use of the word *magic*," she reminded him. The Doctor laughed.

"I suppose the children have won me round to their way of thinking," he confessed.

For a moment the two of them enjoyed the bliss of the accompanying silence, watching the terns paddle along the water's edge. Then feeling the need to get something off his chest, the Doctor spoke up.

"Evelyne, I know that you are quite a perceptive person, and I am aware that you know me almost better than myself, but there is one thing I need to tell you about my true identity," Miss Bagshaw looked at the Doctor with a quizzical expression.

"What do you mean?" she asked, trying to read the Doctor for some sort of clue.

"I've been meaning to tell you for a while, but there never seemed to be the right moment. You see, I am not of this planet. I am of extra-terrestrial origins,"

"An extra-terrestrial? You're file never mentioned that! However, you don't look like one!" she replied with a giggle. The Doctor laughed, almost choking on his food.

"Thank you!" he said trying to recover his breath in between bouts of coughing.

"You see, I am as human as the next man, but I have lived so many lives that I have the stars running through my veins."

"I knew there was something different about you from the moment I met you!" declared Miss Bagshaw, cocking her head, eager to hear more.

"You're not put off by what I have told you, are you?" he asked looking at her nervously.

"No, why should I? You're the most kind and caring person I know," she replied.

"Hah – but therein lies my weakness!" sighed the Doctor pushing his cap back on his head.

"You see, I have the ability to feel so much more than ordinary humans that is why I live such a solitary life. For when someone feels pain, I feel it for them; when someone feels loss or heartache, I feel that too. That's why life here on Earth can be difficult for someone like me."

"Oh Oban, you're such an inspiration!" remarked Miss Bagshaw taking hold of his hand and squeezing it tightly.

"Tell me what was it like on the planet that you used to live on?" she said, coaxing the details out of him. The Doctor scratched his forehead while he thought about it.

"The last one before my life on this planet?"

"Yes, your last one," she replied.

Removing his cap from his head, the Doctor placed it down on the blanket as he prepared to tell Miss Bagshaw what life was like on another planet.

"Firstly, my name wasn't Oban. I was called Ammanah-ahha..."

"Oh...what a lovely sounding name," said Miss Bagshaw affectionately as the Doctor continued to tell her about his past life.

"...and secondly the name of my home planet was Osephius, which is about two billion light years from Earth. Osephius is not unlike earth in so far as it had water on it and plants and animals like we do here. However, we had four moons that orbited the planet, which made for some spectacular skies I can tell you!" noted the Doctor fondly, feeling the edge of his cap and running it through his fingers as he told his story.

"But we didn't live like humans do here, all divided. We lived as one, one people, free to come and go whenever and wherever we pleased. In fact, people had long ago given up living on the surface of the planet,"

"Where do they live then?" asked Miss Bagshaw excited to hear more.

"We lived in giant floating cities made of crystal that encircled the planet, roaming wherever we felt like."

"Gosh, that must have been something to see," she exclaimed.

"There were no cars, no dirty, filthy air and everything was recycled using nano technology so there was no waste and the best of it was there were trees as big as skyscrapers, which attracted all sorts of wildlife. The planet was like one giant game reserve full of amazing creatures," revealed the Doctor as he put his hat back on and pulled it down tight.

"But not all of us lived on Osephius. Many of us spent our time visiting other planets to study other life forms, and I can tell you from experience, there's nowhere quite so strange as Earth," remarked the Doctor with a smile.

"Your story is fascinating," said Miss Bagshaw, taken aback.

"But as much as you tell me about how amazing your home planet is, I still think I'm an Earth girl at heart," she said, returning her gaze to that of the ocean.

"Mmm…Earth, it is truly an oasis in space," muttered the Doctor in agreement.

After sitting in silence for a minute he rummaged round in his bag and brought out a flask of tea.

"Fancy a cuppa?" he asked waving it about and encouraging her to join him.

"Why not?" she said as he laid out some plastic mugs on the blanket.

"I've got to say one thing about this planet though. There's nothing like a good cup of tea to raise the spirits, eh?" he said digging out the angel cake that he had brought with him.

Handing her a mug of steaming hot tea, the Doctor offered her a slice of his cake that he had kept as a surprise.

"When did you make this?" she asked.

"I made it especially for you, one night when I couldn't sleep," he told her. Miss Bagshaw was taken aback that he had gone to all that effort to make a cake specially for her.

"How thoughtful!" she exclaimed as she looked adoringly at him.

The sun was now dropping over the ocean and the light was catching on the water turning it into a golden mirror.

"I could stay here forever," she said wistfully.

"Why don't we?" she said taking Oban by surprise and grabbing him by the arm.

"We could live in your grandfather's cottage, and we could spend the rest of our days here."

"What a wonderful idea. I could fix up the house, give it a lick of paint and you could give me a hand to re-thatch it. We could grow our own veg in the plot behind the house and just watch the changing of the weather," said the Doctor.

"There is just one problem though," he confessed.

"I can't leave Jonathan and Liz alone with the Positive Thought Accumulator just yet; they don't know how to use it." Miss Bagshaw looked disappointed.

"Don't be down," he said, trying to cheer her up.

"I'm sure we'll get to live out our dream one day." With that the Doctor looked out at the setting sun and, beholding the beauty that was the Earth, vowed to himself, one day he would make that dream come true.

Suddenly they found themselves in the dark of the Doctor's greenhouse. With only the light from the Positive Thought Accumulator to guide their way through the clutter of equipment, they picked their way through the old plant pots and garden tools that lay strewn about the place. With the fizz of electricity in the air he rummaged around in search of the light switch.

"Thank you for a most pleasant evening," said Miss Bagshaw full of praise for the Doctor as he turned on the lights.

"It was nothing" he replied clomping around in his wellies and roll neck sweater, looking like a salty sea dog.

"The pleasure was all mine," he said escorting Miss Bagshaw through the greenhouse and out into the grounds.

Leading the way through the tangle of bushes and overgrown shrubs; she followed the light from the Doctor's torch as it shone down on the ground. Once they had made their way back to the house, he offered to walk Miss Bagshaw home.

"It's very kind of you Oban, but I think I'm alright."

"No, no, I insist!" said the Doctor quickly nipping in the back door to change his footwear.

Gladly accepting his kind offer, the two of them walked arm in arm together chatting about all sorts of things when the Doctor said.

"Evelyne, I have something to ask you?"

For a moment, they stood looking at one another under the orange glow of the streetlights.

"Yes, what is it?"

"Well, I've been thinking," said the Doctor nervously.

"It seems rather silly, me living in a great big mansion all on my own, and I thought it might be more practical if you move in with me. After all, I have lots of spare rooms."

Miss Bagshaw was over the moon to be asked to live with him but trying to conceal her delight, she remained tight-lipped not wanting to sound too keen.

"It's alright, I don't expect an answer straight away," he said not wishing to seem too presumptuous.

For a while they walked along together, neither of them saying much of anything in case either one of them should seem too eager to embrace the idea. But when they finally reached Miss Bagshaw's home, she could no longer hide her enthusiasm.

"Oban," she said underneath the light of the lamp post.

"About your idea. I'd love to," she said. Well, the Doctor did not know what to say. For a minute he stood there speechless before declaring what a marvellous idea it was. Wishing her goodnight and giving her a peck on the cheek, he walked the mile or so home to his house without his feet even touching the ground, such was his unbridled excitement of having someone to share his life with.

-20-

A Great Success

W HEN MISS BAGSHAW moved in to Sunshine Villa, she made sure that the Doctor put his energy to good use. Having him connect the whole house to one of his new-fangled power generators, it was no longer the cold, uninviting place it once was, it now resembled a warm welcoming home.

She had even run the old sit-on mower over the lawn so the Doctor could use his old putting green again instead of the one on the roof. Even going so far as to employ a gardener to cut back the jungle like garden outside.

"How are we going to afford him?" The Doctor moaned while sat at the kitchen table, unsure as to how they were going to pay the bills.

"I'm sure that one of your new inventions will come good and we shall have no cause to worry," said Miss Bagshaw, confident that they would get by somehow.

Elbow deep in cake mixture, she couldn't help but comment favourably on Jonathan's new plan.

"What an interesting idea it was, to have the Positive Thought Club?" she said while busy baking cakes and buns ready for the first meeting.

"It certainly was," he agreed with his laptop out and a set of blueprints for his next invention laid scattered across the table.

"I know the Tickles make excellent dreams but it's nice of you to let the children get involved," she said mixing up another batch of cookie dough. The Doctor looked up over the top of his glasses in a dubious manner.

"We haven't had the little blighters round yet… who knows what sort of mayhem they may cause," he chuckled under his breath.

"Now, there's no need to be like that," she said telling him off as he showed her his latest invention.

"What does it do?" she enquired looking at the strange drawing that had all sorts of pipes and various glass flasks attached to it.

"It creates a grey gloopy substance, which contains all the essential proteins, vitamins and carbohydrates needed to give nourishment to the human body."

"Urghh…it doesn't sound very appealing. I'm not sure that will catch on," she said pulling a face.

"It's not meant to be a culinary delight," said the Doctor, defending his work.

"It is meant to provide the human body with just what it needs to survive." Miss Bagshaw didn't seem sold on the idea.

"And what's wrong with my cakes and buns?"

"Nothing, nothing, it's just I'm thinking more along the lines of it being practical for space travel."

Elsewhere, the children at school had been talking about nothing but Jonathan's Positive Thought Club.

"What do you think it will be like?" they asked one another.

"Is he making it all up?" asked others casting doubt on the whole matter, but the proof was there to see when the following Wednesday a small group of children were standing outside the gates of Sunshine Villa waiting to join the club.

"Have you seen this?" asked Jonathan as he peered out from behind the curtains of the Doctor's front parlour.

"Oban, come and have a look at this," said Miss Bagshaw, urging him to get up out of his armchair.

"I was just getting comfy," he grumbled as he strained to get up. With his hands in his cardigan pockets and sucking on a boiled sweet, he made his way over to the window.

"My, my!" he exclaimed upon seeing a group of ten or more children stood waiting outside his house.

"I've got to say I wasn't expecting this many children to turn up. I was only expecting one or two!" he said sucking hard on his boiled sweet and rolling it over with his tongue.

"Have we got enough tea and cake to go round?" he enquired of Miss Bagshaw as she went to go check.

With his hands behind his back like an officer on parade the Doctor strutted back and forth in the bay window, wishing to ensure the children knew the one and only rule of the Positive Thought Club.

"Remember, Jonathan. Not only do they have to have a dream for themselves, but they must have a dream to make the world a better place, is that understood?" he said, checking Jonathan knew what was expected of them.

"And what about you eh Liz? What have you got in mind to make the world a better place?" asked the Doctor, putting an affectionate hand on her shoulder.

"I just want people to be kind to each other," she said in a mouse-like voice.

"Bravo!" declared the Doctor, standing bolt upright and waving a clenched fist in the air as if he meant business.

"See Jonathan, that's the sort of thinking we're after," cheered the

Doctor crunching his boiled sweet between his teeth. Meanwhile, Ajna was lying on the rug in front of the fireplace being watched over by two, pot King Charles Spaniels that sat either side of the hearth.

"Ahh…look at the old fellow. I'm sure if Ajna was a human being, he'd be thinking the same thing, about people being kind to each other," remarked the Doctor staring down at the ginger mog who was fast asleep.

"And what about you Jonathan? What's your dream for the world?" the Doctor wanted to know, but before Jonathan had time to answer Miss Bagshaw returned.

"There's no need to worry Oban, we have plenty of cakes to go round plus I've made some extra cinnamon buns just in case."

"Cinnamon buns!" said the Doctor pawing at his bottom lip with his thumb and forefinger in anticipation.

"I love a cinnamon bun!" he enthused.

"We were just talking about what our dream for the world would be weren't we?" Said the Doctor relaying to Miss Bagshaw what they had been talking about.

"And Jonathan was just about to tell us his,"

"Shouldn't we let the children in first though?" she said looking at the queue outside the gate. The Doctor cast his gaze at the clock on the mantelpiece.

"We're early; it's not quite time yet," he said nodding to the glass encased clock. Dipping into his cardigan pocket, he pulled out another boiled sweet and offered it around.

"Where was I…ahh…yes, that was it! I was just asking Jonathan what his dream for the world would be," he said patting him on the back and encouraging him to divulge his innermost thoughts.

"It's easy. I'd like to live in a world where there is no litter on our streets and our oceans are free from plastic."

"Good lad, that's what I like to hear," said the Doctor sucking hard on his sweet and rocking back and forth proudly on the balls of his feet. It was then that the clock on the mantelpiece began to chime.

"Right, we better let this lot in!" he said raising his eyebrows not knowing what he was letting himself in for.

Opening the front door, Jonathan and Liz showed them in. There was Tammy Northland and all her friends, Kelly, Mahdiya and Saachi; Jacob who had brought along Ben from his football team and a few other children that Jonathan didn't recognise from school. At the very end of the line was Naza Hav'em and his sidekick Dazzler.

"Err…Hello, Naza…" said Jonathan not expecting to see him.

"Hello, space boy. We've come to join the club," he said as Dazzler stepped up behind him to show his face. Jonathan was slightly nervous. Even though Naza had changed his ways and had given up being horrid, he was aware that the Doctor didn't take kindly to bullies.

Standing by the door the Doctor was counting the children in as they filed past him.

"Nine, ten, eleven… oh yes twelve, thirteen," he counted as they made their way past him and into the great banqueting hall where Miss Bagshaw was serving out tea and cakes.

"Wait a minute. Don't I know you two?" Aren't you the one's that gave Jonathan a thumping?" he said rubbing his chin whilst trying to remember. The two children looked down at their feet shame faced.

"Yes," they replied remorsefully.

"Tell me, why should I allow you two bullies to join the Positive Thought Club eh?"

"Well, it's like this. We thought if we gave up bullying, we might be able to…err… have a go in your flying car," said Naza.

"Oh, did you now?" Replied the Doctor. It was then that Jonathan whispered something in his ear. Nodding as if he understood the Doctor looked down at the two children with a suspicious gaze.

"Well, Jonathan here tells me you have changed your ways but before I let you in, I want to inspect your dreams to see if they are suitable. Come on let's have them," said the Doctor motioning for Naza to hand them over. Adjusting the glasses on his nose, he studied what he had written down.

"Mmm…" he muttered as he read the first one quietly to himself. Then as he read the second dream, a smile appeared on his face, and he began to laugh out loud.

"How wrong I was to judge!" he said, chuckling away to himself and slapping his thigh in amusement.

"What's your name, my lad?" he asked as he bent down and put his hand on the young boy's shoulder.

"Nigel, but everybody calls me Naza,"

"Well, Nigel, that's one of the best dreams I've read in a long while,"

"Anybody who wants to put an end to bullying in the world is alright in my book," he said, removing his glasses to chew the end of them while he considered what the impact of a dream like that would have on the world. Motioning for the two lads to go through, he held back for a moment insisting Jonathan to do the same.

"Did you know his dream is to put an end to bullying?" he asked Jonathan, looking pleased with himself.

"He mentioned it at school, but I wasn't sure whether to believe him or not."

"Well, it seems like our friend Nigel is quite serious about the matter. Who'd have thought, eh?" remarked the Doctor, closing the door behind them and rubbing his hands together excitedly.

"Here comes a brighter future!" he giggled as he did a little dance all to himself in the hallway.

In the dining room, Ajna was busy greeting his new-found friends by rubbing himself up against any leg that he could find. Meanwhile, Miss Bagshaw was handing out juice to the children in the finest cut crystal glasses.

"Are you sure you want me to use the best China and cut glass for the children? After all they are rather precious," she remarked, questioning the Doctors thinking.

"Nonsense!" he spluttered taking a slurp of tea from a priceless Ming dynasty cup.

"They are only cups and saucers, and I say if you can't use something for which it was originally intended then it is worthless. Look at this lot," he said nodding in the direction of the children.

"They're the most priceless things I could imagine," he said watching the children play with all the suits of armour and other oddities that his family had collected over the years.

Helping himself to a cinnamon bun, the Doctor took another mouthful of tea before addressing the children.

"If I could have your attention, please," he said in a loud voice. The children stopped what they were doing and turned to look at him.

"May I first thank you all for coming. However, before I go any further, I would like you to give Jonathan here a round of applause, as he was the one who came up with the idea for the Positive Thought Club in the first place," There was polite clapping from everyone as Jonathan, embarrassed by having his name mentioned went red in the face.

"I would like to say that dreams are the source of all good things," he told them as if he was an authority on the matter.

"Here at the Positive Thought Club, we like to ensure that no dream is wasted and that everyone gets the chance to go home happy," the Doctor assured them. Mahdiya then put her hand up to ask a question.

"Jonathan says that you can make dreams come true, is that right?" she asked the jolly old inventor. With a glowing smile, the Doctor was more than happy to answer her question, buoyed up by the company of inquisitive children.

"Correct! You see for years I have sought out a way in which to make people happy. That is why I invented my machine – the Positive Thought Accumulator. It harnesses the power of dreams and sends them out into the world ready for people to dream."

"I've got a dream!" shouted out Dazzler interrupting.

"It's for my football team to win the cup final,"

"Yes. Very good, young man," replied the Doctor wagging his finger, but our main aim is to write dreams that everybody can share in, do you understand?" Dazzler shook his head.

"Have you got another dream that you have brought along with you?" he enquired. Rummaging around in the pocket of his shorts, Dazzler pulled out a crumpled-up piece of paper.

"Read out what it says, please," said the Doctor inviting him to share his dream with everybody.

Standing up straight with the piece of paper in between both hands Dazzler did his best to read aloud what he'd written.

"It says I want an end to bullying in the world."

"Really, did you write that yourself?" the Doctor asked in a questioning manner, suspicious of the origin of the idea. Aware that he had been found out, Dazzler admitted to pinching the idea.

"I copied what he wrote," he said pointing to Naza.

"That's very good, very inspirational, but how about you come up with something of your own next time," said the Doctor.

The Doctor then looked around the room as if seeking a fresh idea.

"You," he said pointing to one of Tammy Northland's friends.

"What's your name?"

"Kelly," replied the girl.

"Well Kelly, what sort of dream have you got that could help the world become a better place?"

"I thought about filling the deserts with water so that people could grow more food."

"Marvellous! Now that's what I'm talking about. That's the sort of thinking that the Positive Thought Club needs," he said setting his cup and saucer down before proceeding to tell them how his machine worked.

"What I have created is a self-aware quantum computer which enables you to live out your best dreams and wishes. Some dreams may be just that, dreams but with others, you might find them creeping into real life. It all depends on what you wish for."

"What do you mean?" asked Jacob who was busy finishing off his last bit of cake.

"I mean like Dazzler here. He may dream of a new football and his father, out of sheer coincidence, might buy him one; on the other hand, you can live out any dream you choose, whatever you want. It can be something completely abstract, something totally wild and outrageous that wouldn't be possible in reality; it really doesn't matter." Realising that he had been talking for far too long, the Doctor decided it was time to conclude his little speech.

"I could bore you for hours about the projected quantum field that it creates or the calculations that it takes to make something like this work, but I think you've had enough of me waffling on for now…" he admitted.

"… I think it best if I take you outside to meet the Positive Thought Accumulator yourselves."

Showing them to his makeshift laboratory, the children gasped in awe at all his equipment as he ushered them through to the central rotunda. Miss Bagshaw, offering a helping hand, made sure everyone was squeezed inside so they could hear what the Doctor had to say. However, Naza, hung back, bringing up the rear.

"Are you alright dear?" she asked noticing that the boy was looking a little nervous.

"I'm scared," said Naza looking up at the great machine.

"It's alright, there's nothing to be scared of," she said trying to reassure him as she put her arm around his shoulder.

"Tell me what's the dream that you would most like to come true?" Naza seemed reluctant to tell her.

"Come on, you can tell me; I won't say a word."

"It's embarrassing," muttered Naza not wanting to be overheard. Miss Bagshaw promised that only she would look and that nobody else would see.

"Alright," he said agreeing to tell her. So, without anyone seeing, he handed his piece of paper over to her. Sensitive to the boy's wishes, she kept it from the prying eyes of everyone else. Reading it she couldn't help but to be moved by the young boy's plight.

"Dear Dream Machine." It read. "Could you please make it possible for me to have a giant teddy bear. It would be the best dream in the world to have someone to cuddle up to on a night. My mum and dad are nasty to me and hit me lots and the only person that cares for me is my granny." Miss Bagshaw nearly wept when she read this and gave Naza a big hug to try and make up for things.

"Don't worry, Nigel. I'm sure we will be able to help you," she said, trying to comfort him.

The Doctor then put the Positive Thought Accumulator into full power and the machine sprang into life with a gush of steam and a hiss of Wartle valves.

"Who's first?" he asked inviting Saachi to step up first and taking receipt of her dream.

"Now, let's see what have we got here?" he said holding the piece of paper at arm's length to see better and adjusting the glasses on his nose.

"Your dream is for a world where no one goes hungry, everyone has a roof over their heads, and has access to clean water and sanitation. Mmm…I like that. Have you been reading my mind?" the Doctor asked looking down at the young girl and chuckling to himself.

"That's a very fine dream," he commented as he fed it into the Positive Thought Accumulator.

"And tell me, what dream have you brought for yourself?" the Doctor asked as she handed over another piece of paper.

"You want to fly with pink-winged unicorns…I see," he said with a look of surprise on his face.

The Doctor then explained to her that all she had to do was believe in her dream and she would be transported there, and that whenever she wanted to come back all she had to do was think of the ocean.

"It's that simple," explained the Doctor.

"Remember all dreams start and end with the ocean," he told her as she stepped up to the machine.

With a majestic hum from the quantum computer, Saachi suddenly vanished right before everyone's eyes and the remaining girls let out a scream.

"It's alright," the Doctor assured them, raising his hand, and trying to dispel their fears.

"She hasn't gone anywhere. She is still here in the same space time continuum; but in a higher reality than us," the girls were unconvinced by what the Doctor had to say, so Liz offered to go next. She was the next to disappear into thin air.

"See? There's nothing to it!" the Doctor reassured them. Still nervous about what was going to happen, Jacob, Ben and some of the other children went next. Watching everybody take their turn, the girls were finally convinced that everything was fine and plucked up the courage to go next. Finally, there was only Naza left.

"Well, Nigel what can we do for you?" asked the Doctor. Miss Bagshaw stepped forward and showed the Doctor Naza's dream

"I take it you have you seen this?" whispered Miss Bagshaw trying to be as discrete as possible. The Doctor nodded.

"Dreadful, isn't it? Come here, Nigel," he said reaching over and putting his hand on Naza's shoulder.

"Now I see that you've asked for a giant teddy bear. Well, that sort of dream I can make come true standing on my head. So, in the meantime, I think you deserve one of my best dreams. One that I save for when I feel I need a little inspiration," Naza looked hesitant.

"Don't worry, Miss Bagshaw will come with you," he said nodding in her direction. Taking him by the hand they both stepped up to the Positive Thought Accumulator.

"She'll take you on a ride you'll never forget, one of giant waves, psychedelic skies, vast mountain tops and rainbows dripping with stars," smiled the Doctor picturing his best dream. Then with a sudden flash they were gone too.

While the Doctor sat there awaiting everybody's return, he read Naza's dream again letting out a despondent sigh.

"What on earth makes grown-ups do that sort of thing?" He said shaking his head in disappointment. Rooting around his laboratory, he laid hands on one of his many notebooks and tore out a sheet of paper to write on. Then, sitting down in an old deck chair, he put pen to paper.

He began by jotting down a few ideas. Scribbling away he thought he would write the best dream he could imagine for young Nigel.

It wasn't long before the first of the children started to arrive back from their dreams giving him just enough time to scribble down some wonderful dreams.

"How was it?" he asked them excitedly as one of the boys told him how he had seen a whole bunch of purple-spotted dinosaurs.

"Impressive stuff," remarked the Doctor listening intently to what he was being told. Then Dazzler suddenly appeared back in the room.

"Two-nil, two nil," he was singing as he waved his football scarf around cheering his team's victory in the cup final. Then, there was a sudden rush of children as they all arrived back in rapid succession. Seeing them laughing and with beaming smiles on their faces, the Doctor didn't need to ask if they enjoyed their trip.

"Can we have another go?" they begged pulling at his sleeve. Shooing them away like naughty mice, he told them that they would have to wait till next time.

There was so much laughing and cheering that the Doctor could hardly hear himself think. Finally, Miss Bagshaw and Naza returned from their dream.

"How did it go?" the Doctor asked Naza as he returned with a smile on his face and clutching Miss Bagshaw's hand.

"It was amazing! Is that what it's like in your head?" he asked. The Doctor gave him a reassuring smile and patted him fondly on the head.

"Sometimes," he said giving the boy a knowing wink.

Counting everyone back from their adventures, the Doctor insisted that they all stand still. Once satisfied that everyone was accounted for, he asked Miss Bagshaw to escort everyone back to the main house. After the children collected their belongings, he and Miss Bagshaw thanked everyone for coming, wishing them a goodnight as they stood by the front door.

"Will there be another meeting next week?" asked Saachi, eager to return.

"I have not given it much thought, but judging by the success of this evening, we may venture into the possibility of holding another meeting next week!" he remarked looking quite pleased with himself.

"Remember, there can never be enough good dreams in the world!" he called after them as he waved them goodbye.

Once everybody had left, Miss Bagshaw let out a great big sigh.

"That was fun! Exhausting, but fun!" she said, closing the door behind her and leaning against it as if she was completely shattered.

"Jonathan, you should be proud of yourself!" remarked the Doctor pinching Jonathan's cheek with his thumb and fore finger and giving it a gentle tug.

"Who'd have thought that so many children would turn up... and Liz? That was so good of you to show those children that there was no need to be scared."

"It's alright," said Liz whose dream had been water-skiing in a lake filled with custard under purple skies and marshmallow clouds.

"So…" said the Doctor inviting comment.

"How about we do the same next week?" he asked looking for agreement. All three put their hands up.

"Good, good, that's what I like to see. Think of all those dreams and positive thoughts going out there into the world; it will certainly put a shine on things," remarked the Doctor rubbing his hands together in a proud manner.

After packing up and seeing Jonathan and Liz home, he and Miss Bagshaw settled down for dinner. Sat at opposite ends of the kitchen table, the Doctor wanted to discuss Naza.

"While you were all gone Evelyn, I decided I'd have myself a little dream all of my own," he remarked cheekily in between mouthfuls of her homemade curry.

"Oh, did you now?" replied Miss Bagshaw with a telling smile on her face, as if she knew what he was thinking.

"Let's put it this way. I don't think young Nigel will be having any more trouble with his parents from now on," he said giving her a sly wink.

"Why what have you done?" she asked.

"Oh, I like to think of it as just a bit of caring magic. Something that will make Nigel's life better from now on," said the Doctor chuckling to himself as he helped himself to another popadom.

When Naza got home, he found a large truck pulled up outside his house and his granny stood on the doorstep waiting for him.

"Where's Mum and Dad?" he asked wondering what was happening. His granny explained that the police had taken them away for fighting and that they wouldn't be coming back anytime soon, so he would have to live with her from now on. Naza was happy as he really loved his granny. Then as they were about to go in the house a man got out of the truck and approached Naza.

"Are you Nigel Hav'em?" asked the man with a clipboard in his hand.

"Err…yes," Naza replied hesitantly.

"I have a delivery for you young man!"

"A delivery?" said Naza completely flabbergasted by what it could be.

"You entered a competition, didn't you?" remarked the delivery driver.

Naza had no idea what the man was talking about. He couldn't even remember ever entering a competition.

"What competition?"

"The competition to win a lifetime worth of giant teddies," the man told him. Naza couldn't believe what he was hearing and stood there completely dumbfounded.

"Did you say a truck load of giant teddies?"

"That's right," replied the delivery driver jumping up into the back of the truck to unload them.

"Where do you want them?" Naza was so excited that he didn't hear a word the man was saying.

"Granny, have you heard? I've won a truck load of giant teddy bears!" he said unable to contain himself.

"Oh, that's wonderful news, Nigel," said his Granny pleased for him as the delivery driver began unloading them and taking them into the house.

The Doctor was on his third popadom when an image suddenly flashed through his mind of Nazza jumping up and down in excitement and rolling about in a house full of teddies. Smiling Miss Bagshaw sensed that he was picking something up and asked him what it was.

"Let's put it this way," replied Oban.

"I think we've sent a little boy home happy tonight," he smiled as he tucked into his dinner. The rest of that evening Miss Bagshaw and the Doctor chatted away in the kitchen, talking about all the amazing dreams the children had brought with them and how, with the help of the Positive Thought Accumulator, the world was going to be a fantastic place to be.

"I can't wait to see the future!" exclaimed the Doctor.

"What an exciting place it's going to be!

-21-

A Bright New Future

NEWS TRAVELLED FAST at school, and the following week there was an even bigger queue outside the Doctor's house. Week by week the numbers began to swell until children from all over the area were coming to join the Positive Thought Club.

"Something's going on over there," said Jack to his wife as he stared out of his living room window at the line of children gathered on the other side of the road.

"Oh, it's probably nothing dear," remarked Margaret busy crocheting yet another blanket.

"Nothing?" fumed Jack, pointing to the line of children stretched all the way along the road.

"Have you seen that? I'm going over there to see what's going on." Marching out of the house in his slippers, Jack was keen to find out what all the fuss was about.

Across the road at Sunshine Villa, even the Doctor couldn't believe the length of the queue that was lining up outside.

"What are we going to do?" he asked scratching his head, unsure how they were going to accommodate so many children.

"It'll be alright," said Miss Bagshaw trying to reassure him as he paced back and forth in the window, biting his nails, and worrying how they were going to cope.

"I never envisioned the Positive Thought Club becoming this popular," he remarked.

Meanwhile Jonathan was staring, open-mouthed at the hordes of children that had turned up.

"I just thought there would be a few children, not the entire neighbourhood!" said Jonathan shaking his head in despair. However, Liz wasn't quite so worried as her brother.

"Well, at least we'll be making lots of positive thoughts for the world!" she said with a more upbeat outlook on the situation.

"Look at them! How on earth are we going to manage?" the Doctor wanted to know, pointing to the ever-growing queue. Miss Bagshaw who was somewhat more composed than that of the Doctor, suggested they let them in.

"Let them in, let them in, we'll be overrun!" remarked the Doctor running his hand anxiously through his hair and looking at his watch to see what time it was.

"Don't worry," Miss Bagshaw reassured him.

"I can supervise the tea and cake in the dining room, and you can run the Positive Thought Accumulator, while Jonathan and Liz can ferry small groups to and from your laboratory." The Doctor sucked on his lip while he thought about the matter.

"Do you think it will work?" he asked scratching his ear nervously.

"I'd hate to turn away a child and spoil their dreams,"

Meanwhile Jack had made his way across the road. Scratching his head as to what they were up to, he asked the children what they were doing.

"We've come to join the Positive Thought Club," said one of the girls.

"The Positive Thought Club?" What's that?" he asked.

"It's a club where you make your dreams come true," said her friend as Jack looked down the road unable to believe the length of the queue.

"Can anyone join?" he wanted to know, scratching his chin thoughtfully.

"Apparently so, but you can't just have a dream for yourself; you have to have one that makes the world a better place," said one of the girls looking at him as if an old man was not capable of such fantastic imaginings. Intrigued to know more he took his place in the queue, patiently waiting to see what all the fuss was about.

Back in the front parlour the Doctor looked at his watch. Giving Jonathan the nod for the Positive Thought Club to start Jonathan went to let everyone in, leaving the Doctor to ponder just how they were going to cope.

"One at a time please!" Jonathan shouted. The children filed past him making their way into the cavernous hallway when Naza and the old gang showed up.

"What's up Jonathan? Do you need a hand here? You look busy," asked Naza seeing that he was struggling with the large number of children that had turned up.

"Please, Naza. Could you stand here and make sure everyone behaves themselves while I go help Dr Fife," said Jonathan relieved by his offer of help.

The banqueting hall was a riot of noise as more and more children piled through the doors. Ajna who had been sitting in the parlour watching the children pour through the gates decided he was much better off elsewhere. So, with all the haste of a scalded cat he disappeared upstairs to one of the unused bedrooms to have himself a nice little nap.

Elsewhere Liz was busy helping Miss Bagshaw serve juice when she spotted Jack. Standing at the back of the hall he waved to her trying to get her attention.

"I've come to see what all the fuss is about," shouted Jack as he navigated his way through the crowd of children. Finally reaching Liz he asked if he could help. Pointing to the empty cups she handed him a jug of juice and he began to fill them as fast as he could. As he did so he explained what he was doing there.

"I saw the line of children queuing up outside and wondered what was going on, and I knew the Doctor must be up to something. So, here I am I've come to join the Positive Thought Club."

Seeing another adult in the room, Miss Bagshaw went over to introduce herself.

"Hello, do you need any help?" she asked thinking he might be lost as he was still wearing his slippers. Liz explained that Jack was a friend of theirs from across the road.

"So, you've come to help?" Miss Bagshaw enquired keen to enrol him as a volunteer.

"Why not? I'm not so old that I've given up on the idea of dreaming of a better world." Rushed off her feet, Miss Bagshaw suggested that he could take the first group of children out to the Doctor's laboratory.

Pointing him in the right direction, Jack marched through the garden with a party of children following on behind, when he came across Jonathan stood by the entrance to the greenhouse.

"Jonathan!" Jack called out, eager to get his young friend's attention. Jonathan was surprised to see him.

"What are you doing here?" he enquired, shaking the old man's hand.

"You know me, I'm a big kid at heart and I just had to come and see what the Doctor was up to." said Jack wrapping his arm roughly around the boy's shoulder and giving him a bear hug.

"Is this the magnificent machine then?" he asked all excited, looking up at the smoky mirrored disc that stood towering over them.

"My, my, that truly is something to behold, isn't it?" he said shielding his eyes from the late afternoon sun that was catching on the disc. Showing the children in, Jonathan stayed behind to talk to Jack.

"You'll have to meet the Doctor. You'll like him," Jonathan said.

Negotiating their way past the children, as well as shiny electron micro-scopes, oscilloscopes that fluttered away rhythmically and petri dishes full of all sorts of horrible-looking organisms, the pair finally made it into the centre the greenhouse. There, in front of him, Jack was amazed to see chil-dren disappearing into thin air faster than you could say "Unumpentium."

"Where are they going?" he asked, taken aback by what he was seeing.

"They're living out their very own dreams," Jonathan replied as if it were an everyday occurrence.

Squeezing through the throng of children they found the Doctor busy working flat out. Stood by the console wearing a white lab coat and with a pencil tucked behind his ear he was busy muttering away to himself.

"Hello, Oban," said Jonathan, distracting him for just a second. The Doctor was so engrossed in his work he did not look up to see Jack stood there right by his side.

"Can you just count how many children we are processing? I don't want to lose any," said an overworked Doctor when he suddenly looked up and noticed Jack.

"Oh hello," he remarked looking Jack up and down, wondering what another adult was doing in his laboratory.

"This is Jack, who saved us from Naza when he was bullying us," said Jonathan introducing him.

"Oh yes, I remember now," replied the Doctor, preoccupied with what he was doing.

Realising that he wasn't really paying attention, Jonathan told the Doctor what a fantastic train set Jack had in his garage.

"A train set!" exclaimed the Doctor coming alive at the very mention of such a thing.

"Well, why didn't you tell me earlier!" said the Doctor admonishing Jonathan for not telling him sooner. With a head full of trains, the Doctor introduced himself putting Jonathan in charge of the Positive Thought Accumulator. The two men then struck up a conversation about the glory of steam trains and all things that little boys love.

"This really is some undertaking you've got here," said Jack praising the Doctor's efforts as he looked up at the giant mirrored disc.

"What do you hope to achieve with your machine?" asked Jack curious to know. The Doctor sighed for a moment as he thought about the question that was being asked of him. Chewing the end of a pencil he replied.

"My aim is to make the world a better place," he said idly tapping at his teeth with a pencil as he elaborated on his ambitions.

"One day, I hope to get people of all races, colours, and creeds to see the beauty in each other and the world around them and put their differences behind them," he said envisioning a better world for everybody. Impressed by his devotion to his project, Jack heartily slapped him on the back taking him by surprise.

"I admire a man with vision like that," he said congratulating him.

Seeing that Jack was clearly a dreamer just like him, the Doctor suggested a way in which he could help.

"Look, the whole reason I built the Positive Thought Accumulator is so that we can build a brighter future for everyone. Why don't you have a go? It's easy, all you have to do is feed positive thoughts into the machine and let it go to work." said Doctor encouraging him to have a go. Handing him a jotter he suggested he write his ideas down.

While Jack scribbled away, the Doctor tasked Jonathan with bringing him some juice from the house. Manifesting all those good dreams was thirsty work and he needed something to wet his whistle with. Upon his return the Doctor thought he'd take a break and let Jonathan run the machine while he had a look at what Jack had been writing.

"Let's see what you've got there," said the Doctor taking possession of the jotter and proceeding to read out aloud.

"Number one, looking after nature. Number two, random acts of kindness," the Doctor continued. "Three, helping plant a forest, four, clean water for everybody, five, making homes for bumble bees, six, making friends with strangers…" the list went on and on.

"…giving a home to the homeless, restoring eyesight to the sick, enough food for everyone, clean air to breath… and my personal favourite!" declared the Doctor.

"World peace!" The jotter was filed with so many positive ideas that there was no more room left in the book.

"This is truly remarkable," said the Doctor moved to tears by the sheer imagination and thought that Jack had put into it.

"It's like a work of art," he added, applauding what he had written.

"In fact, it's so beautiful that I am loathe to put it into the Positive Thought Accumulator, but ideas cannot be squandered or wasted they must be acted on," argued the Doctor tearing out the pages from the book and feeding them into the slot on the control panel.

As the weeks went by, it was becoming clear that the Positive Thought Accumulator was having a noticeable impact on the people in the neighbourhood. People were smiling more and stopped to say hello, while complete strangers were happy to pass the time of day with someone they didn't know. Car drivers would stop to let pedestrian's pass. Cafe and restaurant owners would give out free meals to the homeless; tough guys had given up picking on people and had taken to doing the shopping for old-age pensioners. While everywhere, people were planting trees to make their world a little greener and, in the process, giving a home to birds. Even thieves had given up stealing. Despite all this there were still some small-minded people who only thought about themselves.

Around the neighbourhood, parents were beginning to hear rumours about the Positive Thought Club and were getting concerned. They had taken to writing nasty things on social media about what was happening at the Doctor's house, and they labelled him as some oddball scientist.

"Who is this man?" Mr Choudhry asked his son looking at the tittle tattle and rumours on the internet, while Mrs Timms at number six Britannia Way, and mother of Lesa Timms demanded to know what her daughter did at the Doctor's house.

"It's all about making the world a better place to live," she told her mother, who unfortunately like all the other adults was suspicious of anything new and different.

It was pretty much like that for all the other children who wanted to join the Positive Thought Club. Mr Akhtar argued with his daughter over whether he was going to let her go, while Mr Greaves wanted to know why his son, Leo, wanted to go to the Positive Thought Club instead of football practice.

"What's wrong with kicking a ball about, son?" he asked scratching his head.

"Football is so yesterday, Dad; it's all about making a better world for us to live in," Leo replied.

"Making a better world?" scoffed his father.

"Who wants to bother with that old rubbish when you can kick a ball about?" Leo looked at his father and rolled his eyes.

"Running around chasing a leather ball with the intention of kicking it between two posts is not my idea of fun, Dad," replied Leo who was now starting to wind his father up. After a lot of huffing and puffing on his father's part and trying to sway his son with the power of argument, Mr Greaves finally allowed his son to go to the Positive Thought Club, but on one condition, that he was to accompany him.

Back home, even Jonathan and Liz's mother was getting worried about the amount of time that they were spending at the Doctor's.

"I know the Doctor's a nice man and all that but are you concentrating enough on your schoolwork?" she would say whenever they returned from the Doctor's. Jonathan would just smile and tell her that the Doctor had been teaching them all about the simultaneous equations and all the other difficult sums there was to learn, which silenced his mother and put an end to her questioning.

It seemed that the parents of the children going to the Positive Thought Club were not quite so positive as their children. Intent on putting an end to the club, a group of small-minded adults spread nasty rumours on social media about what was going on.

The Doctor, however, was unaware of what was taking place behind his back, until several weeks later. Sitting at home in his parlour he was waiting for the Positive Thought Club to start when Jonathan called him over to the window.

"Errr…Oban, there seem to be a lot of angry-looking grownups marching up your drive with their children." From his laid-back position in his chair, the Doctor looked at him puzzled.

"Grownups, you say?" he said questioning what Jonathan had to tell him.

"Yes, lots of them," replied Jonathan reporting back. Shooing Ajna off his knee, he asked Miss Bagshaw to take a look for him. Peering round the corner of the curtain, she confirmed what Jonathan had to say.

"Jonathan's right…and they don't look very friendly."

Standing up and brushing the cat hairs off his trousers, the Doctor fumbled around for his glasses. Blindly groping about the table, he made his way over to the window where he cast his gaze on the scrum of angry parents marching up his drive.

"Good gracious!" he exclaimed as the swarm of adults made their way up the steps, accompanied by their children who were being forcibly dragged along.

"What are we going do?" said Miss Bagshaw, looking to the Doctor for direction.

All of a sudden, a loud banging could be heard coming from the front door as the children's parents demanded to be let in.

"Close the curtains!" the Doctor urged, instructing the children to dive for cover behind the sofa.

Unsure of what he was going to do, he paced back and forth in front of the fireplace trying urgently to think of something; all the while the banging on the door grew louder and louder.

"We're going to have to do something Oban!" Cried Miss Bagshaw fearing that at any moment the door would come crashing in.

"Yes, yes, I know," hastened the Doctor, who was well aware of the need for action. With his finger resting on his top lip, he decided there was only one thing left for it.

"We're going to have to let them in,"

"Let them in?" replied Miss Bagshaw sounding unconvinced by his idea.

"Yes, let them in; I have nothing to hide," he confidently proclaimed.

The braying on the door was thunderous. On the other side, they could hear the voices of angry parents yelling and screaming. Bracing himself, the Doctor opened the door while Miss Bagshaw stood behind him for moral support.

As soon as the door opened, there were shouts, jeering as well as angry fists being raised.

"What have you been doing with our children?" the mob of angry parents demanded to know.

"One at a time please," said the Doctor trying to bring order to the situation.

"You have nothing to fear," he tried explaining, but he was shouted down. Raising his voice, the Doctor told them that he was simply running a club to help make a better world.

"Rubbish!" someone shouted while another parent yelled "cobblers."

"Who cares about a better world? You're just selling our children silly fantasies," one cried out.

The Doctor tried explaining that it was dreams that made the world go round, and all he was doing was inspiring their children to greater things.

"Have you not noticed over the passing weeks and months that people have been getting friendlier and kinder towards each another. Has that not gone unnoticed?" asked the Doctor.

"And with all that kindness, have you not marvelled at how those less fortunate have benefitted from all the positive thoughts going around the place." There was a begrudging silence from the crowd of angry onlooking parents.

"Yeah, but what about us?" one of them shouted.

"We want a go on this Positive what's a thingy?" they demanded. The Doctor let out a regretful sigh.

"I am quite willing to let you inside, and we can discuss this matter further over tea and cake," said the Doctor offering the irate parents his hospitality. Opening the door wide, the Doctor allowed the wave of disgruntled parents to sweep inside, showing them through into the banqueting hall.

Jack, from across the road, had also turned up. He too had seen all the commotion going on and wondered what was going on.

"Don't worry, Doc," he assured Oban.

"If it gets lively, I'll sort them out. You're a good sort, never mind what all these small-minded people say," winked Jack with the sleeves rolled up to the elbow as if ready for a tussle. Managing to raise a half-hearted smile Oban took reassurance from Jack's kind words.

Once inside, there was a lot of finger-pointing and accusations flying about as the parents focused all their negativity on the Doctor.

"We want to see if this so-called dream machine of yours is suitable for our children." the parents muttered as they greedily grabbed at Miss Bagshaw's cakes that she had made for children.

Once they'd had their fill, the Doctor invited everyone to follow him down to his greenhouse. With parents and children alike crammed into what little space there was, the Doctor explained to them how his machine worked.

"You see, in order to make a better world, we need positive thoughts and that's where your children come in," he said addressing the crowd while behind him the Positive Thought Accumulator hummed merrily away to itself.

"Who gave you permission to mess with our children's minds?" shouted Mr Levenski angrily, unhappy that his daughter should dare think for herself.

"Please, if you allow me to explain," said the Doctor trying to keep a lid on things.

"I'm not messing with your children's minds. I am just giving them the ability to visualise their own dreams. You see, in return for making their dreams come true, we ask that they come up with a dream, one that can make for a better world, a more harmonious world where we can all live in peace,"

One of the parents, who was standing at the front with his arms folded, demanded that he should be allowed to make his dream come true.

"Who cares about world peace! I want to be a millionaire," he said abruptly.

"Me too," shouted another as they all laughed and made fun of the Doctor's aspirations. Then another demanded that he should be allowed to have a sports car.

"I want to own my own football club," shouted Mr Levine raising his hand and trying to make himself heard.

"Well, I want the most expensive pair of shoes money can buy," one mother yelled.

"Yes, and I want a diamond-encrusted watch," shouted another woman while Mrs Hussain demanded that she have her house completely remodelled.

It was at this point the parents began squabbling over who should have their dream granted, totally forgetting about the true purpose of the Positive Thought Accumulator.

"It should be me; I should go first," argued one father as he grabbed another of the parents by the collar and threatened to punch him.

"My dream's the best!" shouted Mr Evans, who wished to never work another day in his life again while grabbing hold of Mr Dhillon by his tie and rudely pointing in his face.

"No, my dream's the best!" Mr Dhillon snarled back pushing Mr Evans in the chest.

"I want my own private yacht, so I can go to the most exclusive resorts in the world," another shouted.

The adults had no understanding of how the Positive Thought Accumulator worked; they were so self-centred that they only thought about themselves and not the world and everybody else in it. Like a virus, all that negativity became contagious as the adults bickered with each other, threatening each other with violence.

It didn't take long for things to spill over. Mr Choudhry was knocked to the ground and that's when things really got out of hand. Everything erupted into fisticuffs as all the parents began fighting over whose dream was best and who should be allowed to go first.

It was a terrible sight to behold. Windows were being smashed; the Doctor's equipment went flying. Meanwhile, the children who had come to the Positive Thought Club had to stand by and watch their parents make a spectacle of themselves. Jack, worried for the Doctors safety stepped up to protect him while the terrible scene unfolded before them.

"Look at them, they're behaving like animals," Jack cried out, expressing his disappointment at the sight of grown adults fighting.

Jonathan was incensed at seeing all the Doctor's hard work being smashed and destroyed. There were mothers pulling at one another's hair and scratching each other's faces, while fathers were sprawled on the floor kicking and punching each other. The fighting had got so bad that Jonathan had to do something. Summoning up all his energy and clenching his fists, he demanded they listen to him.

"STOP FIGHTING!"

He yelled, taking them by surprise that a little boy had such a big voice. All of a sudden, the adults stopped what they were doing and turned round to see who it was shouting.

"Can't we all just get along?" asked Jonathan pleading with the adults to behave themselves.

"It doesn't have to be like this," he told them with his arms folded tightly across his chest.

"That's right," said Jack, who had his fill of all this nastiness and unpleasantness.

"You should listen to this little boy; he knows what he's talking about," said Jack ushering Jonathan to step forward. For a moment Jonathan wasn't sure he had the courage to speak to all these people, but he felt so strongly about how the adults had been behaving that he had to say something.

"The Positive Thought Accumulator was built so that we could all get along, not so we could spend all our time fighting, Dreams are not about fancy cars, big houses, and designer clothes; in fact, the best dreams come from inside of you…" Jonathan told them.

"…and the best dreams are ones that we can all dream together, like wanting a peaceful world, a greener planet as well as making sure people who are less fortunate than us are looked after," said Jonathan enlightening them as to the real purpose of the Positive Thought Accumulator.

Mr Choudhry, suddenly ashamed of his behaviour dusted himself down and got up off the floor.

"I think the boy's got something there," he said all shame faced.

"He might be right," remarked Mrs Hussain who was busy straightening her hair after all the carry-on.

"I mean what are we fighting for? After all, we're all human, aren't we?" she said looking around for agreement from the other adults.

"Look, I would like to show you something," said the Doctor stepping forward.

Flicking a few buttons on the console of the Positive Thought Accumulator, a bright blue hologram of the earth appeared floating above everyone's heads. Inviting the adults to take a closer look, he pointed out the images of happy shiny faces beaming back at them.

"Those smiles, those are a direct result of your children's dreams," he said. The adults suddenly felt ashamed of their behaviour.

"What can we do to help?" asked Mr Ashley sheepishly who had brought his son Noel and daughter Emily with him.

"It's not hard…," said Jonathan.

"…all you've got to do is think good things, write it down on a piece of paper and think of the Positive Thought Accumulator," he said pointing up at the great mirrored disc that sat atop of the machine.

"I'll give it a go!" said Mr Muhammed raising his hand and stepping forward to set a better example to his son and daughter. Urgently the Doctor searched around for a piece of paper.

"Here you are!" he said fumbling around for one of his jotters. Handing him a piece of paper, he offered him one of his pens from his top pocket.

"Here, try this. I've written some great dreams with this one," he said with a knowing wink.

Mr Muhammed stroked at his beard while he thought of something.

"Do I have to tell you what I'm dreaming of?" he asked looking up at the Doctor.

"No, just let the circles in your mind fill the world with colour," enthused the Doctor. While Mr Muhammed was busy writing his daughter asked him what his dream was. He looked down at her and spoke.

"I dreamt of a better world for you, just like that little boy said over there," pointing to Jonathan.

It didn't take long for the rest of the parents to join in, and soon there were more fantastic dreams being written down than could ever be imagined.

"Do we have to come here to make our dreams come true?" asked one parent. The Doctor told him that it didn't matter where he was as long as they thought of the mirrored disc that sat on top of the Positive Thought Accumulator; then, all their dreams would come to life.

"It's that easy," replied the Doctor, who was in desperate need of a sit-down and a good cup of tea after all the excitement.

EPILOGUE

The Positive Thought Club had become such a success that the doctor had to run it every night of the week. People came from miles around to stare in wonder at the great mirrored disc and wish for a better world; watching the dreams fly out into the night. Filled with a genuine desire to help their fellow human beings, there was no more fighting, and people were content and happy to help each other out. However, all the hard work had got a little bit too much for the Doctor, and he decided he needed a good long rest.

So, along with Miss Bagshaw and Ajna he moved to his grandfather's cottage on the quiet Island of Tamaree to see out the rest of his years, leaving Jonathan and Liz in charge of the Positive Thought Accumulator. With the help of the Tickles, they made sure that plenty of positive dreams went out into the world, making it a brighter place to be.

For the Doctor he spent his days getting up late, enjoying a well-deserved lie in. After breakfast he would sit on the bench outside the cottage with a cup of tea in his hand and his favourite biscuit. There he would take in the views of the crystal blue waters and pure white sands of the Westerly Isle.

In the afternoon, he would take Miss Bagshaw sailing in his little dingy and on their return home Ajna would be sat by the water's edge waiting for them. After watching the sunset together, they would both return to the cottage where Miss Bagshaw would cook up a hearty meal by the glow of an open range and the Doctor would play his grandfather's accordion for her.

Having invented so many amazing things in his life, he no longer needed the money and gave it all away along with all his many inventions so the whole world could benefit from his work. There, on the island he could live a simple life without having to worry about Wartle valves or Boggrobblers ever again.

As for his old house, Sunshine Villa, Miss Bagshaw suggested he hand it over to the council to run as a museum, so everyone could come and see all the interesting things his family had collected over the years.

However, life for the Positive Thought Accumulator was a whole different matter. So many people had heard of its amazing abilities that the quantum computer was struggling to cope with all the wonderful dreams. In need of its wattle valves replacing and a bit of fettling here and there, the Doctor came up with a plan. Realising something needed to be done, Oban began work on a new project. Never one to sit idle, he drew up plans for a new improved Positive Thought Accumulator, and after speaking to Jonathan and Liz's parents, he enlisted their help.

The Bawtry family moved to the nearby island of Mullaach where work on a brand-new positive Thought Accumulator was taking place. Oban had to do very little of the work himself as the Positive Thought Accumulator being completely self-aware had designed and built itself without the aid of any human help at all.

Perched on the craggy peaks, it was taller than the highest skyscraper ever built and was so tall that clouds billowed round its lofty heights and planes had to fly around it to avoid crashing into it. Radiating out good dreams into the night, it was a constant beacon for the whole world to live by.

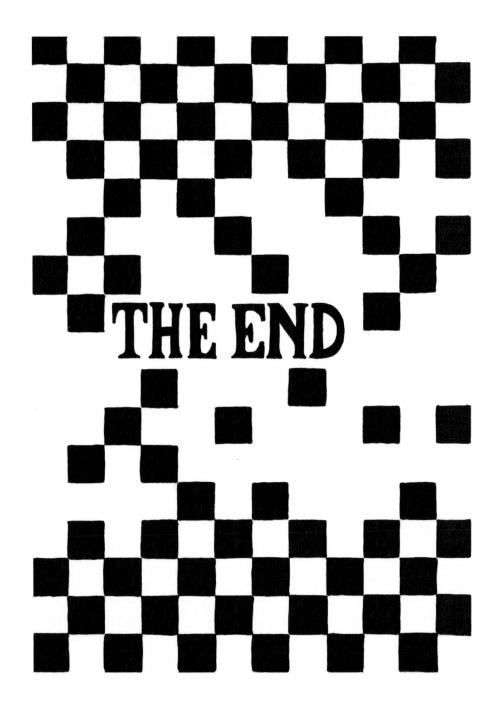

THE END

Printed in Great Britain
by Amazon

81011636R00160